PRAISE FOR

Things Too Huge to Fix by Saying Sorry

Edgar Award Nominee

★ "Combining middle-school mystery and civil rights history with reflections on dying, friendship, and the ethics of writing another's story from a racially different perspective, the novel is ambitious, thought-provoking, and very readable."
—*Booklist*, starred review

★ "Vaught brings history to life as she connects the past with the present, showing how acts of violence, betrayal, and courage both color and blend the histories of two families."
—*Publishers Weekly,* starred review

★ "A provocative, sensitive, and oh-so-timely read."
—*Kirkus Reviews*, starred review

"[A] story of who can tell whose story, and what constitutes appropriation of another's story—certainly a timely issue within the children's literature field. . . . [T]he novel takes its young audience seriously, grappling with complicated issues and covering an important chapter of the civil rights movement."
—*Horn Book*

Also by Susan Vaught

Footer Davis Probably Is Crazy
Super Max and the Mystery of Thornwood's Revenge

Things Too Huge to Fix by Saying Sorry

SUSAN VAUGHT

A PAULA WISEMAN BOOK

SIMON & SCHUSTER BOOKS FOR YOUNG READERS
NEW YORK   LONDON   TORONTO   SYDNEY   NEW DELHI

To Autumn Cook, who loves books.
To Missy and Camille and Sandy and Bonnie,
still holding down the fort in Oxford.
To Jennifer Fritz, for opening her heart and holding my hand and
Gisele's as we walk toward our own little piece of equality.
To Karen Forester, who always loves us anyway.
To Square Books, because it rocks.

SIMON & SCHUSTER BOOKS FOR YOUNG READERS
An imprint of Simon & Schuster Children's Publishing Division
1230 Avenue of the Americas, New York, New York 10020
This book is a work of fiction. Any references to historical events, real people,
or real places are used fictitiously. Other names, characters, places, and events are products of
the author's imagination, and any resemblance to actual events or places or persons,
living or dead, is entirely coincidental.
Text copyright © 2016 by Susan Vaught
Cover illustration copyright © 2016 by Jim Tierney
All rights reserved, including the right of reproduction in whole or in part in any form.
SIMON & SCHUSTER BOOKS FOR YOUNG READERS
is a trademark of Simon & Schuster, Inc.
For information about special discounts for bulk purchases, please contact Simon & Schuster
Special Sales at 1-866-506-1949 or business@simonandschuster.com.
The Simon & Schuster Speakers Bureau can bring authors to your live event. For more
information or to book an event, contact the Simon & Schuster Speakers Bureau at
1-866-248-3049 or visit our website at www.simonspeakers.com.
Also available in a Simon & Schuster Books for Young Readers hardcover edition
Book design by Krista Vossen
The text for this book was set in New Caledonia
Manufactured in the United States of America
0717 OFF
First Simon & Schuster Books for Young Readers paperback edition August 2017
2 4 6 8 10 9 7 5 3 1
The Library of Congress has cataloged the hardcover edition as follows:
Names: Vaught, Susan, 1965– author.
Title: Things too huge to fix by saying sorry / Susan Vaught.
Description: First edition. | New York : Simon & Schuster Books for Young Readers, [2016] |
"A Paula Wiseman Book." | Summary: "A family mystery leads Dani Beans to investigate the
secrets of Ole Miss and the dark history of race relations in Oxford, Mississippi"—Provided by
publisher.
Identifiers: LCCN 2015025579| ISBN 9781481422796 (hardcover) | ISBN 9781481422819
(eBook)
Subjects: | CYAC: Families—Fiction. | Vendetta—Fiction. | Race Relations—Fiction. | Civil
rights movements—Fiction. | Oxford (Miss.)—History—20th century—Fiction. | Oxford
(Miss.)—FIction.
Classification: LCC PZ7.V4673 Go 2016 | DDC [Fic]—dc23
LC record available at http://lccn.loc.gov/2015025579
ISBN 978-1-4814-2280-2 (pbk)

The past is never dead. It's not even past.

—William Faulkner (*Requiem for a Nun*, 1950)

1

THE LAST DAY

———

Excerpt from *Night on Fire* (1969),
by Avadelle Richardson, page 2

In 1960, Maud Butler Faulkner died, and two of her grown sons didn't survive another three years past her last breath. One of them, you won't know. The other, a fellow name of William Cuthbert Faulkner, him you might remember.

That boy dropped out of high school, failed his military physical to become a pilot in World War I, and impersonated a British citizen to join the Royal Canadian Air Force for a few years. Then he went and got himself fired from his job as postmaster at Ole Miss. While all that was going on, though, William Faulkner wrote himself a few books and plays.

"The sun, an hour above the horizon, is poised like a bloody egg upon a crest of thunderheads," he said

in As I Lay Dying. *"The light has turned copper: in the eye portentous, in the nose sulphurous, smelling of lightning."*

That book was published in 1930, but Faulkner's ghost might as well have penned those words in 1960, about Oxford, Mississippi. Poised on a crest of thunderheads. That's what we were, no mistaking.

A squall line had formed from the Gulf of Mexico to the Mason-Dixon Line, and the storm threatened to kill anyone caught in its path.

Talk to them in public, but don't bring one home.

Thou shalt not sow thy field with mingled seed.

They got strong backs, but they ain't as smart as us.

That's what the best ones said. The best White folks. What the worst had to say, that doesn't bear repeating.

What the worst would do—

Well.

That's the stuff of hurricanes and Armageddon.

I SUCK AT PREDICTING THE future, and I am so not the queen of witty comebacks. If I needed any proof of either of those facts, which I really, really didn't, I got it from Mackinnon Richardson at exactly 3:17 p.m. on the last day of eighth grade, at my locker at Ross-Phillips Academy, Oxford, Mississippi, in front of ten thousand people.

Okay, okay. Maybe it was only a handful of sixth-graders—

but it *felt* like ten thousand people. And ten thousand people, or even a bunch of sixth-graders, that's way too many folks to be paying attention when a big chunk of your life turns from sunshine to sewage, and you realize that not one thing in life is exactly what you thought it was.

"Dani Beans," Indri Wilson intoned in her best vintage actress voice, "you *are* the cornado."

I snorted at her as we started the next and probably last cornhole inning. The score was twenty to three, in favor of me. Even if I kept a cowpie on the bright red board, I'd win. Since I couldn't play any other sport known to humanity, I didn't feel guilty for pummeling Indri at cornhole. After all, it was the last day of school, and the sun was out, and everything had gotten warm and relaxed. The teacher policing the cornament had wandered off, and nobody was trying that hard. Indri and I had the pit to ourselves, bookended by two groups of seventh-graders playing a round of doubles.

Indri wiggled her eyebrows over her yellow cat-eye sunglasses as she lined up her next shot. "Mac likes you," she said as she threw a screaming eagle so far to the right, she smacked one of the seventh-graders in the shoulder. He caught the bag, glared in our direction, saw the pretty girl in the bright golden sundress with the clover crown woven through her long black hair, gave her a stupid grin, and pitched the beanbag back to us. Indri waved at him, adjusted her sunglasses, and gestured for me to take my turn.

3

Just as I was about to throw for the win, Indri said, "What I mean is, I bet that's what Mac wants to talk to you about. He likes you. As in, *likes* you."

My bag smacked the board and skittered hard left, clipping a different seventh-grader on the other side of the cornhole board. He wheeled around, saw the short girl in the jeans shorts with the wild frizzy hair, and aimed the beanbag right between my eyes.

I caught his pitch with one hand and pointed the bag at Indri. "Mac doesn't like me that way, and you completely exploded my toss on purpose. No fair."

She shrugged one delicate shoulder. "Throw again. It's what, twenty billion to nothing? And you've got five minutes before you meet Mac."

I gave her a look, then lined up the white bag, ready to give it a gentle underhand.

No way did Mac like me. Well, he was my friend. That's how I liked him, and how he thought of me, and that was pretty amazing given that our grandmothers were mortal enemies. Our parents didn't even totally approve of us hanging out. So the friends thing, it was kind of a victory.

I adjusted the bag. Took a breath. Thought about Mac. Took one more breath. Mom always told me I dwelled on things and had a . . . what was it? Oh, yeah: tendency toward the dramatic.

"Are you going to throw that stupid thing or give it a sloppy kiss?" Indri grumbled.

She was the one with the tendency toward the dramatic. Plus, she had an attitude because her mom—who was my mom's best friend—was an archeologist at Ole Miss, and she had named Indri for the largest living lemur in the world. It was a species native to Madagascar. When you're named for a lemur, you have to do some serious compensating.

I kept my eyes on the hole at the far end of the board. Mac didn't like me the way Indri was talking about. He didn't, even if Indri was usually right about all things connected to human beings. Understanding people and relationships was her special talent. I didn't have any special talents, except maybe winning cornhole games. The hot afternoon sun heated my cheeks and my whole face, because I wasn't blushing. I didn't care if Mac liked me or not.

Indri sighed. "This century, Dani?"

Okay, okay. If I got the bag in the hole, maybe Mac did *like* me, like me. If it just hit the board, he liked me a little bit. If I missed everything, he thought of me like a sister. The early summer air smelled like grass and felt like magic, and I tensed, relaxed, lined up one more time, and tossed.

The white bag sailed in a smooth, perfect arc toward the board. When it dropped through the hole without even brushing a bit of wood, I stared at the space where it disappeared.

Indri stuck her arms in the air like I made a touchdown and yelled, "Swish!" Then, "Thank every god in the whole world this idiotic game is finally over! I'm going to clean out my locker. I'll come over to your hall when I'm done."

5

Before I could even finish collecting the beanbags, she was gone. I shook my head at the skipping streak of yellow with clover in her hair. Indri moved like she was in ballet class all the time. Kinda better than my clumsy stomping, but I guess we both got where we were going.

Mac doesn't like me. Not like *me, like me.*

I had known Mac since fifth grade, and known about him way before that. Who didn't? He was the famous writer's grandson. The famous writer that my grandmother—another writer, respected in her academic field but not exactly famous—famously didn't speak to. "The Magnolia Feud." That's what journalists called the relationship between Ruth Beans, scholar of American history and civil rights, and Avadelle Richardson, novelist extraordinaire. "One of the enduring mysteries of our time."

Neither my grandmother nor Mac's would say a word to anyone about why they didn't talk to each other. They swore up and down they weren't angry and it was much ado about nothing, but they had been friends once, very close friends, and then they weren't. When I was seven years old, my grandmother actually left the Jitney Jungle grocery store downtown to avoid ending up in the same aisle as Avadelle.

With that kind of build-up for why Beans people didn't mix with Richardson people, I figured I'd despise Mac on general principle, but he was quiet and funny and he played electric guitar in a band, and I liked listening to their music while I did my homework.

6

I let out the breath I kept accidentally holding as I walked back to the nearest building, where my locker waited. Mac's locker was close to mine. This morning, he had texted that he wanted to talk to me right here, right about now, before school let out. That was weird, because we usually saw each other in school and after school too, but I hadn't seen him all day. Why had he gone to the trouble of setting up a meeting? What if Indri was right? What if—

I chewed my bottom lip and pushed the thought out of my mind. He'd probably say hi like always. I'd say hi like always. He'd ask if I wanted to go get ice cream like always. Regular and routine and nothing new.

No sign of him yet. I started clearing out my locker. This weekend, I planned to wake up whenever I wanted to, and all week, and maybe the week after that, too. Then I'd start Creative Arts Camp at Ole Miss, with Indri and Mac. I was terrible at all things art, but maybe I would finally find *inspiration* (yeah, yeah, talent wouldn't hurt either) and start making masterpieces like my grandmother.

In years to come, people might say about the summer before I started high school, *That was when it happened. That was when Dani Beans started changing the world.*

Artists really could change the world. My Grandma Beans did it with books she wrote about history and politics, back before she got Alzheimer's disease. Mac's grandmother had changed the world with *Night on Fire*, her novel about Southern life that some reviewer said "opened eyes and shattered stereotypes"—and she was the meanest person in the entire universe. If Avadelle Richardson's hateful old butt could change the world with one book, I could do it ten times over. I just had to find that . . . thing. My special talent. My muse. My medium. Something. I didn't know what it was, but I knew it would morph me from wannabe brilliant transformationist to unstoppable creative force (you can shut up now, brain, *transformationist* can be a word if I want it to be).

I dumped the last of my pencils and erasers into my carry-home bag, then stood and closed the door to my dingy red locker. That's when I came face-to-face with Mac Richardson.

"Oh!" My breath caught, and I almost dropped my bag. "You scared me."

Mac didn't say anything. He stepped away from me, then stared at his feet. He stuffed his hands in his jeans pockets, and he wiggled one foot back and forth. The foot looked like it might be trying to claw its way out of the nasty black sneaker that was strangling it to death. Mac wasn't much on fashion. He was a T-shirt guy, and he kept his brown hair long, so it hung in his face.

I suddenly got too aware of the old red lockers and the cinder block walls, and the way the big square floor tiles seriously needed mopping. A lot of sixth-graders had shown up while I was cleaning out my locker. They were digging through their own lockers, chattering and glancing at us, and the air blowing through the hallway seemed warmer than it had been a minute ago. Why was my heart beating all funny and fast? I made myself grin, even though Mac still hadn't looked at me.

Some of the sixth-graders giggled. I knew some of those girls thought he was cute.

He doesn't like *me*.

Since Mac kept not talking, I thought I would help him out. "I'm sleeping until noon tomorrow, and Sunday, and all next week. Want to come over Monday and walk down University Avenue with Indri and me? We can eat ice cream until we explode."

Mac's foot kept tapping its escape code. "I . . . uh. Um. It's . . ."

He stopped. I waited. Mac wasn't a word wizard, despite his grandmother being such a well-known writer. If something made him nervous, his tongue tied itself in major knots.

I got a strange feeling in my stomach, like something was going really wrong. My neck started to sweat. Just perfect. Every girl needs neck sweat to feel extra-special pretty when talking to a boy who might like her.

"Camp," Mac finally expelled. The way he said it, it sounded like a swear word. He glanced at me and shoved his hair out of his brown eyes. He had a lot of freckles, but all this year, they had been joining together to make him look tan and—I don't know. Older, somehow.

"Camp," I prodded, hoping he'd keep producing words without a high-speed come-apart.

"I can't do camp this year," he said. "I have to help my

grandmother." Then he went right back to staring at his feet. "Yeah, and . . ."

A second ticked by. Two. Then three.

"I'm not supposed to talk to you anymore," Mac said so fast I wasn't sure I heard him correctly.

"What?" My face burned hot. I wrapped both hands around my carry-home bag and leaned toward Mac, who still wouldn't look at me. "Mac. That doesn't make any sense."

"I know. But I'm not supposed to. It's . . . I . . . my parents." He kicked one ugly sneaker against the other. "They said. My parents, I mean."

"You have *got* to be kidding," I said to Mac. Okay, I probably yelled it. "This is not what's happening here. You were supposed to be talking about liking me!"

Oh, no.

Did I actually just holler that loud enough for the entire school to hear? I wanted to stuff myself in a locker and slam the door and never come out until next year in a totally new school where I didn't know any of these people.

"Sorry." Mac sounded miserable. "That story in the news last week about the Magnolia Feud, they got all worked up about reporters coming down here and stalking us again, and . . . never mind. It's just the way things are right now, Dani."

I banged my head against my locker and glared at the chipped paint instead of him. Then I banged my head one more time and turned on Mac. "So you're letting your parents pick your friends now?"

All the noise and people around us faded from my awareness, and I willed him to quit kicking himself and staring at
nothing and look at me. Look at his friend. The one he was
ditching because he was too much of a weenie to tell his parents no, or just do what he wanted anyway.

He didn't raise his head.

Coward.

My chest actually hurt. *Heart*-ache. Who knew that was
real and not just a metaphor?

"You're pathetic," I said. Yelled. Screeched. Whatever.

Indri chose that moment to sweep up to us like a yellow
sunray. Her smile spread light across the world, until she
looked at us. "Wait," she said. "What? Are you two fighting?
It's the last day of school. Are you both crazy?"

Mac glanced at her. Then he looked at me. As in, really
looked at me. His hair hung in his face again, but I could see
his eyes. They looked wide and sad. I had called him pathetic.
I wanted to say it again, with even more underlines and excla-
mation points that actually hung in the air where he could see
them, but I couldn't, not when he looked like that.

My eyes didn't cry with sadness, I was sure. Mine sparked
and glowed with *pissed off*.

Mac's expression hardened. He looked back at the floor,
grunted something at Indri that sounded like "Bye," and
"Talk to you later."

Then he turned and left, shoving through the sixth-grade
crowd to do it.

"What was that about?" Indri asked me. "What did you say to him? What did he say to you? Why was he acting like that?"

I let go of my carry-home bag with one hand and tried to wipe the sweat off the back of my neck. "We're not friends anymore, according to him."

"What??" Indri sort of toppled into the lockers, looking about as stunned as I felt. "Why?!"

"He said his parents won't let him talk to me anymore. That article in *Time* set them off."

Indri recovered herself enough to stand up straight. "So, the feud."

I shrugged like I wanted the feud, Mac, the wrecking of my day, the staring sixth-graders, all of it, to be no big deal at all. "Maybe he just needed an excuse to walk away, so he took the first one that came along."

And maybe if I tried hard enough, I could believe all of this truly wasn't a big deal.

"Just an excuse," I mumbled. "Indri, I thought—I was sort of—and he blew me off." A tear slipped down my cheek. I hoped no sixth-graders saw it.

But Indri did.

Her eyes narrowed. Then they got more narrow, and more narrow, until she looked like a crazed robot.

"Oh, no he did *not* blow you off," psychotic-robot-Indri said as she turned toward the crowded hallway, even though Mac was probably long gone. "He did not blow *us* off."

Indri had been friends with Mac too—but mostly because of

12

me. I suddenly felt guilty for her getting her feelings hurt too.

"Sorry," I whispered, trying not to let a second tear follow the first one.

"Hey, Richardson!" Indri yelled down the crowded hall. "You're a worm! You hear me? You're less than a worm. YOU'RE WORM DUNG!"

She got hold of my arm, jostling my bag as she pulled me into the ocean of sixth-graders. "Come on, Dani," she said. "Who needs Worm Dung anyway?"

Not me.

Definitely not me.

2

XS AND CIRCLES AND THE DEFINITION OF GONE

———

**Excerpt from *Night on Fire* (1969),
by Avadelle Richardson, page 9**

*"I'd have wasted a lot of time and trouble before I
learned that the best way to take all people, black or
white, is to take them for what they think they are,
then leave them alone,"* William Faulkner wrote in
The Sound and the Fury.

*That book got published in 1929, the same year
I was born in Oxford, Mississippi. My name is CiCi
Robinson, and time was, I wanted to write like good
ole Count No-Count. I wanted to be brave as he was,
talking about Black and White and telling the God's
honest truth about the life I lived and the world I saw.*

*But I was Black, and I was female, and stuck in
Mississippi. The most I could hope for was getting
through the winter in our nailed-together clapboard*

*house with its dirt floor and newspapers and quilts
lining the walls to keep out the wind.*

*Black girls who lived in patchwork houses didn't
dare dream of writing stories.*

MY MOM REALLY DID SEE dead people.

Okay, so she was a coroner.

When my dad saw dead people, he puked. I'd probably do the same thing if Mom let me see the actual dead people, which she didn't, except through the crack in the curtains on the view window at the back of her office, all covered up, just shapes under blue paper sheets.

Dad was an organic gardener, and all about tomatoes, not death. Mom said he was a hippie. As for me, I was a "late in life child," according to Mom. Grandma Beans always called me an "oops baby," or just Oops for short. It really got on Mom's nerves. Grandma Beans moved in with us five years ago, when I had just turned seven. She had a lot of time to irritate Mom before she forgot how to do it.

"Indri called him Worm Dung," I told my mother with absolutely no tears at all, even though I wanted to cry. The alcohol stink in her morgue office burned my nose and eyeballs, but I was trying to avoid the whole dramatic tendencies thing, since she was working extra hours plus teaching a class through the summer, and drama made her cranky. I sat in a chair with my back to the view window and pretended there was no crack in the curtains, and there weren't any dead

15

people right behind me, none at all. No drama, no drama, no drama . . .

Mom didn't respond to me or look up from her papers.

"Worm Dung. That's my new name for Mac Richardson," I said a little louder, and really trying to mean it. "What do you think?"

Mom scooted a bunch of reports into a stack, then laid her pen on top. I was too far away to see what she had been working on, but I knew it was diagrams of a human body with stuff marked with Xs and circles. It was kind of weird, knowing that she turned whole lives into shapes on a page. How could people get shrunk down to outlines and pen scratches when they died? But Mom had to check everything out, to see what went bad inside people and what killed them. Those Xs and circles didn't say a thing about who could play cornhole or understand humans and relationships or write world-changing novels. They didn't tell anybody which people were sad because their mom or dad had to go to war, or tired because they were taking care of a sick grandmother. For all I knew, one of those dead people might have been dumped at a locker too, somewhere in their lives.

"What I really think is," Mom said, "you're too young for a boyfriend-girlfriend relationship, so it doesn't hurt my feelings that Mac's out of the picture."

I managed something close to a respectful frown, I hoped, because Mom didn't do disrespectful any more than she did drama. "You never liked him, did you?"

Mom gave me a puzzled glance and leaned back in her rolling chair, the one with *Ole Miss* stitched into the leather in fat red and blue letters. Her navy skirt and white blouse were perfectly tucked together, but wrinkled at the end of the day. Her makeup still looked flawless, and she had her long brown hair braided into a tight knot on the top of her head. Mom was tall to my short and skinny to my chunky. Her skin paled in the bright blue-white ceiling bulbs, next to my in-between color that was darker brown, like Grandma and Dad. Everything about my mom was beautiful and professional, always, except when she got tired—and she had been tired a lot this past year.

"I barely know Mac Richardson," she said in a voice that reminded me of my third-grade math teacher. "So how could I dislike him?"

My eyes roved around the pine paneling of her office walls, bouncing off her degrees and pictures of her with important people and framed newspaper articles about her work on high-profile cases. "Well, he *is* a Richardson."

"Old Polish proverb, Dani."

I sucked down a sigh. *Old Polish proverb* was Mom-shorthand for, *Not my circus, not my monkeys.* That was one of her favorite sayings, even though she was a lot more Irish than Polish.

What Mom meant was, the fight between Grandma and Avadelle Richardson wasn't her feud, or Dad's, or mine either. People could write news articles all day long about

Beans vs. Richardson, but we didn't have to fight just because they wanted us to.

"I know," I said. "The Magnolia Feud is Grandma's battle."

Mom nodded. "It *was* hers, yes."

My breath hitched. Mom gazed at me without blinking.

Was.

That word seemed to hang in the air like a sad balloon tethered by Mom's silence. She was waiting for me to get something, but—

Oh.

That Grandma Beans wasn't able to feud with anybody anymore.

I had a sudden image of the day Grandma moved in with us, how she drove up in her huge black Lincoln, threw open her door, and stretched her arms wide for me to run into her hug. Then she spouted off a quote and waited for me to tell her the author, novel, and year it was written. That's how she was with me, my whole life—before.

Now, if Mom drew one of her outlines of my grandmother, there would be a big X where Grandma's brain should have been, because that's what was going bad inside her. It would kill her too, probably pretty soon.

I spent a few seconds studying my feet, and when I lifted my eyes again, Mom looked twice as tired, and somehow more wrinkled than she had a second ago, and I knew it might be my fault. I thought about Dad, and how while I was at school, he had worked all day looking after Grandma and his garden and the house. When he went to the doctor last month, his blood pressure had been just awful.

This isn't going to be easy, Dani, Mom had told me when Grandma Beans came to live with us. *We'll all have to make sacrifices. From this day forward, our family has a pact to do whatever it takes to make the rest of her life comfortable, and only focus on* real *problems.*

When I thought about Mom and Dad and Grandma Beans, and sacrifices and doing whatever it took to help family when they needed it, my stomach got tight. Worm Dung didn't seem like something to discuss anymore, so I put him on a table in the back of my mind and covered him with a sheet, and scrawled a giant red X on the picture. There. Done with him.

"Can we get dinner on the way home?" I asked, thinking of ways to make stuff easier for my tired parents.

Mom got up and smoothed her wrinkled shirt as she shook her head. "Your father's cholesterol doesn't need a hamburger."

"What about a salad from Living Foods? They're all locally grown and organic, right? So it's like cooking out of Dad's garden, only somebody else does the work."

"You know what? That's a good idea." Mom straightened and actually smiled at me. "We can splurge every now and then. Last day of school is as good of an excuse as any."

"And when we get home," I said, "I'll do the first check on Grandma."

"Mac dumped me," I told my grandmother, because she had never minded hearing about my life and what happened, even if it wasn't her circus or her monkeys.

Grandmas were special like that.

"Only, he didn't dump me, because we weren't going out or anything. He said we can't be friends anymore."

Grandma Beans didn't say anything back, or give me a kiss, or squeeze my hand. She lay in her hospital bed, covered with a white sheet instead of a blue one, and she barely moved at all.

"He says it's because reporters are trying to stir up stuff about the Magnolia Feud, but that's ridiculous. The last time reporters bothered any of us was three years ago, when that tabloid guy tried to hit you up at the hardware store." Late-afternoon sunlight played across my fingers as I rested my hand on her chest, really light, no pressure, to feel the up-and-down movement of her breathing.

"Everything okay, Dani?" Mom called from down the hall, as if she knew I was having dramatic thoughts.

"Yes," I said. "Grandma looks fine."

"Give her a kiss, then, and go eat your dinner. I'll feed her in a bit."

"Okay." But my hand didn't move, and my attention drifted to the room's open window. The curtains swayed in a soft breeze. That window was always open, rain or shine, hot or cold, because way back when we all talked with Grandma about how she wanted things. "When the time came," she told us, she wanted a lot of fresh air. Since then, we'd had to move her four-poster bed out and replace it with this hospital kind. It sat in the middle of the floor, along with the temporary cabinets Dad had built to hold sheets and incontinence pads and washcloths and wipes and medicine. We could have kept her regular furniture, but Grandma thought this way would be easier on us.

You're going to let me die at home. Least I can do is be considerate and not ruin the furniture.

Don't be silly, Mama.

I'm never silly, Marcus. That would be you, with your big ole grizzly bear head and that hippie beard.

Back when she remembered us every day, Grandma liked to laugh and pick at Dad and spend hours working on her latest paper while I played on the floor at her feet. My eyes darted to the few tables lining the walls, where we kept her papers even though she couldn't write anymore. Before Grandma got Alzheimer's disease, she taught elementary school for thirty years, then taught sociology and civil rights at the University of Mississippi—Ole Miss—for fifteen more. She wrote a lot of books and articles on stuff like *The Social Implications of the "Magical Negro" in Folk Tales* and *Whitewashing History*.

I tried to read a couple of them last year, but I had no idea what they meant. Mom said Grandma was a "fire-breather." Dad said she was relentless. Grandma called herself a "jaded realist." That was over a year ago, when she still talked plain and made sense. Now—well, now the times when Grandma still felt like Grandma didn't happen hardly ever.

Heavy sadness settled in my chest, and I blinked fast to keep from crying. No use thinking about Grandma when she could write and talk to me and hug me. That was just more drama. The papers blurred out, then came back into focus. I turned away from them and bent over and brushed my lips against Grandma's soft cheek. She smelled like baby oil, and she didn't have wrinkles like a lot of old people, even though she was so scrawny her skin should have hung on her like an oversized football jersey.

The hospice doctor had given us a booklet, *Gone from My Sight: The Dying Experience*, written by Barbara Karnes, R.N. The booklet told all about what Grandma's dying would look like. But with dying, nothing was that certain.

When it's natural, people die on their own schedule, the doctor told us. *To quote an old proverb, death always comes too early—or too late.*

In the "One to Two Weeks Prior to Death" section, the booklet described a bunch of changes, like pulse getting faster or slower, sweating, trouble breathing and congestion. The hospice nurses had taught me how to check her pulse, so I did it every day, and I looked for changes. This evening, Grandma's pulse was seventy-five, right where it usually was. I watched her breathe a few more times, and didn't hear any rattling. When I scooted my hand off her chest and touched her fingers, they were warm. For now, she was okay.

Sooner or later, Oops, we're all gonna be okay. Grandma used to tell me that whenever I got upset. It always riled me up. Now, it made a weird sort of sense. Grandma's eyelids twitched as I pulled away, and she muttered, "Marcus?"

"It's me, Grandma. It's Oops. Dad's the giant guy with the beard to his chest."

"Marcus," Grandma muttered again.

Her clouded eyes opened, and she stared at the ceiling. Her knobby fingers worried the sheet pulled up to her chest, and she sighed. A tear leaked out of her eye.

My heart broke a little bit, and I kissed her cheek again. "Don't cry, Grandma. Dad's downstairs. I can get him if you want."

This time as I pulled back, her head swiveled slowly in my direction. Her gaze stayed cloudy and far away, like she could see into a thousand worlds I didn't even know existed. After a few minutes, her lips pulled upward, and I knew she was smiling. Her next word came out garbled, but I could tell it started with an *ew* sound.

I grinned back at her even though I really, really felt like crying instead. "That's right. It's me. Your little Oops. I love you, Grandma."

Her right hand shook as she tried to lift it. I picked it up for her and I put it on my face, along the side, where she had always patted me. She kept smiling for a second, then another tear slipped out of her eye and plopped down on her pillowcase.

She started whispering, and I had to lean in close to hear her say, "I'm gone, Oops. I'm all gone."

I kept my ear right in front of her lips. "No, you're right here, in the house with me. With us."

"Gone," she muttered, and her eyes closed, but her face looked like she'd swallowed a mouthful of lemon juice. I knew that face. She was upset, and I hated that.

I leaned closer. "Can I do something for you?"

"Get the envelope," she told me. "Take the key. It's for you when I'm gone. I'm gone, Oops."

Envelope? Key? What was she— Probably nothing. "You're not gone. Everything's okay, Grandma."

Grandma turned her head side to side until I stepped away from the bed again. I didn't want her to stay upset or get so worked up she had to have medicine.

"I was there," Grandma said. She coughed. "You get that stuff out of my bag, you hear me? Get the key. I gave it to history. I let the ghosts keep it for you."

"Dani." Mom's voice came from the bedroom doorway, sharp enough to make me twitch. "I told you to go eat your dinner."

"Sorry, but Grandma's upset about something. She's talking."

Grandma stirred in the bed, more than I had seen her move in days.

"It's time I tell you. It's time I tell her." She let out a little sob. "I'm gone."

When I glanced at Mom, she looked surprised. After a few seconds, she murmured, "Go on now. Eat."

My first urge was to argue with Mom that I wanted to stay and listen. When hospice first came in, they suggested staying in the moment, going from feeling to feeling and memory to memory with Grandma. They talked about how she might have things to resolve, and how we should help her.

I was there . . . get the key. It's time I tell her. It's time I tell you.

That sounded like something to resolve. But what did it mean? Something about an envelope and key in her bag—she probably meant one of the purses hanging in her closet, but those were her private property. We didn't go into her bags and things, even now, and didn't plan to, not until she really was gone.

Grandma told me to, though. She said to get an envelope and a key from her bag.

"Time to eat, Dani," Mom said. "Before your lettuce wilts and you get a mind to go for macaroni and cheese instead of something healthier."

As Grandma calmed back into silence, Dad loomed in the doorway and came to stand beside Mom. He was made out of muscles from years in the Army and all of his gardening, and he had on his black T-shirt and his work-in-the-yard jeans. Sweat glistened on his forehead, from when he was outside earlier.

He looked at his mother, then Mom, and then Dad's eyes fastened on mine. He could probably see how much I wanted to stay, and he shook his head once.

Close that mouth, the head-shake told me. And, *Your mom is stressed enough,* and, *Don't worry, I got this.*

To Mom, he said, "Love you, Cella," and kissed the side of her head.

Mom relaxed into Dad's kiss, and that fast, I found myself smiling. It was the first time since the cornhole tournament that I'd felt a little happy. Grandma was completely peaceful again, the house quiet except for the sound of everyone's breathing.

As I left the bedroom, I went past the table where some of Grandma's papers lay waiting, with a heavy miniature Liberty Bell weight holding them down so they wouldn't blow around if some of Grandma's fresh air got frisky.

I'm gone, Oops.

My hand was still on the knob of Grandma's bedroom door.

Gone.

I used to think *gone* meant *dead*, but that was before I understood there were sicknesses like Alzheimer's disease that could eat away a person's mind but leave their body behind.

So what did gone *really* mean?

"Mom told you to go eat," I muttered out loud, to get my own attention. Everything inside me wanted to go to Grandma's closet and go through her bags. Instead, I went downstairs like I was supposed to. I even sat down and took bites of my salad, tasting nothing much as I crunched away on the greens, which had gotten kind of soggy after all.

But mostly I thought about Grandma's closet and her bags. *It's for you when I'm gone.*

"Just talking out of her head," I mumbled to myself. I ate more limp healthy organic salad, but when I tried not to think about the purses and what might be in them, I thought about Mac. Five minutes of that was absolutely enough, so I got up and fetched the gigantic *Webster's Encyclopedic Unabridged Dictionary of the English Language* Mom kept in the living room and lugged it to the kitchen.

Surprise, surprise. *Dead* was like, the fifth definition of the word *gone*. Before that came "past participle of *go*; departed, left; lost or hopeless;" and "ruined."

Wow. By that definition, Grandma *was* sort of gone already, and she *did* say it herself.

"I'm gone, Oops," I repeated her words aloud, to the few pieces of tough broccoli and cauliflower left in my bowl. My grandmother with all of her quote games and world-changing books, and the Magnolia Feud, and the weird thing she said about writing something down, and whatever was in her purses that she left for me for when she was gone—whatever *gone* really meant—and a disease that robbed her of the ability to explain it all to me—yep. It was a big ole mystery.

I just had to figure out where to start to solve it.

3

GHOSTOLOGY

———

**Excerpt from *Night on Fire* (1969),
by Avadelle Richardson, page 23**

Nothing matters but breathing, to be alive. My father forgot about that one rainy September day, when he and his crew pulled up too much wet tobacco during the big harvest. He was drenched from his hat to his shoes when he got home, and fell down drooling and sweating and throwing up. He died before Mama could bring the lady from down the road, who knew about cures and plant medicine. Two men on Daddy's crew died the same way before the night ran out, even with the Granny Woman's help.

Green Tobacco Sickness.

If the farmer had waited a day or two, until the leaves got dry, they'd all still be alive—but that would have cost him plants, and cost him money. More than my father was worth, I guess. More than all those lives. Work, or get fired and get no pay, and let your family starve.

It wasn't even casual cruelty. That's maybe the worst part, thinking back on it now. Not meanness, or spite, or the darkness of human nature.

It was just life in Mississippi, holding hands with Jim Crow.

WHEN I WAS SURE I had eaten enough salad and organically raised cage-free boiled chicken eggs to please Mom and Dad both, I cleaned up after myself and lugged the dictionary back to its table in the living room, and went upstairs. I wanted to talk to Indri.

I checked my charging phone, but I had no all-clear text from her, which meant she hadn't spoken to her dad yet. He was serving in Afghanistan, and they barely got any time to speak at all, so I couldn't tie up her line. She was still off limits, like Worm Dung and Grandma's purses, only Worm Dung wasn't here, and the purses were in a closet right next to my room.

After a few minutes of staring at the wall and trying to ignore the purses' existence, I changed Worm Dung's ring and text tones and unfriended him on every social media account I owned. That felt pretty good. Except none of that made the purses go away. I went over to the little refurbished school desk in the corner of my room, lifted the lid, and took out a book I hadn't started. The cover was cream-colored with a picture of a witch riding a unicorn on the front. She was supposed to be a good witch, I guess, because of the unicorn and her glittery golden dress.

I tried to read a few pages, but I couldn't concentrate. I put back the book and paced up and down across the open part of my room, in front of the windows, going from my closet door past my rocking chairs to my long dresser, the one with my socks in it. Maybe Grandma wrote me a story, and that's what I'd find in one of her bags, hidden deep in her closet. I'd probably regret it if I read it now.

Closet door. Rocking chairs. Sock drawer.

What if it was a finished manuscript we could sell for extra money to help with her care? Mom wouldn't have to work two jobs then, and we could hire more help, and Dad could relax, and his blood pressure would probably get better. Grandma might have thought ahead that way, and trusted me to dig through her purses at just the right moment.

Sock drawer. Rocking chairs. Closet door. My socks scooted on the hardwood as I walked.

By the time Grandma moved in with us, she was already getting a little paranoid. I didn't understand that when I was younger, but I had learned that her suspicion was part of her Alzheimer's disease. When she lost things and couldn't remember where she put them, she thought people were hiding her stuff. When she forgot to pay her electric bill and her power got shut off, she thought the utility company was out to get her. She talked about persecution and plots a lot, and stuff she thought she did—so maybe she just *thought* she hid something in her purses for me to find, or wrote about plots and conspiracy theories or other nonsense.

Nonsense I wasn't supposed to touch until she was gone, which sort of seemed like a promise even though I never made it. That word again—*gone*. Was she *gone* enough for me to see what she left me?

Closet door. Rocking chairs. Sock drawer. Rocking chairs. Closet doors.

I could hear my parents speaking softly to each other as they left Grandma's room. Last year, I would have heard Grandma too. I would have come home and told her all about Mac, and cried, and she would have wrapped her arms around me and held me tight, and she never would have said I was being dramatic, or getting upset over something that wasn't a real problem.

I stopped at my rocking chairs and sat down, heavy with remembering what life was like before my grandmother's mind hopped a bus for parts unknown. Or maybe I was just waiting until my parents' voices got quiet and I knew they had gone to bed for the night. Because once they had, it took only a second for me to sneak into Grandma's room.

Wait, wait. Not sneaking. Sneaking meant doing something wrong, and I wasn't exactly— Oh, never mind. I was sneaking. On tiptoes and everything.

Grandma lay in her bed, breathing quietly. She didn't even

twitch as I beelined for her closet and creaked open that door as quietly as I could. The inside light flicked on, pitching everything behind me into soft blue shadows just as the smell of her clothes hit me full in the face—light, almost sweet, like flowers, but sharper. It was her perfume, something old she had worn my whole life, called *Oh! De London*. It made me think of Grandma in pantsuits and lipstick, her hair perfectly in place, fixed up to go write at her favorite desk in her favorite carrel at Ole Miss's library.

Tears popped into my eyes. I wiped them with the bottom of my shirt, then my face, and did my own quiet breathing. It took me a few seconds to blink away the idea of crying and fix my attention on the section of the closet where her purses hung.

Feeling halfway out of my own body, I opened one bag after the other, glancing inside and feeling around in the pockets. If I didn't find anything envelope-like, I moved on. The sixth purse, the seventh—maybe this was just stupid, and I'd be standing here smelling perfume flowers when Mom or Dad came in to check, and they'd give me the look, and I'd feel awful, and—

And there. Purse number eleven. My fingers ran across the top of an envelope, and I pulled it out. Hands shaking, I brought it into the light and stared at it. White. Standard business size. The top of it was a little dusty, so I swept it off with my fingertips. There was one word written on the front of the envelope:

33

Oops.

I tried to breathe, but my throat pinched shut. For a few seconds I could hear the *whump-whump* of my own heartbeat. My fingers traveled up and down the edges of the envelope, tapping the corners. So, Grandma hadn't been just talking out of her head. There really was an envelope in one of her purses, and it had my name on it. It felt like it had papers inside and maybe something else, something heavier than paper and all lumpy.

I walked backward out of the closet and let the door shut. It made enough of a noise that my eyes shifted to the bedroom door, and I imagined my parents coming in again. They'd be here to check on Grandma soon anyway. They probably would *not* approve of me going through her stuff, least of all to get an envelope she had left for me to read when she was "gone."

Assuming they didn't kill me straight off, Mom would be all, *You're being dramatic again. You've gone to this trouble, so just open it, Dani, have a look, and be done with it.*

Dad would be like, *She said that's for when she's* gone. *Does your grandmother look* gone *to you?*

And Mac would say, *Open it. Jeez. What are you waiting for?*

And Indri. She'd think about it, and use her relationship talents to divine what my grandmother really meant, and she'd say something like, *How about a compromise?*

Just glance at what's inside, maybe read a little bit of it, and get an idea what it's about. That would totally be Indri.

I liked that idea best of all, but I didn't like it either, because I just didn't know what I should do. So, I snuck out of Grandma's room, still on tiptoes, put the envelope on my bed, covered it with my bedspread, and went and took a shower.

Ghostology
By Ruth Beans

Seriously, that's all the first page said.

So much for imaginary-Indri's compromise. I talked to her after she Skyped with her dad, but we stayed on the subjects of how good her dad was doing, what presents he was sending her, and Worm Dung and her various ideas for getting even with him. I kinda liked the anonymous website involving several embarrassing photos of donkeys, but only in the abstract. I wanted to tell her about Grandma's envelope, but the words wouldn't come out.

Until I couldn't sleep, and everyone else—even my grandmother—could. The entire city of Oxford seemed to be snoring, and I was awake, and I opened the envelope marked *Oops*, even though I felt totally, completely guilty.

The first thing I got out was the lumpy thing, which was a golden key. It had three loops on the end and a long barrel, like old-fashioned door keys, except smaller, and it was too

35

big to be a diary key. I stared at it for a while and turned it around and around in my palm, wondering what it unlocked. Finally, I tucked it under my pillow, figuring I'd know more about it after I read what Grandma wrote. If I even did read it before, you know, she was actually *gone*.

Only—what I found on the first page—who even knew what to make of that?

Ghostology.

I sat on my bed in the dark and used my phone to shine light on the first page of the papers inside my grandmother's secret envelope, and just kept looking at the word. The world hadn't stopped spinning or exploded when I opened the envelope, but I swear it was like my grandmother was teasing me. If she still had all her wits, she'd probably be laughing her butt off and telling me how much I deserved this confusion and giving me some quote to look up about ethics and conscience, or maybe karma.

I couldn't go down to the living room to get the dictionary without waking up the whole house, so I used my phone to Google *Ghostology* and hoped for the best.

Apparently, the writer Nathaniel Hawthorne made up the word in a book called *Septimius Felton, or The Elixir of Life*. After he invented it, nobody much used it, until in the last few years, when it got related to *ghostlore*, or the scientific study of ghosts and the supernatural.

Just thinking about ghosts made my heart beat a little too fast, and I had to spend a few seconds shining my phone all around my dark room, chasing away all the shadows.

"Ghostology," I whispered to keep the silence away from me. Why would Grandma write about ghosts? She didn't really like fiction books all that much, and she always teased me for reading so much about creepy things and other planets and magic.

I turned the phone's light back to the page I had pulled out of the envelope. It looked like the beginning of a manuscript. With a sigh, feeling something between surrender and guilt, I pulled out the second page.

The text wasn't dense. It looked more like a poem than a story. As I read it, my eyes opened a little wider.

For My Granddaughter

I couldn't find my car at the shopping center, and I walked around for an hour, looking for it and getting madder and madder—and scared, too.

That's how it starts, Oops.

You don't think much about it that first time, even if you've never had a problem finding your car in a parking lot before.

*You don't worry when you lose your wallet,
or you can't put your hands on the keys
you know you left on the table, or when you
call a friend by somebody else's name.*

Then it gets worse.

Then it gets more.

Then you know.

And then you're gone.

—Ruth Beans

At the very bottom of the page, I found a date. It was the year my grandmother found out she had Alzheimer's disease, before she ever moved in with us. I didn't think twice before pulling out the next page. In the eerie light of the phone, I read the first page of the thick letter she left for me.

So, my little Oops, it's like this.

*Today, after a bunch of tests, my doctor
told me and your father that I have*

38

Alzheimer's disease. There's nothing they can do for it. It'll take me in bits and pieces, until I'm no more than a ghost of myself, like in those science fiction and fantasy stories you're always reading.

I don't know what to say to my boy, because when my doctor explained it to us, Marcus cried. You're too young to understand right now, but your father realizes that before I die, you'll all learn the details of Alzheimer's disease, Oops. He understands that you'll know my face, and my eyes, and my arms and my hands, and my fingers and my toes. You just won't know me, and I won't know you.

So, I want to leave a little bit of myself for you to find. I want you to know me, Oops. The real me, not that ghost you'll come to call Grandma, and the subjects that are most important to me—our history, and the parts of it that are being forgotten like the United States itself has gotten Alzheimer's.

That's why I sat down to write this, so you'll have it, so you can share what you think should be shared with your parents and your friends, even with the world if that's what you decide. But it's harder than I thought it would be.

If you could write about yourself and tell your favorite person who you are, what would you say? You should try that sometime, because I have as many pages as I can stay myself to write—and it seems like way too much and not enough, all at the same time.

For now, I'll just tell you I'm scared.

I'm going to forget everything, but maybe if I get some of myself on paper, you won't forget me, or how much I love you.

Bear with me, Oops. I don't want to be just a ghost to you, so I'm going to do the best I can.

Tears made the words look funny, and with just the light of my phone, I couldn't stand how everything blurred. I smoothed the three pages I had sort of stolen from my grandmother's closet, and I carefully tucked them back into the envelope. I put the key back inside the envelope too, and I slid the whole thing under my pillow to keep it out of sight, but close to me. Then I shut off my phone and snuck into my grandmother's room again.

She lay in her hospital bed, motionless and quiet. A nightlight glowed beside the table where we kept the supplies we needed to change her, just enough light so that she wouldn't be totally confused and scared if she woke. Moonlight blazed through the open window, spilling across her feet, and a warm breeze still moved her curtains.

I went to the chair next to her bed and put my hand on her chest. She didn't stir at all. A second or two later, relief washed through me as her breathing moved my palm up and down. I checked her pulse. Seventy-seven. For now, she was okay.

Sooner or later, Oops, we're all gonna be okay. I could hear her voice, like she was whispering in my ear, but her eyes stayed closed.

Sometime after that, my own eyes closed. I slept right there until Dad found me. I remember him kissing the top of my head as he carried me to my own bed.

4

Best Friends Never Speaking to Each Other Again

———

**Excerpt from *Night on Fire* (1969),
by Avadelle Richardson, page 74**

Mama and her youngest sister, Aunt Jessie, kept trying to talk to me about school. I was past fourth grade. I could earn money if I went on to work in the fields, or cleaning houses. But I wanted learning. I wanted to stay in school.

"You so stubborn, you could argue with a fence post and win," Mama grumbled as Aunt Jessie nodded.

School might not have taught me everything, but I knew when to keep my mouth shut. I clamped my teeth so hard my jaw hurt from it, tight and ready in case Mama turned loose one of her skin-stinging slaps.

"I don't have time for this," she said. "I have to go to work." She pointed her finger in my face. "And the

sooner you start training like I did, the better."

By training, she meant to farm or clean. That's what she did, all day, every day, sixteen hours, eighteen hours—it never ended for Mama. Aunt Jessie had lost a foot to the sugar already, so she couldn't do much other than see to me and the house. Both of us watched Mama walk to her room and slam the door behind herself.

Later, after Mama left to walk to work, Aunt Jessie started on me again, waving her fist as she spoke. "The roof leaks in that school, and the floor's gonna fall in soon. I heard a boy got blood poisoning from a rat bite last week."

"I don't care," I told her. "The books are at school."

"Old books. Hand-me-downs from some White child who'd spit on you soon as she'd look at you. One teacher for fifty of you crammed into a firebox waitin' on a match—what's the point, CiCi? You don't even have a desk. Only the little ones get desks, right?"

I folded up my arms and glared at my aunt. "Just you wait. One day, I'll write a book like William Faulkner. I'll write a dozen!"

"Now ain't that a big bunch of silly dreams." Aunt Jessie laughed at me. "Your teacher ain't got a degree in nothin', and they can't pay her—how long you think she'll stay?"

I WANTED TO TELL MOM or Dad or both of them about Grandma's envelope. I wanted to tell Indri, or talk to Mac about it, but two weeks ago Mac had turned into Worm Dung, and nobody talked to people named Worm Dung. And Dad's blood pressure had been going up and down a lot, and Mom was still trying to get used to working her regular job with all the dead people, and also working a second job teaching a class about all the different ways people can die.

Indri—well, she was Indri, but her yellows and pinks had been more blues and browns the longer her dad stayed deployed. Everybody had their own tough stuff to deal with, and they didn't even ask for their troubles, like I asked for mine by taking things from Grandma's purse fourteen days ago.

More than anything, I wanted to read more of what Grandma had to say, but I felt guilty about even touching the paper and the key, because it was like admitting I thought Grandma was already a ghost.

The day you were born, Oops, it was the best day of my life. Now don't tell your daddy that, because you know he thinks his birthday should be the best day. Oh, but you, little girl—you had curls the second you popped into this world. You screwed up your pretty face and yelled yourself purple, and all I wanted to do was kiss your little baby forehead. As of the day I'm writing this, I still see the future shining out of your round brown eyes.

"Are you dressed?" Mom yelled from her bathroom down the hall.

I jumped at the sound of her voice and quickly put down the page, neatened it up, and tucked it back inside Grandma's envelope. Then I slipped the whole thing into my pack. In a big hurry, I pulled on my green Creative Arts Camp T-shirt. Vanilla and coconut filled my nose, Mom's getting-ready-for-work smells. They fought off the attack of alcohol and cotton from Grandma's room, where the hospice nurse was finishing Grandma's morning bath. I usually helped with the bath, but I had gotten up late.

"Danielle Marie Beans," Mom called again. "Quit day-dreaming and answer me."

I glanced at my clock: 7:03. I didn't have to be at the Creative Arts classroom until eight, and the campus was only a five-minute drive during summer session. From August to May, about forty or fifty thousand people lived in Oxford, Mississippi. By the middle of June, like now, twenty thousand college students bugged out for the vacation months, and traffic jams went poof like some fairy touched a wand to the roads.

"I'm ready," I told Mom. Then I checked the full-length mirror in my bedroom to be sure I wasn't lying. Yep. Jeans fastened, shirt on, tennis shoes tied. Hair—oh. Hair. Where was my comb? I spotted it on my beside table, grabbed it, and ran it through the flat part of my hair as best I could. It wouldn't matter. My hair always stuck out in every direction, but I tried to make sure I didn't have any obvious rat's nests. I didn't want Mom doing the job.

"I have to be at Shoemaker Hall by eight," Mom said. "Monday morning anatomy lab waits for no one—not even the teacher. Give your grandmother a kiss and let's hit the front door in five minutes."

"But we have plenty of time," I said. "Dad might be right that you need to let that class go. Two jobs is making you all stressed out."

The sound of my father clearing his throat and mumbling something to my mother echoed against the house's old wooden walls.

"Give your grandmother a kiss, Dani," Mom said like she was talking through her teeth. It sounded funny when she did that.

I worked on my hair for a few minutes, trying not to think about the envelope I had crammed in my pack to take to camp, or secrets or ghosts or Dad's health or Mom getting so cranky for the whole two weeks I'd been out of school, or whether or not Indri would be in a brown mood or a yellow mood today. Finally, I gave up on my hair and pulled it into a ponytail. Then I went to Grandma Beans's room and knocked on the door.

"We're finished," the morning nurse told me. I couldn't remember the nurse's name, but I knew it would be on her yellow Sunlight Hospice badge. As I pushed the bedroom door open, I squinted at the badge.

Cindy.

"Thanks, Cindy," I said, slipping inside quiet-like, in case Grandma was having a bad morning. But she seemed to be lying in the bed, peaceful and quiet despite the bath. I eased over to the edge of her white, cotton-smelling sheets, gave her a kiss, and waited for her to breathe. Then I touched her hand—warm—and took her pulse.

Everything seemed okay.

"Eww," Grandma mumbled, and I thought she might be trying for *Oops*, but her eyes were closed, so I didn't say anything.

Cindy patted my shoulder. "It's fine to answer her. She's agitated off and on, but I can give her some medicine if it gets too bad."

I glanced up at Cindy, who looked friendly enough with her nurse's coat on and her short blond hair and her big thick glasses.

"It's better that she doesn't have the medicine," I told her. "It just makes her more confused."

"Eww," Grandma said. "Key."

Her eyelids moved up, and she stared out, seemingly at nothing. A second later, she started crying, and I wanted to kick myself for bothering her.

"Key," she whispered. I glanced around to see where Cindy was. Good. All the way across the room.

"What do you need me to do with the key?" I asked her very quietly, rubbing the back of her knuckles. "What does it unlock?"

She didn't answer.

"She probably doesn't understand much of what you're saying, sweetie," Cindy said from somewhere else in the room. I tried not to be mad, because Grandma might think I was mad at her. I just ignored the nurse and stayed where I was, holding Grandma's hand to my face.

It sounded like, "I wrote it down," what Grandma said next. I couldn't make it out. Then, "Take the key, Oops."

"Everything's fine, Ms. Beans," the nurse chirped. I knew she was trying to say helpful, nice things, like the nurses from hospice usually did. Some of them knew Grandma pretty well, but this one didn't. Not her fault. She was new.

"Something's bugging her," I said. "She's been crying off and on for almost two weeks."

"That can happen," said way-too-helpful Cindy. "Lots of times, near the end, folks have things they need to work out."

"You been doing this long?" I asked the nurse. "This hospice thing?"

Cindy beamed at me. "About six months now."

"Yeah, well, I'm only twelve, but Grandma's been living

here and dying of Alzheimer's for four years, so I know all that stuff you're saying. It's in the pamphlets. You don't have to repeat it."

"Dani." Mom's voice came from the bedroom doorway, sharp enough to make me twitch. "That wasn't very polite."

When I looked at her, I could tell she was past ready to leave. Her makeup seemed perfect, her hair had been pulled into a bun, and her black skirt and white blouse were spotless and creased in the right places. Her expression looked a little pressed and creased too.

"Sorry I was rude," I said to Cindy, my hands fiddling with my hair to smooth it. To Mom I said, "Grandma's upset and trying to talk again."

Mom took a breath in slowly, then let it out. "I'll let your father know. I'm going to be late to teach my class. Work's being patient enough, letting me come in at noon to do it—I can't push my luck any more than that."

"Yes, ma'am." I moved away from Grandma's bed and followed Mom immediately, which seemed to be the right thing to do, except Mom still looked seriously annoyed—and I had to ride with her in the car to Ole Miss.

"You understand why I'm working two jobs right now, don't you, Dani?" Mom's hand scooted back and forth on top of the steering wheel, even though she kept her eyes straight forward. She bit at her bottom lip and waited.

"Grandma needs a lot of extra supplies insurance doesn't

cover," I said, remembering how she and Dad explained it. I took a deep breath, enjoying the closer scent of Mom's coconut and vanilla. When she came home, she'd smell like formaldehyde. "Dad's doing his best selling produce from his gardening and cutting our grocery bill to help with expenses, and after three wars and three decades in the Army, he's earned his retirement."

He's earned his retirement.

Mom said those last words with me. It was what we told everybody about Dad living on his army retirement and not having a paying job, because that's what he wanted us to say. He didn't like talking about the fact that he didn't sleep well, and sometimes he just couldn't stand to be around anybody but us. His plants and his dirt made him feel better when the wars bothered him, so Mom wanted him to garden as much as he needed to, and so did I. Besides, somebody had to look after Grandma in between the hospice nurse visits. Dad was kind of a reverse babysitter now.

I stared out my window, watching University Avenue whiz past, house by house. Some were old like ours, with columns and steep roofs and spindly railed balconies off upstairs doors. Other houses seemed way too new, crammed on top of bits of grass like somebody barely fit the foundations to the yards. Oxford had turned into a weird mix of really old stuff and really new stuff, since a lot of people decided to come live here. Dad told me that when all the newcomers started building houses, nobody thought about protecting historic homes and buildings that didn't get burned down when a Civil War general's soldiers got drunk and torched the town square in the 1800s.

Houses gave way to trees and more trees, and then sidewalks, and then we passed by the brick gate that said *University of Mississippi* and *1848*. Not long after that, we passed two people that made me go stiff in my seat. Just a boy my age, dressed in jeans and a navy T-shirt, and an old lady like Grandma. She was wearing jeans too, and an obnoxious black and yellow striped shirt, along with a fedora that didn't match anything at all. She leaned on the boy's arm, and used a cane too. Aw, how cute. That's what poor unsuspecting fools would think if they saw the two of them walking, and they didn't know.

They would be *so wrong*.

Mom cleared her throat, and I jumped. I realized her eyes were darting back and forth to the rearview, and she squinted. "Was that Avadelle Richardson and Mackinnon?"

"Yes, ma'am," I said, only my voice cracked on the *ma'am*, and my face flushed hot.

The navy T-shirt was probably the one with the glow-in-the-dark skull on it. He liked to wear it when he played his electric guitar at school band club. Music meant everything to Mac, or so he'd told me. But he also used to say I was his friend. Who knew if anything Worm Dung said was the truth?

Mom only missed two beats before she said, "No boy is worth all this grief, Dani, especially not at your age."

My face got even hotter as I closed my eyes. We swept around University Circle and plunged into the flickering shade of the big oaks and magnolias. I knew where we were from the dark-light, dark-light, dancing off my eyelids.

"Worm Dung isn't a boy," I muttered. "I mean, like a boyfriend. It's just—I thought he was my friend. Almost a best friend." I gestured at the car window. "Best friends are supposed to be like you and Ms. Wilson, or me and Indri. Best friends aren't supposed to turn into people who never speak to each other again, like Grandma and Avadelle. Stupid feud. I mean, did you see any reporters following Avadelle and Worm Dung around? It was just one article—and it's not even our circus or our monkeys, right?"

"I see," Mom said, but I didn't think she did. Her tone made me worry she was going to launch into another lecture about age-appropriate relationships with the opposite sex.

Thank goodness she didn't. I wanted to keep my eyes clamped tight, but it was making me carsick, so I watched as Mom turned again, this time to move past Ole Miss's signature building, the Lyceum, with its six white columns gleaming in the morning sunlight. She angled us down the road toward Bondurant Hall, then said, "You think Avadelle might be on her way to talk to Creative Arts Camp?"

"What? No! I mean—" My pulse leaped like I'd seen a zombie. Oh, no, no, no. That would be horrible. Like, the worst thing ever in my summer camp life, if you didn't count when I was eight and fell asleep with honey on my fingers at

Sardis Lake Swimming Week and woke up covered in fire ants. "Um, I hope not."

"Well, *Night on Fire* was an amazing book. Can't deny her talent."

I grabbed the handle over my head with my right hand and held on like I might get sucked into a black hole. "She throws whiskey bottles at squirrels *and* people, Mom. Awards or not, I don't think anybody's going to invite her to speak at a camp with kids."

"Dani. Stay civil. Remember, not our—"

"Circus, yeah, I know. Thank gosh her daughter is a *lot* nicer, and not responsible for creating Mackinnon."

Worm Dung was the spawn of Avadelle's youngest child, her son, one of the town's doctors. I couldn't blame Naomi Manchester, Avadelle's daughter, one of the booksellers who worked for Square Books, for his existence. The car slowed to a stop in the parking lot next to Bondurant Hall, and Mom waited for me to give her a kiss. I did, then grabbed the backpack with Grandma's papers in it and got out of the car. Mom started to put the car in gear, then stopped and kept looking at me. "I always hoped Avadelle and Ruth might patch things up before your grandmother passed. It's hard to think about best friends never speaking to each other again."

My hand froze on the edge of the door, and my mind danced across Grandma's tear-streaked face.

I wrote it down . . .

Grandma and Avadelle *had* been good friends, maybe best friends, just like Indri and me (not thinking about Worm Dung, not not not). Then they stopped speaking. That's what everyone said about the Magnolia Feud—and all anyone knew, even Dad. He told me Avadelle and Grandma had dinner on Wednesday evenings at six o'clock, every week when he was a younger kid. Then, a month or so after Avadelle's first novel came out, the dinners stopped. Something about that world-famous book seemed to have punched their friendship dead in the nose. Journalists had been analyzing the book for decades, trying to guess what secrets were hidden in those pages, what started an argument so bad it never ended.

Grandma wouldn't talk about it, and Dad said he didn't have the guts to ask Avadelle anything about anything, then or now. Thirty years in the military, three wars, and Dad was more scared of that old woman than bullets or drill sergeants.

I wrote it down. Grandma might have been talking about her spat with Avadelle, right? About whatever happened between them to cause the feud.

I kept the smile on my face so Mom wouldn't worry, and knew, finally, that even if my grandmother wasn't really gone, I should read the rest of what she wrote to me, to help her pass in peace.

Oh God.

What if I had to face down the Wicked Witch of Ole Miss? What if I found out something I needed to talk about with her? And Worm Dung . . . never mind.

"Have a good day, Mom." There. That sounded all cheerful, right?

Mom grinned. "You and Indri don't get up to too much mischief, okay?"

"Yes, ma'am."

"And promise you'll walk straight home if I run late?"

"Promise," I said, figuring a swing by the Grove to feed squirrels and a trip to grab ice cream would still be sort of straight home, with a few small detours thrown in. "I have my phone." I tapped my pocket. "I'll call you or Ms. Wilson if there's trouble."

I burst through the front doors of Bondurant Hall. Indri had seen me coming. She was standing just outside of class, her brown eyes wide and her mouth open.

"Did you see a ghost?" she asked immediately, clutching her Stephen King book to her chest. Stephen King wasn't exactly considered "appropriate reading" for our age group, but Creative Arts parents had to sign a waiver that short of X-rated material, we could read anything we chose. Indri and I loved ghost stories and not-totally-gross horror, and science fiction and fantasy, too. Ghosts the most, though. Bonus that we had been assigned to read some for this week.

"No," I said. Then, "Yes." Then, "Kind of? Worm Dung and Avadelle were walking down University Avenue. Mom thinks Avadelle might be coming here to talk to our camp."

Indri's eyes got even wider. I had seen pictures of the lemurs Indri's mom had named her for, and right now, with her long black hair swept back and her black and white shirt and black jeans, and that shocked expression on her face, Indri really looked like one of those lemurs. If I told her that, she'd beat me in the head with her Stephen King book, so I kept my mouth shut.

She eased the book down from her chest and came over to me. In a low voice, she said, "We staying, or we bolting?"

Best. Friend. Ever.

I slid my fingers up and down the strap of my backpack. "Staying for now," I said. "But keep the bolting option open."

"Roger that," she told me. Military-speak. That, plus the black motif of her clothing, let me know that her dad was weighing heavy on her mind today. I would have asked her about it, but Indri didn't like to talk about her dad. My backpack seemed to pull at my shoulder, reminding me of what lay hidden inside, and the fact that we might *have* to talk about Avadelle Richardson and her stupid, moronic grandson, for my grandmother's sake.

"Inside, ladies," called Ms. Yarbrough, the Creative Arts Camp director, like she could sense the escape plans zipping through my brain. She was only five feet tall, but her voice gave her a few extra inches of authority. When I didn't move, Indri laced her arm through mine, and I leaned in to her, holding my breath.

"Campus ghost stories," Ms. Yarbrough called out as she clapped her tiny hands together. "Gather round, gather round! We have a guest speaker, and she's in my office, getting ready now."

I sagged against Indri, and she sagged right back against me. Safe.

Whoever the speaker was, it wasn't Avadelle. Avadelle Richardson wouldn't be caught dead talking about anything paranormal. I could breathe again. And—ghost stories!

"Let's go," I said to Indri, but she had already started for the classroom door, pulling me along with her.

5

Things Too Huge and Awful to Fix by Saying I'm Sorry

Excerpt from *Night on Fire* (1969), by Avadelle Richardson, page 111

Funny how fast years can go. One minute I was ten and fighting with Mama about school, and the next, it was 1960, and I was thirty-one years old and widowed and back in Oxford with a boy of my own, taking care of Mama and still listening to Aunt Jessie's loud mouth.

"That's about the whitest White girl I ever did see," Aunt Jessie told me as she stuffed papers into envelopes at the Mt. Zion Church office. She nodded her big head toward a straw-haired kid hanging with the registration trainers.

"Hush your mouth." I gave her plump elbow a pinch. "That child came down here to do the right thing."

*Aunt Jessie grunted. "She came down here to die.
She just don't know it yet." She wiggled her fingers
at all the students from up North, who had crowded
into the front of the sanctuary. "None of them really
understands Mississippi, or what they gettin' into,
CiCi. It bothers my conscience."*

*I ignored my aunt's opinions and kept my eyes on
the girl. After a few minutes, she just looked scared.
My own conscience nudged me. I stood, then closed
the few steps between myself and the girl, and I stuck
out my hand. "CiCi Robinson," I said. "I teach school
over in Holly Springs."*

*"Leslie Marks," the girl said as we shook. "I just
graduated from Ohio State University. I moved down
here to help."*

*You're White was about all I could think, but I
couldn't for the life of me understand why I was thinking that, because I wasn't prejudiced, at least I didn't
think I was, but I couldn't seem to help myself. "Come
on, then," I told her. "Work on these mailers with us."*

A CHILL RIPPLED THROUGH THE silent classroom, and I
shivered. Air conditioner. Had to be. But . . .

No sunlight crept around the heavy drapes pulled over the
windows, and a rolled blanket across the bottom of the door
blocked any glow from the hallway. The air smelled like dust
and perfume and turpentine from soaking paintbrushes. Indri

and I sat cross-legged on our floor mats, gripping each other's hands as Naomi Manchester from Square Books shined a flashlight under her chin. She had brown eyes and dark, arched eyebrows. In the spooky light, her M-shaped mouth looked huge, and her teeth seemed way, way too white.

"The year was 1862, and Mississippi writhed in the grip of the Civil War." Her quiet words sat in the air around her, and I imagined cannon smoke, the flash of rifle fire, and men shouting and running for their lives. I held my breath. I was pretty sure Indri was holding hers, too.

"Eighty miles northeast of where we're sitting, twenty-four thousand Americans lay dying on the battlefields of Shiloh, Tennessee." Ms. Manchester's dark hair glittered in the yellow beam of the flashlight. She had it pulled into a bun, and her cheeks flushed as she shifted her gaze from me to Indri to the next person in the listening circle. "Confederate troops limped back to Corinth, Mississippi, then fled farther south, to this campus."

I glanced to my left and right. This building was old. Had the soldiers come here? Was I sitting in the exact spot where some guy bled to death, or had his brains run right out on the floor? Another fit of shivers made my teeth chatter.

"Why did the North and the South fight like that anyway?" Sheila behind me asked before Ms. Manchester could start talking again.

"Duh," said Bobby, who was sitting on my left. "Over slavery. Everybody knows that."

Ms. Manchester looked around the room as she answered. "There were many, many reasons for the Civil War, but disagreement over the moral soundness of slavery was a big one."

"Why did they have to kill each other, though?" Sheila said. "Couldn't the people who had slaves just release them and apologize?"

"I think there are things too huge and awful to fix by just saying *sorry*," Indri said. "Like kidnapping people and making them into slaves, and torturing them for three hundred years just because they were Black instead of White."

"Be niiice," I whispered to Indri.

"That *was* nice," she shot back.

"Indri has the gist of it," Ms. Manchester said. "The problems between northern states and southern states had grown so deep and gone on so long that they couldn't be sorted out by talking—or at least that's what everyone believed. So the war began. Then, in May 1861, Company A of the 11th Mississippi Infantry Regiment in the Confederate Army was formed, leaving only four students at Ole Miss." Ms. Manchester held up four fingers, wiggling one at a time. "Four. That's all. The college closed, but was soon forced to open its doors again as a hospital for the wounded and dying. They came on horseback, carried by friends, carried by wagons. Two by two and three by three they came, dozens, and dozens more, and then hundreds. The Lyceum filled to capacity, so the wounded spilled into other buildings, like this one.

I choke-gripped Indri's fingers until she yanked her hand away and smacked me on the shoulder.

Ms. Manchester's eyes traveled slowly around the circle. There were twelve of us, and she looked each of us in the face as she spoke. "Nurses and townsfolk did what they could, but most war wounds don't heal. Moans echoed through these walls. Men suffered, and men died. Bodies lay stacked in the fields outside. Back then, nobody burned the dead. They put them in the ground."

She lifted her arm and pointed one finger over our heads, like she could see the exact spot where the bodies got planted. "Hole after hole, prayer after prayer, those men were buried right over there, behind our football stadium. A hundred. Then two hundred. And it wasn't over, no, not even close. Before the year was out, General Grant himself pitched a tent in Oxford's town square, a few feet from Square Books where I work now. There were more battles, and more wounded, and Union dead joined Confederate dead until the cemetery held the remains of more than seven hundred soldiers."

Indri glanced at me, eyes bigger than a Madagascar lemur.

"Souls of the dead killed in battle, now they're restless at best," Ms. Manchester said. "Townsfolk brave enough to walk by the graves at night told tales of whispering and moaning and distant screaming. Some said they heard cannon fire and rifle shots. And then in 1900, workers sent to cut grass and weeds moved the markers. Once the cemetery had been cleaned, nobody knew where to put the gravestones, and seven hundred soldiers lost their names."

Well, that about sealed it. That graveyard would so totally be haunted. Judging by the way Indri squeezed my fingers, she thought the same thing.

"How would you feel if you died for your country, got buried in strange ground—and then somebody went and lost your marker so your people couldn't even pay their respects?" Ms. Manchester looked at each of us again, and she nodded at the frowns on our faces. "That's right. Angry. And sad." She leaned into her flashlight, turning her cheeks almost translucent. "And *restless*."

She paused. The air conditioner rattled in the background. My own breathing sounded too loud, so I held the air in my lungs until the darkness around Ms. Manchester seemed to pulse.

"All that remains is a single monument, put up later to list as many names as we could find." She shook her head. "But I don't think that monument appeased the offended dead. I heard tell once of a student, we'll call him John Smith. Brave John, he took it on himself to show his fraternity brothers that Ole Miss's cemetery ghost stories were nothing but tall tales. So he dragged his sleeping bag out to that monument, to spend the night."

Stupid. Why were people in scary stories always so dumb? I'd have glued my feet to the floor before I went to a graveyard in the middle of the night—for any reason, much less to prove there weren't any ghosts. People who tried to show ghosts didn't exist always got eaten by something fanged and nasty. The second anybody in a spooky story laughed at ghosts, you *knew* blood was gonna flow.

My teeth ground together as I waited for the worst to happen.

"Idiot," Indri whispered about Brave John.

Ms. Manchester's eyes drifted in Indri's direction, and Indri clamped her mouth shut. "His fraternity brothers went halfway to the graves with him," Ms. Manchester said. "But they stayed back, respectful and scared."

"More like smart," Indri whispered.

I nodded.

Ms. Manchester's eyes narrowed.

We both got very still.

"After a time, the night moved on, and the fraternity brothers fell asleep." Ms. Manchester let us imagine that, then leaned into the flashlight's beam again. Her voice dropped. "The first brother woke hollering and ducking, saying he heard rifles shooting right over his head. The second woke running away from the ear-bursting boom of cannon fire. As for the third—"

She shifted away from the light, so far back I could only see her mouth moving.

"The third brother said he heard something screaming . . . but it wasn't human. More like a war horse, maddened from battle, bellowing as it charged. He heard hoof beats, then they all heard hoof beats, hammering the ground, coming straight for them, thundering down the unmarked graves, and they ran, and they ran, and they didn't look back."

Ms. Manchester moved.

I couldn't see her face at all, just the flashlight beam blaring in a column all the way to the ceiling. When she spoke again, she was nearly whispering. We had to lean toward her to make out the words.

"Come the morning, when Brave John didn't show up at the fraternity house, his friends went looking for him, and what do you think they found?"

She waited.

Nobody said a word.

"BONES!" she cried, and we all yelped and shrieked. "BLOOD AND BONES!"

The flashlight clicked off, pitching us into total darkness. Up turned to down and down turned to up, and I almost fell backward because I couldn't figure out where I was. Indri started giggling like a psycho nutjob in a bad horror movie.

"Might have been sharp hooves that did him in," Ms. Manchester said, each syllable slow and quiet in the cavelike nothingness. "Might have been splintering wagon wheels. And maybe, just maybe, it was the rough heels of seven hundred pairs of war boots."

Pictures flickered to life on the cinder block walls around us. A black-and-white photo of a stone monument. An oil painting of a Civil War battle scene, complete with blood-stained grass and a sky blackened with smoke. A surreal digital picture of a Confederate officer riding a huge black stallion with devil-red eyes, its mouth wide and steaming. A graying, grainy shot of Oxford's town square and its courthouse, surrounded by dozens of white tents and covered wagons. The pictures faded, until only the last one remained.

"Is that real or Photoshop?" Indri whispered to me too loudly.

"Real, I think," I told her.

The classroom lights clicked back on, blinding me as Ms. Manchester said, "This is the only known photo of General Grant's occupation of Oxford, Mississippi, during the Civil War." She stood by the picture, and the gray light covered half her face. "So yes, Indri, this picture is real, and not Photoshopped. What's also real is the cemetery with seven hundred unmarked graves, and the fact that the campus closed for the Civil War because almost all the students were fighting as the University Grays—and those boys never came home."

"What happened to them?" Mavis Simpson asked.

Ms. Manchester favored her with a smile. "On the last day of the Battle of Gettysburg, the University Grays reached the farthest point in Pickett's Charge up Cemetery Ridge and established what became known as the high water mark of the Confederacy. That achievement came at the cost of one hundred percent casualties. Every single soldier was either killed or wounded."

My mouth came open. Indri squeezed my hand, and her

brows pulled together. She really didn't like to hear about military men getting killed in battles. I wanted to grab her and hug her and tell her not to listen, that everything was going to be fine with her dad, but she wouldn't like that. It would make her go all weepy in public. *Soldiers' kids don't cry.* She had told me that a hundred times. I didn't think that was true, or even good for her, but it was what Indri wanted. So I just let her murder my fingers until Ms. Manchester moved on with her storytelling.

"The buildings at Ole Miss actually did serve as an infirmary to the wounded and dying from Shiloh and other battles," Ms. Manchester said. "And the campus didn't reopen for classes until 1865. Now, as for Brave John, him and his tale are all my creation." She tapped her chest and grinned. "Local legend has it that on dark, dark nights, you can hear hoof beats in the cemetery, as the ghost of a general rides his patrol—but he's never killed anybody."

Indri let go of my hand before my fingers went totally dead, and we clapped along with everyone else as Ms. Manchester gave us a deep, courtly curtsy. I knew she was around the same age as my mom, but she looked younger somehow. Maybe it was working in a bookstore instead of cutting up dead bodies.

When we settled back on our mats again, Ms. Yarbrough switched off her iProjector, shutting down the creepy picture of the town square full of little white tents. Then she turned back to us with her hands clasped in front of her.

"So who can explain why people tell ghost stories?" she asked.

"To scare themselves silly," Indri muttered.

"That's right." Ms. Yarbrough smiled at her. "For entertainment. A good scare can be fun, and that's the primary purpose for many spooky tales—excitement and entertainment. Why else do people tell ghost stories?"

"To explain things they don't understand," Sheila said, and Ms. Yarbrough nodded her approval.

Bobby came up with, "To warn people about evil, and bad choices. You know, scare them into acting right."

That got approval from Ms. Yarbrough and Ms. Manchester, too.

Indri poked her hand in the air and said, "To help themselves not be afraid of what happens after death, 'cause if there's ghosts, then there's something, and we don't just disappear."

Ms. Manchester gave her the thumbs up.

I wanted to say that people told ghost stories to make sense out of what really was their circus and which monkeys they should worry about, but I figured all that would get me would be a trip to the campus infirmary. So I raised my hand, and when Ms. Yarbrough pointed to me, I said, "People tell ghost stories so they don't forget the past."

Or their grandmothers.

Double nods for me, and then Ms. Yarbrough said, "Who can tell me what story-telling elements and techniques Ms. Manchester employed to make her tale dramatic?"

Hands went up, and the discussion took off again until Ms. Manchester had to go back to work.

Ms. Yarbrough told us another campus ghost story about a fraternity boy who got killed in a car wreck in the 1960s coming back to campus from the LSU–Ole Miss football game. Apparently, he was mad about dying, so he haunted Saint Anthony Hall, the Delta Psi frat house. Ms. Yarbrough didn't use a flashlight, and her story wasn't that scary. She wasn't as good as Ms. Manchester at making all the words sound interesting.

People started doodling on papers and reading other books and fidgeting with their phones while Ms. Yarbrough talked. I felt a little sorry for her as she blabbered out a third tale that started in the 1960s, about screams coming out of the Lyceum part of the old steam tunnels that ran under the campus. Could I tell a story as good as Ms. Manchester? I could write a little bit, like poems and short stories, but I didn't think my writing was smart like Grandma's had been, and definitely not like Avadelle Richardson with all her awards.

According to Mom and Indri, I had an "expressive face." Maybe that would help me scare the snot of people if I decided to tell spooky tales.

I had a sudden image of Grandma, asleep at home in her hospital bed, her thin fingers gripping the white sheets like they were all that kept her from floating up to Heaven. My throat tightened. Grandma always thought I was smart and special. My parents said that stuff to me, but Grandma really made me feel it, whenever she looked at me and smiled at me. Back when she remembered me, anyway.

I really, really missed her, even though she was still alive. Sort of. Jeez, even thinking stuff like that made me feel guilty. I slid my pack into my lap, and carefully eased out the page from Grandma's packet that I had been reading this morning.

. . . On your second birthday, I gave you a magnetic alphabet board with big purple letters, and your daddy about had kittens when you threw those letters every which place and they kept wrecking his vacuum cleaner. You were running ninety miles an hour up and down the halls, and you could say so many words, but NO and WHY were your favorites. By the next year, you were spelling all kinds of things on that alphabet board, and I told everybody how you'd take after me and write for a living. . . .

"Earth to Dani." Indri poked my shoulder.

When I looked at her, I realized she was getting to her feet. Everyone was. Reality seeped back into my brain, and my legs felt like concrete. Worse than that, I had a seriously

bad case of mat-butt. I tucked the pages back into the envelope and put it in my pack.

Indri yawned and stretched. "Lunch time. And then we're
going to the Grove to draw or take a break if you don't want
to sketch."

I pushed myself off the mat and stomped my feet to wake
them up. Indri was good at sketching, not me. But my grandmother thought I'd take after her and write books. That made
me happy. She was telling me again how smart she thought I
was, even though she couldn't really talk to me anymore.

How awesome was that?

6

An Implied Promise

Excerpt from *Night on Fire* (1969),
by Avadelle Richardson, page 163

"I took a class in peaceful resistance," Leslie Marks
told me a few weeks later as I held a dropper over a cut
on her right shoulder and dripped Mercurochrome
on the broken skin, staining her bright red.

"Ouch!" she hollered. "That stings."

I blew on the cut just like I blew on my son's
skinned-up knees, to lessen the ache, then I covered
the spot with a Band-Aid strip. "Well, they should
have taught you to duck when people's throwing
rocks."

"I can't believe that happened," she said. "He had
on a business suit. I think he works at the bank where
I put my money!"

"Honey, you're a White woman walking out of Mt.

Zion. He knows why you're here. He knows what you are." I glanced past her to the door to the bedroom where my mother lay sleeping, fighting off cancer as best she could. When I was young and fresh back from Chicago and college with all that I thought I knew, did I try her patience like Leslie tried mine?

Leslie frowned. "He called me some of those names, yeah. He told me exactly what he thinks I am."

I put my first aid kit back together and closed it up with my red-stained fingers. "Just being at my house on this side of town, you know that can earn you a lot worse than a rock to the shoulder."

"I'm not scared of those people, CiCi."

"You should be," I said.

THE AFTERNOON BREEZE FELT WARM on my arms as Indri and I sat at our wooden picnic table in the Grove. The rest of the class had scattered to the other tables, and Indri had a case of pastels open in front of her. She busily shaded the devil-horse she had drawn on her sketchpad, using first black, then a dark, dark red for its eyes and the blood dripping from its mouth. I didn't want to bother Indri while she drew, and I didn't feel like writing, so I kept looking at the canopy of leaves over our head, watching how the shadows danced on the table when the branches moved, and thinking.

The whole friendship ending thing—I hadn't considered it much before Worm Dung pulled his trick at my locker. I knew from listening to my parents talk that people "drifted apart" sometimes when they get older, but I couldn't see that happening to Indri and Mac and me. I thought we'd go to high school together, and college, and then—well, I didn't know what next, but it never occurred to me that we wouldn't still be friends.

Only now, we wouldn't be, because Worm Dung messed everything up.

So, if I had to make a list of what could make best friends just stop talking to each other like Grandma and Avadelle did, the first thing on that list would be one friend being a butthead to the other one and messing everything up, just like Worm Dung. Only to me, one friend would have to do something so bad that saying "I'm sorry" wouldn't be enough to fix things. And the other friend would have to stay so mad, they didn't care if the butthead friend apologized.

It still didn't make sense though. How could two people who really cared about each other be *that* stubborn? How could anything be *that* bad?

Could something make Indri stop talking to me and stay angry with me forever? Something like . . . keeping a big secret? The thought made me sick to my stomach.

I needed to tell Indri about the envelope and key my grandmother left for me. She might be mad that I waited two weeks, but I'd apologize and everything would be fine.

Right?

I had to work to breathe for a minute. When I finally

calmed myself down enough to talk, I said, "I looked up the definition of *grove* once. It means a little group of trees. So this Grove has to be misnamed, because it's like, what, ten acres of magnolias and gum trees and really old oaks?"

"Forty species," Indri said, filling in a spatter of blood near her demon-horse's front hooves. "That's what the website said last time I looked. People take tree tours with that map they can print."

Stop it, I told myself. *Just talk to her. I mean, really. How bad could it be?* Words wouldn't come to me, so I opened my pack and took out Grandma's envelope. I pulled her papers out and laid them on the table in front of me. Indri kept right on drawing, and I didn't interrupt her. I fiddled with the key and waited, getting more and more miserable each passing second.

Finally, Indri sat back and studied her sketch. Then her eyes flicked to me, and to the stack of papers and key in front of me. "What are you doing with all that stuff, Dani? You writing a novel?"

"Um, no." I tapped the key on the papers and tried not to panic. "My grandmother started talking out of her head. At least I thought she was. About papers she wrote for me, and a key, and how I was supposed to get it out of her purse once she was gone. And I couldn't decide if she was gone, or gone enough, you know? But I went to look a couple of weeks ago, and they were really there. The papers. And this key."

Indri's eyebrows lifted, and her eyes slitted down to crazed robot proportions.

I talked faster. "See, she said something about writing it down, and I can't help wondering if it's about what happened between her and Avadelle, but it's hard to read what she wrote so far, so I haven't read much of it, but Grandma's staying upset and she's crying too, and I need to help her, so I thought maybe I should finally read all the rest of this and figure out what this key unlocks, but I can't make myself get past the first few pages because it's so sad, and Grandma's not actually gone, and I wanted to tell you, but I didn't want to bother you when it might just be stupid and really nothing. Here's the key."

I held it out.

Indri's mouth pinched together, but she reached her pastel-dusted hand out and took the key. She glared at me for a second, then studied it. "It's small. And old. Maybe to a door or something? No. Too small for that. I don't know."

She handed me the key, and I put it in my pocket as she looked down at the papers and read out loud. "*Ghostology*. What's that all about?"

"Grandma said Alzheimer's would make her a ghost of herself, and she wanted me to know who she really was and what was important to her. I think she used the word to mean she was giving me a study of herself, before she, you know. Went away."

Indri frowned. "That *is* kinda sad."

She read the first page, like I had done. Then she read the second page. At the end of the third page, she stopped and waited for me to turn over the fourth. I fiddled with the corner of the paper. I wanted to turn it over, but I didn't want to, all at the same time.

"What do you think?" I asked Indri.

"I think she loved you a lot, to have written you just to tell you you're pretty and brilliant and stuff." She looked up at me, frowning. "Why didn't you tell me about this when you found it?"

"I'm sorry. I really didn't want to distract you, with your dad and stuff."

"And I can't believe you haven't read it all already."

"It's sad. And she's not *gone*, really, so I felt guilty, and—" I closed my eyes. "It didn't feel right."

Indri went quiet for a few seconds, and then she said, "Okay." Simple. Stuff could be like that with Indri, when I let it be like that.

After a moment, I said, "I think when Grandma wrote this, she believed everything would go in a straight line. That she'd be herself, then she'd get sicker, and then she'd die. I think she didn't figure on all of this in-between-ness. She thought she'd be a real ghost, not a living one."

"You're probably right," Indri said.

So, Grandma sucked at predicting the future too, just like I did. Why did that make me feel better? "I don't think anybody in my whole family understood how much in-between-ness there would be."

"Right. And now, something's bothering your

77

grandmother," Indri sounded more sure. "I think the best thing we can do is figure out what to do to help her."

I turned over the third page, and Indri and I looked at the fourth page together. It was all about me in first and second grade, and more about everything Grandma thought about my brilliance, and how beautiful and perfect I was.

"I know she's your grandmother," Indri said, "but I gotta say, all this stuff about your wonderful wonderfulness—it gets a little nauseating."

"I think it's sweet," I mumbled, trying not to get all sniffly and make her laugh at me more.

"It is sweet." Indri patted my hand. "But sickening."

We turned the page, and then both of us got very, very still.

I have a lot to say to you, Oops, and not all of it is about how much I care about you and believe in you.

I need to tell you about the falling out I had with Avadelle Richardson. I'm sure it's what you want to know. It's what everyone always wants to know—and that gets old, let me tell you. I've published eighteen academic books and forty-two scholarly articles, and still all anyone wants to hear about me and my history and all that I've learned is, what happened to a friendship I had with a woman I knew for a handful of summers, over fifty years ago, and how much of _Night on Fire_ is really true?

The sad thing is, Oops, it won't make any sense to you unless you understand where I came from and what I was dealing with back then. It's so far away in time now, kids your age, they don't get the facts anymore. They don't learn about what really happened, not all of it. So I want you to read along here on this last manuscript I've been trying to finish, a time line of our state's history and how it relates to the Civil Rights Movement. In the final analysis, this is my history, and it's yours too. Read it carefully before you read about Avadelle and _Night on Fire_. Understand it before you judge me—and before you judge her.

That's all that was on page four. Somewhere in those sentences, my heart had started beating so hard I could feel it at the top of my throat. Indri's mouth had come open, and when she gazed up at me, her eyes had gone all lemur.

"So, she's going to tell us?" she whispered.

"Yeah." My fingers played along the edges of the manuscript. Part of me wanted to snatch up the papers and read ahead fast until we got to that part, but page four seemed to be asking for a promise that we wouldn't do that.

"She wants us—me—to read it all in order so we understand the fight when we get to it. It's her ghost story, right? She should be able to tell her story her own way, like Ms. Manchester would."

Indri groaned, but she nodded. "We should follow her rules and read everything in order—but I have two rules of my own."

The sudden edge in Indri's tone made me grimace, but what could I say at this point, after not telling her about the secret for two whole weeks?

Indri held up one finger. "First, no reading without me. If we don't get it finished today and you read a little ahead, you tell me right away."

Well, that wasn't too bad. "Agreed."

"Second, don't keep any more secrets." Two fingers now, and a glare, right into the back of my eyeballs.

"Um, okay." Was I smiling? That might not be a good idea, but I couldn't help it. This felt like the most normal moment in my life since Locker Horror on the last day of school.

I slid page four aside, and we looked at page five. It had a staple in the corner, and some attached documents. I left them alone and studied what was on the paper. Indri did, too, careful to keep her pastel-stained fingers away from the white paper. It was just a list of dates and events, like a section straight out of our Mississippi history class.

1817 Mississippi granted statehood.

1848 University of Mississippi founded (not called "Ole Miss" until the 1900s).

1861 JANUARY—Mississippi becomes the second state to declare secession from the Federal Union, and to join the Confederate States of America. MAY—Company A of the 11th Mississippi Infantry Regiment in the Confederate Army forms. Only four students stay at Ole Miss, so the college closes for the duration of the war. SEPTEMBER—American Civil War begins.

1862 JANUARY—Abraham Lincoln issues the Emancipation Proclamation. APRIL—The first of 18 named Civil War battles in Mississippi is the Siege of Corinth (April 29 to May 30, 1862). Grant wins and uses his position in Corinth to take control of the

Mississippi River Valley and Vicksburg.

JULY—Last day of the battle of Gettysburg.
Pickett's Charge. The University Grays are
all killed or wounded. Half of the 12,500
Confederate soldiers in the charge die. Possibly
the turning point of the entire Civil War.

1864 The last named Civil War battle in Mississippi is
the Siege of Vicksburg.

1865 APRIL—The Civil War officially ends.
Lincoln assassinated days later.
NOVEMBER—The Black Codes are enacted.

"Some of this stuff is from camp today," I said. "Interesting."

"What are those papers stapled to this page?" Indri asked.

"Looks like a copy of Mississippi's Declaration of Secession and a copy of the Emancipation Proclamation. She didn't write anything on them. Maybe they're just for reference."

Indri's gaze moved over each entry on the time line, until she got to the bottom. "What are the Black Codes?"

"No idea. And what do you think this means?" I showed her a bracket drawn near the Black Codes entry that extended onto the second page full of dates and events. Outside the bracket was a bunch of numbers, written in a straight line:

"1882-1968 42+539=581"

And under that, a name, underlined a bunch of times.

"Fred???"

"Why was she doing math in the margins?" Indri asked. "And who is Fred?"

"These first numbers must be dates, 1882–1968. But the math?" I shrugged. "Fred might mean Fred Harper."

"The goofy old history professor who does the coathook gag?"

"Yeah. Grandma and Dr. Harper worked on other books together. They were good friends, I think—um, without all the fighting and never speaking to each other again part."

Indri scratched her chin, leaving a blotch of red pastel dead center. "Do you think the numbers are important?"

"I don't know what's important and what isn't," I admitted as I laid page five down on the stack and spread my fingers to hold it in place. My insides sank as I realized Grandma might have already been turning into a ghost when she did this. The numbers might be some big deal, or she might have been distracted by me talking about my math homework the night she was making her notes. Who knew?

"She might not have gotten to the end of this," I admitted. "And I know we just agreed to follow her rules, but . . ."

"Nobody made any promises," Indri said with something like confidence. "Well, just an implied promise, maybe."

I moved my hand, then carefully shifted the papers that we had read through to the bottom of the stack. More time line appeared, a lot of stuff about civil rights in Mississippi. We looked at the next page, and the next.

"More time line," Indri murmured.

Another page. And another. Time line. Dates. Who got lynched and when and where and what was known about why. Who was shot and killed for their work for civil rights. When major events happened. Some years in the 1960s took ten or twelve pages to list everything important. But nowhere in there did we find one bit of information about what Grandma and Avadelle fought about.

Around 1968, we ran into trouble.

"What does, 'Putting the garfle in the window' mean?" Indri pointed at the strange sentence mixed into Grandma's typing between "April 4, 1968: Martin Luther King, Jr. assassinated in Memphis," and "Approximately 1,500 people marched in Hattiesburg four days after his death."

"I have no idea," I said. The next line read, "April 11, 1968: President June signs Civil Rights Act of 1968."

Indri and I looked at each other. *President June* should have been *President Johnson*. Grandma never would have made such a mistake. Her writing got worse and worse after that. More and more words were wrong, or spelled incorrectly. She crossed through a lot of things and tried to add notes, but those trailed off too. Sometimes, she just wrote, "I love you, my little Oops." Other times, sentences seemed like total gibberish.

"This doesn't make any sense now," I said. "She must have gotten too sick too fast to finish."

"I can't believe it." Indri banged her hand on the picnic table.

I flipped back and forth through the pages of Grandma's

writing, sadness expanding in my chest, heavy and bitter. I went all the way to the last pages, still just hoping—but there was nothing besides a star on September 1, 1969, which, according to the time line entry, was the day Avadelle Richardson's *Night on Fire* was released. After that, nothing but a blank page with some pen marks.

"There's nothing else here," I said.

Indri stared at the oak leaves above us as I neatened the stack of papers and put them away.

"So much for understanding the feud," she said. "I'm sorry, Dani. I know you really thought she was going to tell us. So did I."

"I'm not giving up," I told her, even though that's exactly what I felt like doing. "There's still the key. It has to unlock something important."

"Or something lost, or a safe full of confused writing—who knows?" Indri sighed. She didn't have to tell me Grandma wasn't right when she hid the key for me, that the key might be completely meaningless.

I spread my fingers out on the stack of papers, and—

A cane smacked down next to my hand, barely missing my thumb.

I jumped so hard I let out a squeak. Indri jumped too, knocking her pastels every which direction.

"What are you doing with those papers?" asked a gravelly, angry voice. "That's your grandmother's writing, isn't it? It's not yours."

I barely had time to process the hornet-colored shirt and fedora before Avadelle Richardson made a grab for Grandma's writing.

Panic helped me swipe the papers sideways out of her reach. Blood pumping so hard I could barely think, I yelled, "It's not yours, either!"

Then, everything seemed to slow down like in the movies. Each beat of my heart echoed in my ears as I became aware of Mac standing beside the table, looking totally unhappy. He shoved a shock of brown hair out of his eyes and tried to get hold of his grandmother's elbow.

"You got no business in Ruth's private papers," Avadelle barked at me. "She's not dead yet, is she?"

"No." I held the papers to my chest and glared at the elderly writer.

"Come on, GG," Mac said. "We should go." He made another grab for her elbow, but she jerked away from him.

GG, his baby name for his grandmother. I remembered that from when Mac sat with me after he played the national anthem at a school football game, picking at the calluses his guitar strings made on the ends of his fingers and explaining why he couldn't go with my parents and me for pizza afterward. *It's my turn to help look after GG. She doesn't get around so well anymore.*

Yeah, and she kept almost getting arrested and sued because she was such an evil old bat. Worm Dung wasn't just making sure Avadelle didn't fall down and go boom. He was doing his shift to keep the world-famous novelist out of the county jail.

I kind of hoped his grandmother would hit him with her eagle-head cane. The wings would make a heck of a mark.

Before Avadelle could grab for Grandma's papers again, I slid them into their envelope and tucked it into my backpack.

"That's right," the old writer grumbled, her blue eyes round and half-wild. "You put those up, and you let them be." Her breath came short, and her face turned red as a summer sunset.

"GG," Mac said again, and this time she let him take hold of her arm. "Why don't we—"

"I can take care of myself, thanks," I snapped at Mac. He actually flinched at my tone, and for three seconds, I felt like a lioness. Roaring wasn't totally out of the question.

"If she was working on a manuscript," Avadelle said to me, "somebody with some real brains might be able to finish it later, if you don't go mucking it all up." The oaks behind her made her look tiny, and a leaf drifted lazily to her shoulder. She didn't brush it off. Squirrels, oblivious to the danger she posed, darted around five or six feet away, jaws jammed with acorns and bits of people's sandwiches.

Then, from out of nowhere, Avadelle asked, "Is Ruth—is she still . . . talking?"

The wildness in the old writer's gaze dimmed to something like sadness, only sharper. Her expression caught me by surprise so badly that I answered her.

"Sometimes."

My attention shifted to Mac, but I jumped off him in a hurry and looked at Indri. She had frozen in place like a Grove statue, color-stained hands poised in midair, lemur eyes and mouth formed into O shapes.

Avadelle breathed in, then breathed out. "When Ruth says things, is she out of her head?"

I dared to look her straight in the face. "Most of the time."

The pain in Avadelle's expression deepened. "That's an evil disease she has, stealing the brain. Taking away the best of who a body's been, and who they might be."

Before I could agree with her, she pointed a knobby, time-blotched finger right into my face. "If she says anything outlandish, you don't pay it any mind, and you don't repeat it. She has a right to her dignity."

"Look," I started, but Indri kicked my ankle so hard under the table all I could do was bark, "Ow!"

A few tables and trees away, I saw Ms. Yarbrough's head snap up. She stood and stared in our direction. I couldn't be sure, but she might have looked a tad horrified as she started toward us.

"GG." Mac dug his feet into the grass and pulled at his grandmother's arm, forcing her toward him. "Your favorite table's free. Come on now. We need to go."

Ms. Yarbrough was one hundred yards away and closing fast. Her eyes fixed on Avadelle, and something in her expression reminded me of Indri's evil pastel horse.

Avadelle gave me one last angry glare, her cloudy eyes

shifting between my face and my backpack, then let Mac pull her away. I watched him try to act tough with her, but I could tell he was being gentle. I would have thought that was nice, if I didn't totally hate his stupid guts.

"Okay, that was weird," Indri murmured.

I couldn't quit watching Avadelle, which of course meant I was watching Mac, too. I really needed to grab a squirrel and let it bite me to bring me back to sanity. "Yeah. Completely."

Time to get my thoughts off Mac. The jerk. Worm Dung. Way past time. "So, since Grandma didn't finish what she wanted to tell me, we'll have to figure it out ourselves."

"I'm in," Indri said. "Where do we start?"

"With my parents, I guess. And maybe with Professor Harper, since Grandma wrote his name down on the pages?"

"Isn't he in Ventress Hall?" Indri asked.

"Yeah."

"Isn't that the most haunted building on campus?"

"Supposedly."

Indri gave me a wicked smile as Ms. Yarbrough reached us.

"I'm in double now," Indri whispered. "I'll get a note from my mom."

1

ALMOST TRUTH COULD BE ALMOST GOOD ENOUGH

———

**Excerpt from *Night on Fire* (1969),
by Avadelle Richardson, page 191**

"This place is so small!" Leslie covered her mouth after she spoke. She did that a lot, blabber, then try to stuff the words back down her throat. Thing is, she tended to tell the truth, and the truth didn't need silencing.

I glanced around my classroom, at the old maps and stacks of worn-out books. "You should see it when there's thirty kids here. It'll be crowded enough with ten or twelve grown people in a few minutes."

She picked up one of the English textbooks, and it came apart in her hands, cover and pages alike. She looked sad, then guilty, then angry. "These should be replaced. But . . . there's no funding, right?"

"There's a professor at Ole Miss, Jim Devon. He gets books for me, new as he can."

She got quiet for a few seconds, then popped out with, "CiCi, how can separate ever be equal? How can anyone become who they were meant to be when they get treated as less than human?"

"People believe in the way things have always been." I shrugged, wondering why I was spending all my time with this girl younger than me, who still didn't have much of a clue about how the world worked itself in Mississippi, even after a whole year of trying to learn. "That's why speaking out and registering folks to vote is so dangerous."

Her eyes met mine, and I knew she was imagining my students sitting shoulder to shoulder in the tiny room, sweating in the swelter, trying to turn pages without books falling to pieces, doing their best to learn despite a world arranged against them. Something flashed across her face, something solid and strong and full of purpose, that made me know why, of all the students showing up in the South to "help," I didn't mind looking after Leslie Marks.

TELLING THE WHOLE TRUTH IS one of those things everybody talks about like it's always the right thing to do, even if it's not easy. But I was starting to think that was stupid.

Watching life leave a person you love, a minute at a time, an hour at a time, a day and a week at a time, can change how you see everything, even what's "right" and what's "wrong" and what's "truth" and what's "fiction." Maybe absolute whole truth wasn't always the right way to go. Maybe almost truth could be almost good enough.

Mom and Dad and I moved quietly around Grandma's room, arranging dinner plates on the blue card table Dad had folded out for us. Sunlight still coated the cream-colored walls, and the ceiling fan turned lazily on low, its big blades stirring the air just enough to keep the room from being stuffy.

Natural light seemed better for keeping Grandma easy, and a little bit of sound. Mom's iPad was on the farthest counter, playing a Grandma mix of Amos Lee, Norah Jones, Dionne Farris, and Jazmine Sullivan. Grandma had worked with Dad right up until last year, collecting music she loved and sorting it into playlists she'd enjoy "later," as in, when her mind and hands wouldn't let her handle tablets and song lists anymore.

As in, now.

My place was closest to Grandma tonight, and I had already done my usual checks. Her pulse was still seventy-five. The tall stool helped me reach her bed, and I put her plate next to mine. Mom had puréed up her pork chops and potatoes and green beans, and we had applesauce too. Four colored pools of food. It didn't look great, but I had tasted the puréed stuff before. It was different, but decent. Kinda like a food milkshake.

Grandma loved applesauce, so after we sat down, I leaned

over to where Grandma lay in the hospital bed. The head had been raised, but her eyes were closed tight. I could tell from the way she was breathing that she was far, far away in her mind, so I rubbed my fingers against her cheek like the nurses had taught me to do.

"Got some applesauce for you," I said.

Nothing happened, but the muscles in her face tightened, like she might be thinking about it.

"Applesauce," I told her again. "Yum. It's got some cinnamon."

Her lips pursed.

I slipped the spoon into her applesauce, and brought the tip to her lips.

"Way to go," I whispered when she ate it, then turned back to Mom and Dad. I put Grandma's spoon down, picked up my fork, and ate a little of my own dinner. Mom had cooked the pork chops with lemon pepper, and I liked the way the spice stung my tongue.

Mom was trying to get Dad to talk about his day, but I could tell right away he wasn't listening. He studied me, then Grandma, then back to me again. "She take it?"

My mouth was full, so I nodded.

In the background, Amos Lee sang about "Keep It Loose, Keep It Tight." That's what we were supposed to do, have as normal a family meal as we could, letting Grandma participate any way she could. The hospice people told us it was the best gift we could give Grandma, and ourselves. It made sense, I guess, but it wasn't always easy to do, especially for Dad.

"Feed her another bite, Dani," he urged.

Mom patted his hand. "She will. Just give her time. We don't have mess schedule and lights-out in civilian life, remember?"

Dad frowned. "Mama doesn't eat enough to feed a bird. She's got to be starving."

Mom patted his hand again, but she didn't say anything. To make him happy, I fed Grandma a few bites in a row, pork chop milkshake, then potato milkshake, then green bean milkshake. After that, another applesauce. When I finished, I dabbed her mouth with an aloe wipe, and turned back to the table to eat.

Dad stared at his food. Mom stared at Dad and looked worried. I wanted to let out a great big sigh, but I didn't. That wouldn't help anything. Dad didn't want Grandma to go. I understood that. I didn't either. Not really. But she was so sick now, and so far gone from the person she used to be, she really was like a ghost. Thinking that—and sometimes thinking that it would be better if she did go ahead and pass away—made me feel really, really guilty.

"Ms. Manchester told us a great ghost story today," I related to Grandma when I fed her another bite of applesauce.

"It was about the cemetery at Ole Miss," I said.

"Ghost stories," Dad grumbled from behind me. "You going to have nightmares tonight?"

He couldn't see my face, so I rolled my eyes. "No, Dad.

I'm not five anymore. Jeez. Do I ever get to live that down?"

Mom laughed. "No, you do not. We had to keep the lights on in the house—*every single light*—for a week after you and Indri stayed up and watched those horror movies."

I gave Grandma some pork chop. "Those were gross. Stalk-and-slash stuff. Today, it was just a spooky story with a lot of history. We heard a few more too, about Saint Anthony Hall and somebody screaming in the steam tunnels around the Lyceum."

"Oxford's history isn't all sweetness and light," Dad said. "The city—the whole state—it's come a long way. Maybe it's time people let go of all that mess from the past and just moved on."

Grandma got green bean milkshake, and more apple-sauce, then I turned to eat some more of my food as Mom said, "There's room for both remembering and forgetting, I think. Moving on can happen even when folks remember everything clearly. Speaking of which," she fixed her eyes on mine, "did you see Mac Richardson today?"

The mouthful of pork chop I was swallowing stuck in my throat, and I coughed and spluttered. My face flushed, and I had to take a big drink of lemonade to get everything down. By the time I finished, both of my parents were giving me that oh-no-you-didn't face.

I wheezed a couple of times, then got myself together enough to say, "Could we not talk about Worm Dung at dinner, please? I don't want anything to do with him."

From the expressions on my parents' faces, neither one of them believed me.

"He's under a lot of pressure," Mom said, "having to help look after Avadelle. Hard as our situation might be, at least Ruth isn't screaming at preachers and being hostile to half the town."

"I don't feel sorry for Mac," I said, even though I sort of did. A little bit. It was so completely time to change the subject. "Dad, did Grandma say anything else this morning, when she was upset?"

He paused, a hunk of pork chop right in front of his mouth. "Not really. She settled down pretty fast after you left."

I turned enough to run my fingers along Grandma's white sheets. Her eyes were closed, but I didn't think she was sleeping. "Do you think she was talking about the answers to her fight with Avadelle?"

"Where on earth would you get that idea?" Dad shook his head. "She said 'Oops' a few times today though, almost."

Mom squeezed her eyes shut. "I vote we move on from *that* piece of Dani's past. I hate that nickname."

I held back a laugh and tried to keep a serious face on for Mom as I said, "It doesn't bother me. I always thought it was funny."

"You were not an oops-baby," Mom said. "We wanted you more than anything."

Dad grinned. "We had just given up on getting you, so you were a great big, wonderful surprise."

"Six pounds, two ounces at birth. I wasn't that big." I shifted my attention back to Grandma, thinking about her gibberish pages. If I didn't ask my parents what they knew about that time in Grandma's life, I'd be completely stuck.

"Do you think Grandma ever wrote something about her fight with Avadelle, and the Magnolia Feud? Maybe something that would explain what could have been so bad that they just stopped being friends? I mean, she might have done that and hidden it somewhere."

Dad clinked his silverware on his plate as he put it down. "Pretty sure she didn't. And it wouldn't be a good idea to stir up that mess again. Mama's taking her piece of it to the grave, and based on how many reporters Avadelle's cussed over asking, she's never going to discuss it either. If they don't want to share their troubles with the world, that's their business."

I put my hand on Grandma's bony, warm shoulder. "Maybe. But what if that's what's upsetting Grandma now? What if she needs to work out her fight with Avadelle before she dies?"

"I can't imagine Avadelle wanting to see Ruth like this," Mom said. "And Ruth sure wouldn't want Avadelle around her when she can't defend herself."

Norah Jones started singing "Come Away with Me." I picked up Grandma's spoon and got her a bite of pork chop. When I touched her cheek, her eyes opened and fixed on a spot on the ceiling. Tears slid slowly down her gaunt face, and her lips moved like she was talking to somebody I couldn't see.

"Grandma, don't cry." I moved the bite so I could lean down and kiss her forehead.

My kiss made her weep harder, and she lifted her hand and pressed it into my hair. "Ewww," she whispered, pushing my head against her face until my neck cramped. "Ewww. Ewwww."

I tried to pull away, but she wouldn't let me go. I didn't want to yank free because I was scared I'd hurt her, so I just said, "Dad, a little help here?"

His chair slid against the wood floor as he got up, and I listened as he walked to the other side of the bed.

"Mama." He slowly worked her hand free from my hair. "Take it easy on the kid. We don't want to pull her head off, even if she does fraternize with nasty slugs like Mac Richardson."

"I don't fraternize with Mac anymore," I protested, my words muffled by Grandma's face.

By the time Dad got me free, Grandma had stopped crying and gone back to staring.

"What do you think that was about?" Mom asked as I sat down.

"Have to admit, she seems unsettled any time Avadelle comes up." Dad went back to his chair and settled in to eat again. "Maybe we shouldn't talk about the Richardsons around her anymore."

"Or maybe we should figure out what happened," I said. "So Grandma can resolve it and make peace, like the nurses told us to help her do."

I got up again, but this time, I went to my room and pulled page five out of my backpack. Then I carried it back to Grandma's room and I laid it on the table, right in the middle, where it didn't touch any of our plates. My parents gazed at the page for a time. Then they looked at me.

In the end, it was Dad who asked, "What's this?"

I gestured to the desk behind him, and told my almost-truth. "It's something Grandma wrote. I found it, and I'd like to figure out what some of it means. I think it has something to do with this whole Avadelle thing."

Dad gave me a yeah-right look. "You think this time line is related to Avadelle?"

"Avadelle tried to take it away from me today," I said. "In the Grove. It bothered her that I had something Grandma wrote, just like any mention of Avadelle seems to be bugging Grandma."

Mom's eyebrows lifted.

"It was no big deal, Mom. She said I had no business reading it, or listening to anything Grandma says if she's talking out of her head."

Dad frowned at the paper. "I want to agree with Avadelle that it's none of your business," he said. "Not because Mama would mind you messing around with her work, but because the history Mama liked to look into—" He shook his head. "Dani, there's a lot of ugliness in old Oxford, in the old South, that you haven't had to deal with up close. The hornet's nests Mama liked to poke could really sting you."

99

I frowned at him. "The past can't hurt me like things in the present."

"I wish that were true," Mom said. "You weren't born until after the worst of it, thank God. What happened in Mississippi back then, so much of it was senseless and violent."

"I've had Mississippi history, and American history." I put my hand on page five. "Both of you have talked to me my whole life, and Grandma told me a lot of stuff too. I know about civil rights."

Dad stared at me, right into my eyes, with a funny look on his face. He took a breath like he might be counting to ten so he wouldn't say something sharp. Mom put her hand on his, and that seemed to help enough for him to come out with, "You *think* you know about civil rights."

"Dani, we talk about police brutality and news stories about racism nearly every day, even though we live next to a university full of educated folks." Mom moved her hand away from Dad, this time covering my knuckles. "Remember when that kid in kindergarten asked you if you were adopted because your skin didn't match your father's or mine?"

My eyebrows automatically pulled together because thinking about that always ticked me off. "Yes, ma'am. I got grounded for a week because I kicked him."

"Exactly. Yes. And your father and I, we chose your schools and activities very carefully after that, so you wouldn't have to put up with as many painful questions and bad attitudes just because your parents aren't the same color. We rarely go into Southern rural areas at all, for the same reason. Times are different, yes, but there are still a *lot* of problems."

I didn't know what to say to that, so I just looked at her. Bigotry and racism and discrimination stayed all over the news, but in my school, there were lots of kids and teachers like me and Indri, and lots of different skin tones. Nobody talked about race very much, and nothing really bad had happened to me, so I didn't think about it that often.

"I hope you never experience the terrible things your grandmother lived through, and your Dad," Mom said.

I heard the concern in her voice. I almost told her not to worry, but something stopped me. I mean, it could happen. I didn't want to think that it would, but—maybe?

Stomach churning a little, I pointed to the *Fred* note, and all the numbers. "Indri and I want to go see Dr. Harper tomorrow and see if he knows what these numbers mean."

"Fred," Grandma echoed.

We all looked at her, and she was weeping again.

"Enough," Dad told me in a tone that meant absolutely, positively no arguing. Then he went back to eating, and he didn't look at me, or at Grandma either.

I did what I could to distract Grandma with applesauce, and waited for my parents to tell me not to go see Professor Harper.

But they didn't.

They just stopped talking about the paper I showed them,

and discrimination, and civil rights, and Avadelle. They stopped talking to each other, and stopped talking to me, too.

We ate the rest of dinner with just the music in the background, and the pitiful sound of Grandma crying beside us.

8

WARS SHOULD NEVER BE SANITIZED

Excerpt from *Night on Fire* (1969),
by Avadelle Richardson, page 238

Aunt Jessie sat in the front of the little schoolhouse night class as I held up a battered civics book.

"Any of you remember reading something like this in school?"

Leslie raised her hand, then put it back down in a hurry. Red colored the edges of her cheeks as her eyes darted around the eleven other folks stacked into the kids' desks. I was teaching in dim light, so nobody could tell we were here, if they looked from outside.

One of the men raised his hand. "That looks like higher grades. Most of us was done by fourth, fifth at the latest."

I nodded. "It's around sixth grade, maybe seventh, but even if you went that far in Oxford, you wouldn't have it. In the South, we aren't allowed to teach from books that show the United States Constitution, or the Declaration of Independence, or the Bill of Rights."

This made Leslie shift in her chair, wide-eyed.

"Well, of course not." Aunt Jessie snorted. "If you read them things, you'll know that government is supposed to be by the people and for the people. All the people. You'll know your rights, and how they being stepped on down here."

After that, Leslie came to my illegal classes every Tuesday night. "'We must be free not because we claim freedom, but because we practice it,'" she told me, quoting William Faulkner from an article we read, in Harper's Magazine four years ago.

Slowly, we worked on teaching a handful of brave folks who wanted to know more about reading and writing and math and civics, men and women who wanted to understand the founding documents of our country, and how they applied to us as Black people— and how they didn't, at least in the South.

LAST NIGHT, WHEN I WAS feeding Grandma, I got some green bean milkshake and applesauce milkshake smeared on my shirt. When I took it off, I saw the greenish stain and I treated it just like Mom taught me—stain remover, a little water, and letting it sit.

But when I got up this Tuesday morning, it still wouldn't

rub out. It's like the color dyed the fabric of my shirt—just changed it forever, so it can't be the shirt it used to be, and I can't wear it in public anymore.

It made me wonder if ghosts and ghost stories were like stains on a shirt that just won't come out. Or maybe some things, like wars and hate and discrimination and violence, those things that Indri said were too huge and awful to fix by just saying "I'm sorry," stain time so nothing can ever be the same again. Did something like that stain the friendship between Grandma and Avadelle, like Mac had stained ours by telling me he couldn't talk to me anymore? Was there any way I could rinse everything out enough to clean it up for both of them? Could I even convince Dad and Mom that I should be allowed to try?

Still way early in the morning, I sat on a bench in our backyard and watched Dad pull weeds out of raised beds full of squash plants and green tomatoes. His hair and beard glistened in the new sunlight, and he was wearing frayed jeans shorts and a white tank, both already soaked with sweat. He stayed bent over, plucking out little green bits and dropping them into a pile near the wooden slats that held the dirt and plants.

I didn't know anything about gardening. Dirt sort of grossed me out. But I liked eating what Dad grew, and I liked watching him be happy. Dad liked that he didn't have to take as much medicine during gardening season, because his nerves got calmer when he could work outside. From March to October, all he had to take was blood pressure pills, and his time in the garden did the rest.

I had gotten ready for camp early, before the nurse came. Mom might actually blow a gasket in shock over my promptness. Before I went outside, I checked on Grandma like I always did. She was sleeping peacefully, and not crying, but I couldn't forget the sound of her weeping the night before. My throat tightened every time I thought about it, so I used Dad's iPad to play him music to weed by while I read a book I had checked out from camp—*Ghost Stories of Oxford*. As Julie Miller's "All My Tears" played in the early light, I read about people thinking they had seen the ghost of a woman at William Faulkner's home, Rowan Oak. A few minutes later, Dad got my attention when he stood and used a blue bandana to wipe the sweat off his forehead. Then he nodded to me. "Tough song."

I closed my ghost story book and focused on the lyrics. *It don't matter where you bury me/I'll be home and I'll be free.*

"Oh," I mumbled. "Sorry." I tapped the pause button. "I'll find something lighter."

"No, it's fine." He wiped both his cheeks, then folded the bandana and tied it back around his head. He had his beard pulled into a rough braid this morning, and he tugged on it as he looked at me. "That's exactly what your grandmother believes. You like this version better, or Emmylou Harris?"

I put down my book and picked up his iPad, scrolled through the song list, found the second version, and played it for a minute or so. "I don't know. They're both good. Do you think Grandma's right? Does all pain end when you die?"

"I hope so, baby girl." Dad came over to the garden bench and sat beside me. He smelled like dirt and salt and wild onions and spices from the oil he used on his hair and beard. He kept his eyes on the beds he had been weeding, but he scooted closer, then folded his hands and squeezed them between his knees like he did when something was really bugging him. "I'm sorry I was short with you last night."

"It's okay—" I started, but he cut me off.

"No, it's not." He patted my leg, then went back to squeezing his hands between his own knees and staring out at the garden. "I want you to understand something. Before your mom and I ever got married, we thought about what our children might go through, on account of us being different races. It never occurred to us we'd end up back here in Oxford. In Mississippi, of all places. But Mama started getting older, and—" He sighed. "Man plans, God laughs, you know?"

I'd heard him say that before, and I knew what he meant. "Oxford's great, Dad. I love it here."

Dad smiled, but he looked skeptical. "I never wanted you to have a rough time of it. Not over me, and the color of my skin—or yours."

I touched my skin, which seemed so light compared to his. "Maybe people just think I'm really tan?"

"Don't joke."

"Okay, sorry. But I haven't had a rough time."

"Then your mother and I, we've done some right things." He stared off into the sky. "What to tell the babies," he murmured. "That's always been a question. When to start. How to warn them. How to make them see."

I frowned at him. "I'm not a baby, Dad." His eyes met mine, and his smile seemed sad.

"My baby," he argued. Dad seemed relieved by this. "I still don't think it's a great idea to go poking around about the Magnolia Feud or Oxford's past, but after watching Mama cry—Dani, maybe you're right and we should try to ease her mind. Maybe your mom is right too. You won't be finding out anything that didn't already happen."

I laid Dad's iPad on top of my book, on the bench between us, and I must have bumped the play button because "All My Tears" started back again, with Emmylou Harris singing. I slid the volume down but left it playing. "You and Mom and Grandma taught me a lot. We really have studied the Civil Rights Movement in class, too. I know it was bad, especially in Mississippi. I know it's happening now, too, with so many people getting shot, and how more people of color go to jail. That's in the news and books too."

Dad kept his hands between his knees, and his jaw looked tight. Finally, he nodded, but he said, "What they write in books can sound clean. Wars should never be sanitized like that."

I thought about that for a few song verses, and my brain hooked it up with the hospice pamphlets and other stuff I'd read about Alzheimer's disease. "So, it's like what people write about dying from what Grandma has? Facts and how-to, but nothing about changing diapers and how stuff stinks—or the drool and how tired everyone gets?"

"Exactly." Dad nodded. "Once the people who yell the loudest and write the most have a chance to clean up history's rough edges, it can look like revolutions happen without horrible hardships and losses. Then it gets easy to lie to ourselves that the same disasters can't happen again."

At that moment, Dad looked almost as far away as Grandma did. My pulse picked up, and the air seemed too hot to breathe. I eased my hand over to his, worrying he'd jump when I touched him. He did that sometimes, if he was thinking too hard about wars and bombs and people he knew getting killed. When my fingers brushed across his, he didn't flinch, and all of a sudden, I could breathe again.

"Mostly, they leave out how much death hurts," he said. When he looked at me, his eyes were wet like he might cry. He tried to smile but didn't make it, then shook his head. "And not just the dying part. Sorry, Dani. It just tears me up to see Mama like she is now."

"I know."

He kissed my forehead, giving me a fresh nose-full of wild onions and garden sweat and spiced oil. For a few seconds, I sat there feeling like I had no ghost stories at all, and like maybe Mom's proverb was wrong, and everything really was everyone's circus, and all monkeys belonged to all people.

"You and Indri don't give Dr. Harper too much grief, you

hear?" Dad interrupted my thoughts. "He's old to be keeping summer hours on top of working till midnight all the time, and he might wear out pretty easily."

"We won't wear him out."

"I mean it. Respect his time."

"I know, Dad."

He messed with my hair a little bit, then gave me a push off the bench. "Go on now. Don't make your mom jumpy this morning."

I slid my book from under Dad's iPad, then picked up the backpack holding Grandma's papers and the key and walked away from the garden, leaving Dad to his plants. I heard the iPad music switch to "Whatcha Wanna Do" by Mia X, the first song in Grandma's attitude mix. I had to smile. That was Dad, trying to change his mindset.

Go, Dad.

Feeling a little better, I went to Mom's car and climbed into the passenger seat, leaving the door open for air.

I read my ghost story book for a while, skipping over the stadium cemetery and Saint Anthony Hall tales I had already heard at camp. Instead, I studied the story from the 1960s, about screams coming from the steam tunnels under Ole Miss. There wasn't much information about it. Just a bunch of people swearing they heard screaming and yelling late at night near the Lyceum, when they were crossing campus alone. If what we learned at camp about why people told ghost stories was true, the steam-tunnel-screaming-and-yelling tale probably had to do with scaring people into acting right. *Don't walk across the campus alone at night*. That made sense.

I put down my book, fastened my seat belt, and closed my eyes, listening to birds and traffic through the open car door.

My grandmother's secrets, they were like a ghost story. Like she was haunted by some ghost or other that only she could see. But she wouldn't feel all haunted just for entertainment, and she was too smart to be haunted by something she didn't understand. She mostly acted right, and didn't tend to try to scare people into doing things her way, and I didn't think she was scared of dying, either. That left something that should be remembered—only, she couldn't remember much of anything now. That had to be it. She needed to remember something, maybe say it, or take care of it.

"Jerk alert!" screamed the phone in my pocket. "Jerk alert! Jerk alert!"

My heart whammed as I jumped and grabbed at my pocket, nearly choking myself on the shoulder strap.

What—? I—no way. I managed to get free from the seat-belt strap and get the phone out of my pocket, because Mac Richardson, Mr. Worm Dung himself, just sent me a message.

I fumbled with my code, finally got the stupid thing unlocked, and read, @ campus with GG 2day. If U see us don't show papers.

Breathe. Air. Must have air.

The phone shook in my hands as I forwarded the message to Indri.

She popped back immediately with, **No way!!!!!!!!!!!** setting off her alert of, "Best friend texting!" Then, **Don't answer WORM DUNG.**

She was right. I shouldn't answer Mac. Or at least I shouldn't answer him right away, right?

Leave me alone, I sent back. Then I put the phone down and glanced at the front door. No sign of Mom. She still had five minutes before we would have to hurry. My eyes went back to the phone. The jumble of emotions in my chest turned circles and bashed into each other until they finally settled on pissed off and . . . of all things, curious.

Crud.

The papers. He didn't want Avadelle to see Grandma's writing again.

"Best friend texting!" **R U talking to WORM DUNG?**

No, I typed to Indri on reflex, then sent a quick **Yes** to make up for it.

"Jerk alert! Jerk alert!" **Just keep papers to yourself.**

"Best friend texting!" **STOP TALKING TO WORM DUNG!!!!!!**

"Jerk alert! Jerk alert!" **Please.**

Wow. Mac wasn't usually one for politeness or extra words. *Please* was a real stretch for him. I almost got a case of the warm-fuzzies . . . but then I glared down at the phone. First he blew me off, then he treated me like I was weak and stupid and couldn't look after myself against a crazy old woman, and now he wanted to tell me what to do?

Blocking your number, I wrote back to him. Then I did it. And a minute later, I unblocked him. Block, unblock. Block, unblock.

I totally needed to beat my head against a great big tree. *Blocked. There. Leave it.*

Mom came out the front door almost at a dead run, and I put the phone on mute and stuck it in my pocket. Too many text alerts got on Mom's nerves in the best of circumstances, much less early in the morning before her third cup of coffee. Plus, if she found out I was just texting Mac, she'd be way less than happy.

"You ready?" she asked as she got in and fastened her seat belt. She reached over and handed me a signed note, giving me permission to go see Dr. Harper during lunch break at camp.

"Sure thing." I took the note and tucked it in my pack, closed my door, and tried to ignore the phone vibrating between my butt and the car seat.

9

HISTORY IS CREEPY

———

**Excerpt from *Night on Fire* (1969),
by Avadelle Richardson, page 299**

*By the time 1960 turned into 1961, Leslie and I
worked like a machine with our teaching, but I could
tell she was frustrated.*

*"Not even seven percent." She tossed the lat-
est figures on my school desk. "That's not even one
out of ten registered to vote in Mississippi, Cici. In
some counties, it's nobody, not even the war veterans.
They're beating any person of color who tries to reg-
ister, much less vote. If they can't vote, they can't elect
anyone who might change the situation."*

*I slid the latest literacy test and poll tax documents
toward her. "These are getting harder. More subjec-
tive. The registrars and clerks are failing preachers
and professors, and letting through illiterate Whites*

with no challenge at all. We don't have a good strategy yet, and we need more help. We need a plan."

Leslie rubbed the sides of her head. "And we need to get more men in our class, and— What?"

She caught the look on my face before I could wipe it clean. Her eyes narrowed, and all of her features went sharp. "What do you know that I don't?"

We'd had these fights before, and I always lost, a testament to the fact that Leslie was really the one who could argue with a fence post and win. I started off slow. "Most of the menfolk here, they're sick or dead since we don't have doctors and hospitals who'll see us close to where we live—or they've joined up with the service for a ticket out of the South, or they're working two or three jobs to feed their families. They can't risk stirring up trouble."

"Or getting beaten or murdered," she said, and sighed, and I thought maybe, just maybe I was gonna get by with it, but then she went all narrow and sharp again and said, "And what else?"

It was my turn to sigh. And then be honest. "Some of them, they're scared to risk being around you."

And I waited, and I watched it sink in.

"Because I'm White," she said.

"Because you're a White woman," I corrected, and I wondered what she heard in those words. My soul heard the sobs of Emmett Till and the shouts and

screams of so, so many others, boys and men, slaugh-
tered for smiling or speaking to or even being near a
White woman like Leslie Marks.

"*Jim Crow,*" *she said, like she was talking to God*
instead of me, and that was good, because I couldn't
do a thing about it, more than I was already doing.

INDRI EYED ME WITH SUSPICION the second I sat down
beside her in the Bondurant camp classroom, and she stuck
out her hand. "Give me your phone."

I forked it over immediately. She knew my passcode, so I
didn't even have to tell her.

Her expression stayed tense as she examined my text
exchange with Mac. After a few seconds, I realized I was
holding my breath, and let it out.

"Fine," she mumbled. "You really did block him. I guess I
won't have to scream at you for interacting with Worm Dung
anymore."

"Um, okay." I smiled at her. "Thanks. Sort of."

She rolled her eyes, and Ms. Yarbrough cut us off as she
breezed by, handing out construction paper and glue.

When she passed the phone back to me, I unblocked Mac.
You know. Just in case.

We had lunch in the Grove, and Ms. Yarbrough let Indri and
me finish our food quickly and head over to Ventress Hall. Mom
had called ahead to Dr. Harper and made an appointment

before she wrote out my permission note to visit him.

We trooped down the sidewalk toward University Avenue without talking much, me toting my backpack with Grandma's envelope and Indri hauling her giant pink purse with all of her art supplies. She had her hair pulled back, and her dark ponytail looked almost blue in the hot sunlight as we broke from the tree cover and turned right, onto the main sidewalk. She was happy today, judging by her pink sun pants and flowered shirt, and she kept smiling as we got closer to the old building. Across the street, six or seven art students sat with sketchpads, and I knew they were trying to capture its angles and spires, and probably the way it looked almost like a church or a small castle.

"Think you could draw this building?" I asked Indri.

"I don't do very well with structures. Better with trees and flowers and nature stuff. But I bet all the ghosts in Ventress are in that turret." Indri pointed up and to the left as we got to the front door. "Where the graffiti is. Do you think Dr. Harper will let us up there?"

I shrugged. "The dean let me look, back before all the renovations. You can peek in the door any time, but you can't see much from the bottom. It's nothing special. Just a windy, twisty staircase with writing all over the walls."

"It's historical." Indri sounded incredulous. "A Civil War vet wrote on the walls—and students since 1911."

"It just looked like scribbled-on plaster and spiderwebs to me."

"You have no artistic sensibilities, Dani."

"I know."

We went inside, and the air-conditioning felt like diving into ice water. I shivered instantly as the door closed behind us. The building's entry hall looked so polished now, with its beige walls and white trim, and the paint still smelled new, even though it was a few years old. The whole building had to be remodeled when I was around nine or ten, after pipes exploded and flooded everything.

Dr. Harper had retired from the history department, and he worked for the College of Liberal Arts now, in student services. In addition to being notorious for his silly gags, everybody talked about how he worked twelve and sixteen hours a day like a new professor trying to get tenure, especially since his wife died. A sign told us his office was up the main staircase, so Indri and I followed the rust-colored carpet runner up the steps. She had to stop on the middle landing, where the stained glass window was, and stare at all the colors. I had seen it before, a lot of times, and it reminded me of being in church, with all the gold and blue glass.

"Hey," Indri said, grabbing hold of my arm. She pointed at the glass. "Those soldiers. I just realized—those are *the* soldiers, right? The ones from Ms. Manchester's ghost story."

I looked at the glass. The gray uniforms, the hats—it was the University Grays, the Ole Miss students who had all died or been wounded in the Civil War, during Pickett's Charge.

"Weird," I said. "I've looked at this glass so many times—why didn't I get that?"

A soldier seemed to stare down at me with wide eyes and round, smooth cheeks. He had a sword over his head that seemed to be made out of blue light, and at his feet, other soldiers lay wounded or dying. The whole scene made my stomach jittery, and I moved away from it, backing up the steps.

"It's amazing," Indri said, then realized I wasn't standing beside her anymore. She hurried up the stairs after me. "What's wrong?"

"Nothing. It's just seeing what they looked like, it's kind of eerie." I turned around, but I felt the dead soldier's glass eyes on my neck, and goose bumps rippled across my shoulders.

"Slow down, Dani," Indri said as we got to the top of the stairs. "It's just more history."

"History is creepy. That whole window—it's probably why this stupid building is haunted. The Grays fought for the Confederate side. The pro-slavery side. I feel like we should be ashamed instead of proud."

"They thought they were doing the right thing," Indri said.

"Well, they weren't." My heart kept beat-beat-beating too fast the whole time we stood there. It didn't help that Indri was giving me a you-big-dummy look. Whatever. I reserved the right to be squicked out by dead soldiers made out of painted glass, and worried about whether or not we should give them a memorial.

"Not that way," I told Indri as we left the stairs and she tried to turn through the first open door. "That goes to the tower." I pointed inside, to an open door behind a desk. A very busy-looking lady sat at the desk on her telephone, typing at the same time.

Indri stared at the tower entrance, and I could tell she wanted to go in really, really bad.

"The lady won't let you go past," I told her. "Sorry. Not unless the dean gives you permission."

"That sucks," she mumbled. "I should have gone up there a long time ago. And I *am* going up there, soon as I can convince my mom to get me the dean's okay."

"It's just scribbles on walls," I reminded her, and she groaned.

We moved down the longer hall and turned in to Dr. Harper's alcove. His office doors were open like he was waiting for us. A patterned rug covered the hardwood floor, and the walls were floor-to-ceiling bookcases, with huge windows in between them, and he had a big meeting table covered in books too.

Dr. Harper was sitting behind his big wooden desk in the middle of the room, bent over some papers. He had an unlit pipe in his teeth, a magnifying glass in one hand, and his shirt sleeves rolled up to his elbows. A pile of books blocked the right side of his desk, but on the left, he had a new tablet sitting up in a case. His famous tweed suit jacket hung on his wingback chair behind him. When he looked up at us, his thick, snow-colored hair stuck out on both sides of his head, and he took the pipe out of his teeth, dropped it on the desk, and broke into a huge smile.

"Girls! Hello!" He pushed back from his desk and jumped so fast Indri startled. He grabbed hold of his suit jacket and struggled into it as he hurried toward us, even though he left his shirt sleeves rolled up. I couldn't figure out what—oh. Oh, yeah.

"Just let me—here. Out here," Dr. Harper was saying.

I gave Indri an elbow, and she moved aside to let him out of the door, which he pulled closed behind him.

"Is he—" Indri started, making the crazy sign by her temple, but I put a finger to my lips, then pointed to the chalkboard beside the door.

Understanding dawned across Indri's face just as Dr. Harper opened the door and walked back in, looking much more organized with his jacket in place and his hair patted down. He beamed at us, his blue eyes warm and twinkly, then he went straight to the chalkboard.

Indri and I waited as he drew a coat hook on the board, and shaded it quickly with yellow, then white chalk. When he finished, he pulled off his tweed jacket and hung it on the chalk coat hook.

It fell straight to the floor.

Seeming delighted, Dr. Harper turned back to us. "Ladies, the day that coat hangs on that hook, I have to retire. Today is not that day!"

We both tried to look tickled, like we had no idea about his gag, even though it was a campus legend.

"Now then. Dani, your mother told me you had some papers for me to look at?" He motioned us to his meeting table, and pushed aside some book stacks to make room.

Indri and I sat down, and I pulled out Grandma's envelope and took out page five for him to read. "Grandma was working on something before she got so sick, and Indri and I have been trying to figure out what some of the notes mean. Your name is written on one of the pages, so we hoped you might be able to help us understand what she was trying to say."

"Really, now." He took page five from me and studied it. "Your grandmother is an astute scholar of history, young lady."

"Yes, sir." I kept a happy expression on my face even though I felt suddenly sad. Grandma wasn't able to be an astute scholar of anything anymore. Guilt prickled in my chest again. Why did I keep acting like she was already a ghost? Grandma wasn't dead.

"It's hard to believe that Ruth's memory has failed her." Dr. Harper put down the papers and made eye contact with me. "Is she up to writing much anymore?"

"No, sir. Not now. But she wrote those pages when her mind was still sharp."

"I see. Well, this time line makes perfect sense." He smiled. "Of course. She always wanted to do this."

"Do what?" Indri asked.

"Ruth thought the history of the Civil Rights Movement, particularly in Mississippi, had gotten too fragmented," Dr. Harper said. "People could read bits here and pieces there, but an organized time line, from start to finish—with *everything* on it, for depth and context—that's hard to come by. She was afraid too much was being lost, so she wanted to preserve the details."

I thought about this for a second, but I still wasn't sure why it mattered so much. "What about this?" I pointed at one of the phrases on page five. "Do you know what the Black Codes were?"

Dr. Harper eyed the passage and touched it with his fingertip. "The Black Codes were laws passed in the South, just after the Civil War, to keep Black citizens from exercising their newly won freedoms."

Indri leaned forward and propped her chin in her hands. "Like?"

"Well, Black people couldn't rent property except within city limits, and they had to be able to prove they had legal homes." Dr. Harper gestured to Grandma's papers. "Otherwise, they could be arrested and forced into low-wage labor agreements almost as bad as slavery. They couldn't quit jobs without arrest and heavy financial penalties. Basically, anything the community didn't like could be used to prove the person was a 'vagrant' under the Codes, and that person could be placed into forced labor as a punishment. The same thing happened to Black orphans and mixed-race children—"

He broke off, gazing at me, and his eyebrows lifted. "Oh—um, sorry, Dani. And Indri. I didn't mean to use a disrespectful term."

Indri grinned at him. "No big deal, Dr. Harper. I call myself blended—as in, perfectly blended."

"It didn't feel disrespectful," I told him.

He still looked uncomfortable. "Is there a preferred term these days?"

I had to think about that. My parents and I had talked about the issue, like Indri and her parents—her mom was from India and her dad was white like my mom. But really, like I told Dad, it just didn't come up. "Multiracial, I guess?"

"Multiracial." He sounded happier. "According the Black Codes, being multiracial was considered an abomination in the eyes of God and the law. If two people of different races tried to marry, they were arrested. The penalty carried a life sentence."

"So our parents would have been felons, just for getting married," Indri said.

Dr. Harper nodded. "They would have been put in prison, and very likely, both of you would have been considered Black, and subjected to the Codes. It was the *Loving vs. Virginia* Supreme Court decision in 1967 that finally put an end to the anti-miscegenation laws—the ones forbidding interracial marriage. Still, Mississippi didn't remove those statutes until the 1980s, and I believe Alabama was the last to erase theirs, in the year 2000."

parents got married before Mississippi even changed its laws." I felt sort of proud of them, and wondered what that was like. Then I wondered why they hadn't told me more about it.

I couldn't wrap my brain around that at all, so I went back to page five. My finger drifted along the page margin until I came to Grandma's math figures. "What about these numbers here?"

"Hmm." Dr. Harper tapped on the figures. Then his smile faded. "Oh. Yes. I think I do know what these numbers stand for."

Indri and I waited, but Dr. Harper didn't say anything. He glanced at Indri, then at me, and his cheeks colored at the top.

"What is it?" Indri asked.

My stomach got a little twitchy. Dr. Harper seemed to be debating something, until finally he closed his eyes and let out a breath.

"Just a moment," he said. "I'll show you."

10

WHEN EVERYTHING WAS STILL A STRAIGHT LINE

———

Excerpt from *Night on Fire* (1969),
by Avadelle Richardson, page 303

*Just when I thought Leslie understood how to behave
herself in the Magnolia State, Aunt Jessie and I made
the mistake of taking her by the Kream Kup on
University Avenue. We chose it because it was close
to Mt. Zion, and because vanilla ice cream just might
have been born inside that old A-frame drive-in.*

*It was gray outside, but not sprinkling yet, and
the air smelled like asphalt and rain. Leslie didn't put
up a fuss when we told her we'd need to park some-
place quiet and walk up separately, because White
and Black in the same car was near enough to cause
a street riot. Once we took to our feet, Aunt Jessie
and I led the way, with Aunt Jessie fanning herself
with a palm-frond fan she saved from Easter Sunday*

service. There were two lines at the A-frame, and we got into the long one on the right.

Leslie looked uncomfortable, but I didn't dare glance at her. With a sigh, she gave up and joined the Whites-Only line on the left side of the Kream Kup. Her line got served first, so Aunt Jessie and I were still five folks back when we heard Leslie order her banana split. She stood at the outside counter waiting for her dish, staring first into the left-hand half of the building with its shiny tile and shuddering window air conditioner and bright lights and White faces. Then she stared into the right-hand side, with its open windows, dim jungle prints, and Black faces. There was a jukebox on both sides, but only the Black side played any music folks could hear, because the windows stayed open to let in a breeze.

"Don't stare at the Colored people," said the woman in line behind Leslie, rattling the shoulder of a girl next to her who couldn't have been more than eight years old. "It isn't polite."

"Why can't we eat over there?" the child asked, pointing toward the open windows where the music played.

"Because," her mother said in a pretend-whisper, "those people are dirty, and they smell. If you lie down with dogs, you'll end up with fleas."

"Everything smells in this heat," Leslie said from

the service window, her back still to the woman and
child. "I know I do." She scratched at the back of her
neck. "Well, now. Is that a flea bite?"

DR. HARPER GOT UP AND retrieved his tablet from his desk, and brought it back to the table. When he sat down, he popped the tablet into place and typed on the keyboard fixed to its case. I was amazed at how fast his knobby fingers moved on the keys.

"Hmm," he said again, moving the tablet around. It looked funny, the shiny new computer in its purple case, mixed in among the papers and all the old books on his table. "Yes. Here it is."

He turned the tablet around so Indri and I could see it.

Indri and I both leaned back at the same time. The screen had a drawing of a Black man hanging from a tree. It looked real, with its swollen face and the tongue hanging out.

"Dr. Harper," Indri said. "What—I mean, that's pretty awful."

He turned the tablet back around. "Hmm? Oh! Sorry. Yes, absolutely awful. But that's what the numbers mean." He scrolled down from the nasty drawing. "There's the information without the graphic."

He turned the screen around, pointing to the figures. "Your grandmother was using this website's estimate of the number of people murdered by lynching in the State of Mississippi between 1882 and 1968." He tapped the tablet again. "It's the ultimate form of mob violence, one of the most vicious tools used to keep one group of people terrorized and under the control of another."

The image of the hanged man flickered in my brain like something I couldn't un-see. It didn't help that the drawing had been of a man who looked like Dad, beard and all. I wanted to rattle my head back and forth to keep myself from putting Dad's face on the drawing. Indri had her mouth pressed tight, like she did when something made her mad. Was she angry about the drawing, or seeing scary stuff in her own head?

Dr. Harper kept right on showing us things on his tablet. "This number here, five thirty-nine, is the estimate of Black citizens lynched in Mississippi during that time period, and this one here, forty-two," he pointed to the smaller number, "that's White citizens, or other races. They were likely lynched for showing sympathy or support to a person of color. The total comes to five eighty-one, like your grandmother noted. The Tuskegee Institute over in Alabama puts the total number much higher. I believe they have a count of five hundred thirty-eight lynchings in Mississippi between just 1883 and 1959—the most of any state."

I didn't know what to say. In school, we had learned about a boy named Emmett Till who got murdered in 1955 down in Money, Mississippi, because he talked to a White woman. I remembered the photo of his ruined body lying in a casket. Some people thought the publication of that photo, and how mad everyone got about it all over the world, marked the beginning of the modern Civil Rights Movement.

"I knew about Martin Luther King and Medgar Evars and Malcolm X getting assassinated," Indri said. "I didn't know there were this many more."

"And many beyond that that we'll likely never know about," Dr. Harper said. He turned the page on what Grandma had written, to page six, and showed us other dates. "May I see the next page?"

Indri and I exchanged looks. Then almost at the same moment, we seemed to come to the same decision, that we needed Dr. Harper's help if we were ever going to find the answer to what happened between Grandma and Avadelle. I reached into my pack, got the envelope out, and carefully removed the next few pages. All of them looked like page five and six—dates, with notations after the dates.

"I'll show you these," I said, "on one condition."

Dr. Harper looked surprised, but he waited. A few butterflies bumped around in my stomach, because I had never tried to put conditions on a grown-up before, much less a professor who was friends with my grandma and knew my parents.

"Uh." I swallowed and gripped the pages tighter. "Yeah—well. Grandma wrote this for me back when everything was still a straight line. I mean, this is—it's mine. She meant it just for me until I decide what to do with it. I showed it to Indri because I needed her help understanding it, and I need your help too, but it's still mine."

"Meaning, I can't use it for my own purposes," Dr. Harper said. He gazed at me like he might be looking at a student in one of his classes, all professerly and stern, but his eyes still twinkled just a bit.

"Yes," I said, "and you can't tell anyone about it."

His look got even more stern, and the twinkle went away. "Like your parents."

"Exactly." I let out a breath, then gulped another before he spoke again.

"A secret." He fussed with his sleeves again, then studied Indri, and came back around to me. "Dani Beans, I don't much like keeping secrets from childrens' parents."

"I don't much like secrets either," I said in a hurry. "So let's consider this . . . a private project?"

"Oh, well." He shoved up one sleeve, about halfway to his shoulder. "That's completely different. I agree to your condition of privacy in full."

Indri gave me a quick thumbs-up when I checked with her, and I handed over the time line.

Dr. Harper moved through the next four or five pages quickly, shifting them between us so I could see they were an ongoing time line, and mumbling out loud about yellow fever epidemics and Spanish flu, and then flooding in the Delta that left almost a million people homeless. "Here," he said, pointing to the center of page eight. "In the 1920s when your grandmother was born, Mississippi schools made it illegal to teach evolution—right around the time her favorite writer,

Mr. William Faulkner, was buying his Rowan Oak homestead. We got a brief stretch of peace, then World War II came along, and we had more unrest and more riots because the military integrated, but the state didn't."

He showed us page nine.

1942 OCTOBER–Lynching of 14-year-old Charlie Lang, 14-year-old Ernest Green in Shubuta, MS, and 45-year-old Howard Walsh in Laurel, Mississippi.

1943 MAY–Members of the African American 364th regiment arrived at Camp Van Dorn in Centreville, and refused to be segregated. Local outrage fueled the shooting death of Private William Walker, killed by a local sheriff during a fight with a base military policeman over improper wearing of his uniform. The 364th rioted. What happened next is unclear. Over 1,200 soldiers disappeared from the rosters of the 364th between that shooting and the war's end. Some historians allege they were killed in skirmishes with heavily armed local citizens in Centreville, and a military cover-up ensued to prevent drop-off in the recruitment of Black soldiers. Other sources indicate many left the South and sought asylum from their local military authorities. The company was shipped out to the Aleutian Islands. If, as Army records indicate, there was no mass killing at Centreville, then between June 1943 until V-J day, an average of one soldier per day disappeared from the rolls of the 364th while they were in the Aleutians, with no explanation of what happened to them. Only 116 survivors have been accounted for to date.

1944 OCTOBER–Lynching of Rev. Isaac Simmons in Amite County, Mississippi

"A maybe-massacre in Centreville," Indri whispered. "How is it even possible that we still don't know if it actually happened?"

Dr. Harper made a pained sound. "What few academic papers I've reviewed were disturbing. For example, Private Walker, the murdered soldier, was listed as separated from service, with no indication that he was killed by a local sheriff, or indeed that he was dead at all. Military officials have indicated that the records necessary to get to the bottom of this mystery were accidentally destroyed in a fire in the 1970s."

"Do you believe that?" Indri sounded as worried and sick as I felt, and I could tell she was thinking about her dad again. Losing him in battle for his country would be bad enough, but losing him in some covered-up horrible crime because somebody didn't like the color of his skin—never finding out what really happened to him—it was unthinkable. I put my hand on hers, and she didn't pull away from me. She wasn't crying, but her eyes had gone wide and glassy.

"I honestly don't know, Indri," Dr. Harper said. "On the surface, it seems preposterous, until you realize how many other cover-ups, injustices, and instances of ignoring race-based murder happened in this country between 1865 and the late 1960s."

The sad thing is, Oops, it won't make any sense to you unless you understand where I came from. . . . Grandma's words echoed through my head, like she had spoken them out loud instead of writing them down. *In the final analysis, this is my history, and it's yours, too. Read it carefully before you read about Avadelle and* Night on Fire. *Understand it before you judge me—and before you judge her.*

I put my hand over Dr. Harper's before he spoke again, and I gave him the first four pages. He read them quietly. Then he read them a second time, and dabbed at his eyes with his fingers.

"I see," he said after a third pass. "I do see."

Indri and I looked at him, neither of us sure what to say, or what to ask. I didn't want to tell him the whole truth of it, that Grandma never got to the part about the fight, because it was so sad, but also because I worried he'd lose interest and stop helping us.

Dr. Harper piled up the papers he had and worked with them until they fell into a neat stack. "The information that may be in here—well, I don't need to tell you, many publishers, both book and periodical, would pay quite a bit of money to have it."

"The stuff about the feud, Ms. Beans—" Indri started, but I hushed her with a warning glance.

"I don't think Grandma wanted a bunch of publicity," I said.

"No," he agreed.

"She wanted me—maybe all of us that were close to her—to understand," I said. "And for me to decide what's best to do with it all. But why did she start way back with Mississippi turning into a state?"

"I haven't heard of any of the people Ms. Beans mentions in those first eight or nine pages," Indri said, pointing to the small stack on the table. "Like Charles Lang or Ernest Green."

"The anonymity of those murder victims was a point Ruth liked to make when she discussed this state's history," Dr. Harper said. "The true human cost of struggles like the Civil Rights Movement can get pushed aside over time. Once that occurs, mountains of progress can erode almost overnight. Ruth didn't want that to happen."

I thought about the stained glass window with the University Grays, and the unmarked graves in the cemetery behind the stadium. I looked at the papers I had shared with

Dr. Harper. A list of forgotten events and forgotten people, murdered because they were Black, or some color other than White, or nice to Black people, or seemingly for no reason at all.

Who had more right to become ghosts and haunt us, the people on this list who died in a war nobody admitted was a war, or the soldiers who fought in named battles but didn't even get their own graves?

Both?

I had no idea. I felt ashamed, and I wasn't sure why.

"How will any of this help Dani and me understand Ms. Beans's fight with Avadelle Richardson?" Indri asked.

Dr. Harper pushed up his rolled shirt sleeves so they rested on his bony elbows. Then he moved Grandma's writing aside, got up and dashed to his desk, and came back with a white piece of paper and a giant box of crayons. Indri and I stared at him as he sat and scribbled on the clean paper with dozens of colors, one right on top of the next. Finally, he took a black crayon and scribbled over the top of the chaos, then smiled at us, and pointed down to the crayon-covered paper.

"What did I just make here, Indri?"

She shrugged and he looked at me. Zero idea. The best I could come up with was "Um, a kindergartener mess?"

He laughed, and it sounded a little like a turkey call. "Indeed. A big, sloppy mess. Let's say all those colors I started with were events. History. Like the items on your grandmother's time line." He touched the black crayon layer. "And this, this is a more recent occurrence."

He reached into his shirt pocket and pulled out a paper-clip, then unfolded it and handed it to me. "Here, Dani. Use the end to scratch your name into this mess."

"Oookay." I did it, slowly, forming the D-A-N-I with careful strokes. To my surprise, my name emerged out of the jumbled darkness perfectly clear, in rainbow hues.

Dr. Harper waited, like he wanted Indri and me to understand what that meant at some deeper level—like his coat-hanging gag.

"Everything underneath makes the color of her name show through and not be just black or white?" Indri said, in what I thought was a valiant first try.

"Yes!" Dr. Harper clapped his hands together and beamed at her. "The colors, the events leading up to the recent occurrence, the moment you scratch a word into it, form *context*. The recent occurrence blocks out so much, and yet when Dani scratches her name, those past events still come shining through. In fact, they determine how her name will look, much more than the darkness of this recent occurrence."

"Context," I muttered. Indri looked completely confused. I picked up a piece of the blank paper, and some crayons. "So, Mississippi gets to be a state." I scribbled a color. "The Civil War happens." I scribbled another color on top of that. "And then the Black Codes." I picked a dark brown for that one. "And lynchings. And the World War II stuff. And the

Civil Rights Movement starts." I added color after color, then layered on the black crayon and scratched Grandma's name into it. *Ruth* shined out at me in a new set of rainbow hues, different from how my scratched name had turned out.

"If all the colors below are the history leading up to Grandma's . . . recent occurrence," I said to Dr. Harper, "what's the recent occurrence? Her fight with Avadelle?"

"I don't know," he said, but something in his voice sounded funny. It made me look him full in the face, and his eyes shifted away from mine.

He cleared his throat. "If I had to make a guess, I'd say her recent occurrence, her biggest event, had something to do with the night of the Meredith riot, when your grandmother got hurt." He frowned, and it made his whole face look sad. "I was so out of touch back then, not paying attention to the world outside the library and my books. I had no idea the campus was in such trouble, and I didn't warn Ruth, you see? She came to Ole Miss with Avadelle to pick up some books from me, for the school where she was teaching, over in Abbeville."

"You think the Meredith riot was Grandma's really big deal, her recent occurrence—not some fight with Avadelle later, after Avadelle's book came out?" I'm sure I looked as clueless as Indri did.

Seeming perplexed, Dr. Harper put his hand on Grandma's papers. "Well of course, I think most serious scholars of the feud agreed that something happened during the riot—perhaps something Avadelle told in her novel, or something she didn't. Otherwise, why would the publication of *Night on Fire* have coincided with the end of the relationship?"

It made sense. And yet, who could know? My brain turned in really fast circles, but I couldn't come up with the next question to ask.

Thankfully, Dr. Harper did it for me. "Ruth never told you about her own experiences the night of the riot?"

I shook my head. "No, sir. She won't talk about anything to do with that period of time, or *Night on Fire*, or the feud. What happened to her?"

"Much of *Night on Fire* has the ring of truth, but Avadelle has always acknowledged it deviates at the point of the riot." Dr. Harper folded his hands as he spoke. "And the friendship seemed troubled after that night. Not as close, if you ask me. Avadelle and your grandmother seemed to get past the night of the riot, until the book was released."

Indri and I stayed very quiet, listening.

"That night, they really were on campus, of course, Avadelle and Ruth," Dr. Harper said. "But Ruth took a fall, and she was laid up a long time—had to go to a hospital out of state. Your dad probably remembers her being away for so long. A few of the Internet feud websites mention it too, but they don't have details."

My mouth came open, but I slowly cranked it shut and tried not to seem freaked out, so Dr. Harper wouldn't stop talking. I had always known, sort of distantly, about the Meredith riot, and that *Night on Fire* talked some about Grandma's past, and involved Grandma and Avadelle and everything leading up to the night of the riot. But I had no idea my grandmother got seriously hurt that night.

I picked up the time line and paged through name after name, and date after date. Lynched people, awful laws, hate groups, natural disasters, riots, amendments—so much. When I got to the 1950s, each year took up pages all by itself. Did more happen in those years, or did people just know to write it down better, with more details? By the 1960s, each month had a page or more. James Meredith's name jumped out at me in a 1961 entry. I put it on the table and pointed so Indri could read it too.

1961   JANUARY 31–World War II veteran James
Meredith formally applies to the University of
Mississippi, stating on his application to the
registrar that he is Black.
FEBRUARY 4–James Meredith receives a
telegram from the University of Mississippi,
rejecting his application.

I looked up at Dr. Harper. "I've never really understood how it went from Mr. Meredith applying to Ole Miss to a riot happening. It seems so—so stupid, a riot because a Black man, a war veteran like my dad, wanted to go to college in his home state."

Dr. Harper still wasn't smiling. He looked misty, like people do when they're seeing things in their heads that bother them a lot. "Some folks consider the Meredith riot to be the Pickett's Charge of segregation in Mississippi—the moment everything began to change."

"And Dani's grandmother saw all that in person with Avadelle," Indri said. "But Ms. Beans got hurt?"

."Yes, Ruth was one of the riot injuries. Two people died and over three hundred were wounded."

Hundreds of new questions flashed through my brain. "But what exactly happened to Grandma?"

Dr. Harper held up both hands. "She never told me, or to my knowledge, anyone. None of the journalists and scholars who have investigated the Magnolia Feud have much information about it. Her medical records are private, and those haven't been leaked. As I told you, most feud scholars think the argument didn't really start until the book came out, but a few, like me, disagree. I think the roots of the disagreement grew sooner. I think the seed got planted the night Mr. Meredith arrived at Ole Miss."

Dr. Harper kept his hands folded. He looked far away, totally lost in his own memories. "Nobody can get answers, from Ruth or Avadelle." He gave a little laugh. "No, especially not Avadelle. If Ruth's told you the truth of the Magnolia Feud in those papers—well. I can't imagine. I just can't imagine."

Indri looked like she was about to tell him Grandma never made it to the feud in her papers, but instead she said, "Dani, we need more information about the riot."

Dr. Harper jumped a little bit, then seemed to get himself completely back under control. "Well, if it's details on the Meredith situation you want, Avadelle's daughter, Naomi Manchester, over at Square Books wrote her thesis on the riot, and she also has books and accounts of what happened. Now, shall we look at the rest of those pages?"

"We should talk to Naomi Manchester next," I said, not wanting to give him the rest of the stack. "Dr. Harper could go with us. If you're willing, I mean, sir."

"Surely," Dr. Harper said. His smile got a little fixed. "But the pages, girls. The rest of what Ruth wrote?"

I might have been imagining it, but he seemed a little too . . . eager. Or something. On impulse, I picked up the few papers I had let him see, then remembered the key I had zipped into the front pocket of my pack. I put the papers back on his table and fished it out, showing it to him on the palm of my hand. "Any idea what this might unlock?"

Dr. Harper stared at the key, his eyes wide and his brows drawn tight together. His face went slowly pale, until he looked like the blank white typing paper on his table.

Indri gave me a look, then glanced back at the professor, who was nervously rubbing his neck. He seemed to realize we were staring at him, and he mumbled, "It's, uh, a bit too small for a door."

His voice sounded thin, and his smile was definitely forced. He reached for the key, but I closed my fingers over it, and quickly put it away.

For a split second his face darkened, like he was angry. My thoughts banged together too fast. My backpack seemed to fight with me as I tried to cram Grandma's papers inside, so I gave up, shouldered the pack, and gathered the papers into my arms. I didn't like having all the lynchings and mysteries and murders hugged tight to my chest, and I didn't like how Dr. Harper had just acted about Grandma's key.

Neither did Indri. She inched away, toward the door. "Thanks," she said to Dr. Harper. "We'll, um, call you."

Or not.

Dr. Harper cleared his throat again and blinked a few times. A little color came back to his cheeks, and he managed another fakey-type smile. "I'll look forward to seeing you at Square Books."

We hurried out of his office.

It was all I could do not to run past the big stained glass window, covering my eyes as I went.

11

NOT WHAT I EXPECTED

———

**Excerpt from *Night on Fire* (1969),
by Avadelle Richardson, page 304**

*Both sides of the ice cream line went motionless and
quiet. Leslie kept her back turned to the crowd. My heart
beat so hard I couldn't swallow. I couldn't even breathe.*

*The White woman didn't say anything else. She
didn't even look at Leslie, just sniffed and humphed,
then waited her own turn. Leslie had enough sense
to take her banana split and walk off, rather than go
into either side of the restaurant.*

*Half an hour later, finishing our own ice cream
cones, Aunt Jessie and I walked back to the out-of-the-
way road where we had left the car. We found Leslie
standing next to my faded red Mercury Marquis. Her
arms were folded.*

"I'm not even speaking to you," I said. "You're completely crazy, and you're gonna get me killed." I threw my ice cream on the grass beside the car, then looked around, suddenly nervous some White person would show up and see us, see me, see everything. "You're gonna get my boy killed, and then I'll just kill you, too. I'll do it myself, with my own two hands."

Eyes wide and pleading, Leslie looked at Aunt Jessie for help.

"Child, what that woman was saying, it wasn't even directed at you." Aunt Jessie held out one big, black arm and pressed it against Leslie's pale, freckled skin. She forced a laugh, trying to make us all feel better, but Leslie refused to laugh along with her.

Finally, Aunt Jessie shook her head. "Now that things are starting to happen in Oxford, you got to be more careful."

"That man James Meredith," I said, "the one who got turned down by Ole Miss because he was Black, well, he filed a lawsuit last month. He means for to be heard all the way up to the Supreme Court. He means to go to school at Ole Miss this fall. Folks like that woman in line, they're scared, and it's only gonna get worse from here."

"Scared people do stupid things," Aunt Jessie

said. "So here's the first, best rule for survival in Mississippi. Don't never trust a scared person, not ever. You understand me?"

INDRI AND I RUSHED TO the entryway and she held the outer door open for me. Together, we spilled through it, jogged down the concrete steps, and made it to the sidewalk. Then we stood there with our backs to the Grove, staring at the building and blinking and breathing, letting the light and the warmth cover us.

After a few moments, Indri said, "That . . . was . . . NOT . . . what I expected. Any of it."

"Me either," I admitted. Talking seemed hard, like the muscles in my mouth didn't want to cooperate. "What was that about, his reaction to the key?"

"It was kind of awful." She gave me a sideways look. "He knew something he didn't tell us."

"Yeah. But what?"

"No idea." Indri shook her head. "All of that creeped me out."

"What are you two doing here?" somebody growled from behind us and I spun to find Avadelle Richardson right in front of me, fedora and all. She was wearing a T-shirt with gold fringes that sort of looked like a lampshade, but it matched the gold threads in her slacks. The slogan on the shirt read, *I hate everybody!*

The snarly look on her face made the slogan all too real.

Bits of silvery hair poked out from beneath the fedora, sticking to her sweaty face as she gazed at the papers in my arms. Her cheeks turned sunburn-red. She raised her cane to eye level and shook it at me. "I thought I told you not to muck in Ruth's work!"

I stepped back from her, cradling the papers, and that's when I saw Mac beside her. He had his hands jammed in his jeans pockets, and he looked tired. His gaze shifted from my face to the papers, and his frown made me feel like a salted slug. I moved backward again, wondering how many more steps it would take for me to be safe from a swing of that cane. Mac would probably stop Avadelle if she tried to smack me with the eagle's head, but he looked so mad I didn't trust him to move fast enough.

"Ms. Richardson," I said, stealing words from Dad and trying to sound as much like him as I could, "this is really none of your business."

"Yeah," Indri agreed, but she backed up with me, squinting at the sunlight glaring off the cane's bird-shaped handle.

I looked at Mac for a long second, then looked away. People moved on the sidewalk in both directions, but nobody seemed inclined to get close enough to Avadelle to help us.

She finally lowered the cane but raised her voice. "What were you two good-for-nothings doing in Ventress? Did you talk to Fred Harper? What did he tell you?"

No way was I answering that. Even if I'd wanted to, I wouldn't have a clue how to explain what just happened in Dr. Harper's office. All I could do was stand my ground, wondering if Indri and I should turn and make a run for the Grove and Creative Arts and Ms. Yarbrough.

"I know you hate me now, Dani," Mac said, "but are you trying to make my life harder?"

"Everything's not about you, Worm Dung." Indri's comeback was almost as loud as Avadelle's raggedy breathing.

"So what if we saw Dr. Harper?" I asked Avadelle. "Why does that matter to you?"

"Worm dung?" Mac asked nobody in particular. "As in worm . . . poop?"

"Worm, caterpillar, snake, maggot." Indri shrugged. "Take your pick."

Avadelle ignored Mac and Indri as she glared at me. She smacked the cane down on the pavement and leaned on it. "I don't have to tell you a thing, girl."

"And I don't have to tell you anything either." My arms were getting sweaty against the manuscript pages, but I didn't dare try to get them into my pack now. "Except this. My grandmother gave these papers to me, not you. Whatever I find out about your feud, she wanted me to know."

"Dani—" Indri started, but she didn't try to finish. It was probably the look on Avadelle's face, three parts fury and one part stunned sadness, that made her hush. I know it shut *me* up cold.

"What happened between me and Ruth," Avadelle said in a deadly quiet voice, "that's old history. She's half dead and I've got one foot in the grave."

She had a point, and even though she was a mean old witch, I felt even more like a slug for upsetting her again. "I'm sorry if it bothers you, Ms. Richardson. I really don't have anything against you. I'm just trying to figure out what's making my grandmother so unhappy, so she can stop crying and be at peace."

Mac had stepped up beside Avadelle, his hands hovering near her cane in case she raised it again. His eyes widened as I spoke, and so did hers.

"Ruth is upset?" she asked, leaning away from me like she was the one thinking about running now.

Something tugged at my pack, and I realized it was Indri, trying to get the strap off my shoulder. I stretched out one arm and let her take it, but I kept my gaze on Avadelle. The breeze blew again, bumping the brim of Avadelle's hat. I heard the zipper of my pack whizzing along its track as Indri got the bag open, but I felt like a bubble had formed around us, freezing the day into so much green and gold stained glass, because Avadelle turned whiter than any of the ghostly soldiers in the Ventress Hall window. Her eyes seemed to hollow out, and her cheeks flattened, and she got one hundred years older in between one breath and the next. Her hand lifted off the eagle-head cane. Her knobby fingers fluttered just above her chest, and right that second, I was pretty sure she had a heart, and that it was hurting her, in more ways than one.

"GG, you all right?" Mac reached to steady her, but she

turned around and marched away from us, smacking her cane with each step.

Indri pulled Grandma's papers out of my arms, and I let go of them without fighting her. As she stuffed the manuscript into my pack, Mac watched his grandmother head up the steps into Ventress.

"We have an appointment with Dr. Harper," he said, sounding confused and surprised.

"Why?" Indri asked as she closed up the pack, protecting the papers from the breeze and my sweaty skin and Avadelle, too, if she changed her mind and came charging back with that cane leading the way.

"No clue," Mac said, turning to face us. "GG gives the orders. I just try to keep her out of trouble." He rubbed both eyes with his fingertips.

Sympathy must have showed in my expression, because Indri nearly yanked my arm out of the socket as she slid the pack strap back into place. I ignored her and asked, "Are you having to take care of her all the time now?"

Mac put his hands back in his pockets. "All last week, and the first part of this one, because Mom has to be out of town."

The world around us seemed more solid now, and I could tell it was getting way past lunchtime since the crowd on the sidewalk was so thin. "Looking after her has to be hard," I told him.

One side of his mouth quirked into a smile, but sort of a sad one. "I guess you do understand how that is."

Leaves rustled in the bushes and trees, and Indri snorted like a ticked-off bull as I came back with, "I'm sorry about her seeing the papers. Dr. Harper got—well. We left Ventress in a hurry, and the papers wouldn't go back in the pack right, and I didn't—just, I'm sorry."

I expected Indri to step on my foot, but she didn't. At least not yet. She just stood beside me, arms folded, the picture of suspicion and no-way-am-I-being-friendly-to-WORM-DUNG.

Mac's gaze flicked to the pack. "What's it all about, anyway? The feud, for real?"

"The first part's just on civil rights," I said. "Sort of. It's bigger than that, really. More like a time line of Mississippi history, but with a lot of stuff we never read about in school." Thinking about my rainbow name shining out from dark crayon, I added, "Grandma wrote about her wars and ghosts, for context. You know, to help me understand whatever happened between her and Avadelle."

Mac nodded as Indri's foot started to tap. "Dani, we're late," she said. "We better get back before Ms. Yarbrough calls our parents."

"I'm sorry GG won't tell you what she knows, if it would stop your grandmother from being upset," Mac said, making me pretend Indri hadn't just told me we needed to leave.

"Do you know what they fought about?" I asked him.

Mac shook his head. "She won't talk about Ms. Beans at all." He pointed to the manuscript. "Except to say that digging up bones doesn't do anything but make angry ghosts."

Digging up bones doesn't do anything but make angry ghosts. That phrase shot into my head and stuck like a dart. All of a sudden, I wanted to know why Avadelle was meeting with Dr. Harper. Had he told her we were coming to see him? Would he tell her what he'd seen in the papers so far, and about the key? What did he know, anyway—about what Grandma was writing, and the key, too?

My eyes shifted to Ventress Hall, and I thought about storming up the steps again, banging on his door, and demanding answers, whether Avadelle was there or not.

"No," Indri said. "Just, no. Going after her won't help anything, and I don't want to be around Dr. Harper again right now."

Mac's face tensed, and his fists clenched. "Please don't follow GG in there. That'll just set her off a thousand times worse."

White-hot noise roared in my mind. Neither one of them had watched my grandmother weep and cry and whisper about the secrets trying to claw their way out of her broken mind. They didn't know. They might not even think it was that big of a deal.

Stop, my better self reminded me. *These are your friends. Well, one of them is, anyway*.

My anger started to ebb as fast as it had crested. Because that was the truth. I wasn't angry with Indri. I didn't know what I felt about Mac, not really, except I didn't want to miss a chance to get more information, just in case Grandma didn't manage to get all of her thoughts on paper. And it wasn't so bad, actually, talking to Mac when he wasn't being an idiot.

"Dr. Harper told us my grandmother got injured during that riot back in the 1960s," I said.

"The Meredith riot? Yeah, I remember GG talking about that." Mac pulled his hands out of his pockets and shoved his hair out of his eyes. "She said she met your grandmother a few years before all that stuff, that she got hurt and had to go to a hospital in Chicago—but I don't know how Ms. Beans got hurt."

He absently picked at the ends of his fingers, scratching the callouses he got from pressing his skin into metal guitar strings. "So," I said, "you still playing your guitar a lot?"

"Every day." He stopped messing with his fingers, like he got suddenly self-conscious about it.

Indri huffed out another few sighs, so fast it sounded like she was blowing gnats out of her face.

Mac looked me in the eye, his gaze steady, his body more relaxed now. "I still have the band, too."

I thought about Indri and me sitting for hours, eating cheese and crackers and drinking Coke while Mac strummed and Ben beat the drums and DeMario played the keyboard. They hammered at the same loud song over and over and over—but really, they didn't suck too bad.

"My parents finally soundproofed the garage so we can practice whenever we want now," Mac added. He took a breath like he wanted to ask me if I wanted to come to their practice again, but he didn't.

"Dani." Indri caught hold of my arm at the elbow and started to tug. "We really, *really* have to get back to camp now."

I looked back over my shoulder. "We need to go to Square Books and talk to Ms. Manchester, and get some details about the night of the riot."

"Aunt Naomi?" Mac nodded. "She knows a lot about that night. Call me when you go, and I'll meet you there." Mac watched Indri tow me down the sidewalk toward the Grove entrance, and then he grinned and called out, "See you then. Um, later."

He waved, and Indri made me turn around. She kept pulling me along, muttering, "I can*not* believe you," and, "Good thing I'm here to be the one with actual common sense," and, "Did we just have a decent conversation with Worm Dung?"

"Yeah, I think so." I caught up with her, and she finally trusted me to keep going and let go of my arm.

"Ew, we did. We spoke to that lowlife." She brushed off her shirt like she had bugs. "I need to go home and take a shower."

"Come on. It wasn't that bad."

"He blew you off, Dani, like you had no meaning at all to him."

"Yeah, yeah. I know. You're right." Somehow, I didn't look back toward Ventress Hall to see if Mac had already gone inside. Indri was probably right.

But I had to admit, for a minute or two there, Mac was the nice guy I remembered him being.

12

SOMEBODY HAS TO DO THE RIGHT THING

———

**Excerpt from *Night on Fire* (1969),
by Avadelle Richardson, page 315**

A week later, I was still mad, but I couldn't explain myself. I felt too weary to try. Just when I thought Leslie truly understood the world I lived in, that my son, Abram, and my mother and my aunt lived in, she pulled some stunt that let me know she didn't grasp reality. Maybe she never would.

Could any White person understand living Black in Mississippi?

We were getting ready for our Tuesday-night class, and I dusted shelves too hard, too fast, and I didn't talk. Leslie had the books ready on the desks, but she kept fiddling with them, trying to get me going. "'All of us failed to match our dreams of perfection. So I rate us on the basis of our splendid failure to do the impossible.'"

She waited.

I heard myself grunt just like Aunt Jessie, and then I sighed. "That's from William Faulkner's Paris Review *interview you gave me. The 1958 one. Too easy."*

"How do you rate me, CiCi?" She turned toward me, and the single bulb in the room underscored the shadows ringing her eyes. She wasn't wearing lipstick, and her hair lay flat against her head. In her drab brown dress, she looked more a prisoner than a woman of privilege.

I quit dusting and leaned against my desk, rag still in my hand. "Say what?"

"How do you rate me? What do you think of me? Really?"

"Oh, Lord." That made me stop a minute. I tried to find the exact right words, but in the end, I said what I felt. "I think you're smart. You're determined. You want to do the right things, and you mean well. You care, Leslie. That's obvious to me."

She took in everything I said, then met my eyes. "Is that enough?"

"Enough for what?"

Leslie bit at her bottom lip. "Am I your friend, CiCi, or am I not?"

"HMM," MOM SAID AS SHE drove us home down University Avenue. "Yes, I remember your father saying something about your grandmother being injured in the Meredith riot—fell into one of the steam tunnels or something."

"Must have been a bad fall, if it laid her up as long as Dr. Harper remembers. Mac said Avadelle told him Grandma had to go to a hospital in Chicago." I stared out my window, watching the campus zing by, old buildings blurring into new buildings, then trees, then the nothingness of the bridge as we drove into town. "And are those steam tunnels even still open? I thought they were closed."

I could see Mom's reflection in my window, and she reached up and fiddled with her braid, then straightened the collar of her lab coat as she answered. "Well, there are the real tunnels and the campus-legend tunnels. Some folks thought there was a network of underground routes that federal marshals used to get James Meredith to his classes once he was admitted, but I don't think those actually exist. The tunnels I've seen are more like utility areas, small and all full of pipes, and they've been padlocked now—well, except for the few under these main roads."

Frowning, I stared down like I could see through the asphalt. "You mean the links between the concrete culverts, where you won't let me explore?"

Mom turned on her blinker. "Not apologizing. There's a lot of graffiti down there that's not appropriate for somebody your age, never mind the people who put it there."

"So did Grandma get hurt in one of the big tunnels, or one of those little ones with all the pipes?"

"That, you'll have to ask your father." Mom started to look at me, then shifted her gaze back to the road. "Did you enjoy your visit with Dr. Harper?"

I stared at the pack on the floorboard, between my feet. It sagged against my leg, feeling huge and heavy. "*Enjoy* wouldn't be the right word. We found out a lot of stuff, though."

"Things that bothered you?" She didn't look at me, but I heard the worry in her voice. I thought about not saying anything else because I hated stressing her out. It's just that I had so many questions in my head, and I didn't have any place left to stuff them.

"Did you and Dad go through a lot, getting married when this state still had anti-miscrimination laws?"

"Anti-miscrim—oh. The anti-miscegenation laws, about interracial marriage." Mom turned in to our driveway. "Those were struck down by the Supreme Court in 1967. Your dad and I were still kids."

I picked at the strap of my pack. "But our state didn't get rid of them completely until the 1980s, *after* you got married. Alabama didn't get rid of theirs until 2000."

In the driveway, Mom shut off the car and turned toward me, her mouth slightly open. "I honestly never knew that."

"So, did you go through a lot?" I kept my eyes fastened on her face, watching for any hint that she was hiding bad things—maybe so she wouldn't stress *me* out. My own breathing sounded way too loud, and it was already getting hot in the car with the air off. Every time I inhaled, I smelled coconut and vanilla, and my brain told me everything was fine, that the world was okay and Mom and Dad were okay, and I was okay, but my heart still beat too fast.

Sooner or later, Oops, we're all gonna be okay.

Grandma's voice seemed loud in my head, as if she was up and fine and completely herself again. The thought made the corners of my mouth twitch toward a smile.

Meanwhile, Mom seemed to be having an argument with herself. She finally cleared her throat and said, "We went through a few rough situations. There are always people who hold on to old beliefs like the sky will fall if they let go. Doesn't matter where you live. Mississippi's no different."

I noticed that she didn't tell me what any of the bad things were. I thought about asking her, but I was flat out of room for awful today. The image of the hanged man on the lynching website jammed itself into my awareness, and I couldn't help a shiver. I popped my seat belt and got out of the car, towing the pack with the manuscript.

Mom was out of her seat before I shut my door, and she asked, "What spooked you just now? Because something did."

I kept a firm grip on the pack and glanced at the house, up to my window. Dad was probably in Grandma's room, getting her ready for dinner. He was the one who had worried all this would upset me too much. I didn't want him to be right.

"The numbers that Grandma wrote down, the ones we took to Dr. Harper, they're about lynchings," I said, keeping my gaze on the window instead of Mom. "Grandma added up how many people got lynched in Mississippi between 1882 and 1968. There were five hundred eighty-one that we know of, and probably a lot more nobody knew about."

Silence.

And then, "I see."

This time, I thought she probably did see, and I was glad. A few seconds later, she asked, "Dani, are you sure you want to take on the things your grandmother studied? Now, at this point in your life, I mean? There's always later."

My eyes watered from staring at the house so hard, not because I was crying. "If I don't know about them, will they stop being true?"

"No. They won't." Mom sounded sad. That didn't help my watering eyes.

I sucked it up and wiped my face with one hand. "If we don't help Grandma find peace, then who will?"

Mom went quiet again, until I looked at her.

"This is our circus," she said, sounding resigned. "These are all our monkeys."

But she was leaning on the car, studying me, like she was trying to decide whether or not to tell me to stop trying to figure out what was bothering Grandma, to leave everything to Dad and her. My fingers ached from squeezing the strap of the pack too hard.

"I need to ask Dad about Grandma getting hurt, and we need to go see Ms. Manchester at Square Books because Dr. Harper says she knows more than anybody about the Meredith riot."

Mom stayed quiet so long that sweat formed on the back of my neck. "I'll talk to your father about that."

Wow. I did *not* like the maybe-this-is-a-bad-idea tone in her voice. "Meaning?"

She pushed away from the car and came toward me. "Meaning, I'm not sure we've done the right thing by protecting you so much from racial issues. And meaning I'm worried about you."

I pulled the pack closer, until I was hugging it. Tears seemed far away now, and I felt sort of mad, and stiff inside, like concrete was filling me up and chasing away any emotion except sureness that I needed to take the next step and go see Ms. Manchester tomorrow.

"Somebody has to do the right thing," I told Mom.

Mom stopped walking a few feet from me. The way-worried look on her face slid into something else, like surprise, or maybe shock.

I glanced down at my clothes to be sure I hadn't torn anything or gotten a big stain I hadn't noticed. Everything looked clear, so I asked, "What?"

Mom folded her arms. "Somebody has to do the right thing." She shook her head. "I wonder how many times I heard your grandmother say that." When I didn't answer, she said, "I guess that was more when you were little, before you can remember—but trust me, it was a Ruth Beans staple, just like her quotation game."

Some other feeling nudged in beside the concrete-stubborn holding me up straight. It felt warmer, and happier, like a little breeze had blown out of Grandma's window, straight to my heart.

"Okay, then," I said.

"Okay, then," Mom echoed as I shouldered my pack. When she reached her hand out for me, I took it, and we walked into the house together.

Gray twilight spilled through Grandma's open window as Dad finished stuffing a wad of bed pads into a big trash bag. "Your mom tells me you want to go to Square Books to see Naomi Manchester about the Meredith riot."

My pulse picked up its pace, and I bit at my lip. "Yes. I think she works at the main store all the rest of this week."

"Your mom also said you dug a little deep today, Dani, that you got into some of the rough stuff and it upset you."

"Kinda rough, I guess." I mopped off Grandma's bed tray with a disinfectant wipe. "What I don't get is, there wasn't anything about five hundred eighty-one people being lynched in Mississippi in our history book last year. And that's just this state, so you know there's a lot more who died if you add up all the states. How could the Civil Rights Movement be just one chapter in any book?"

Dad tied his trash bag. "When you get to college, you can take whole courses. Middle school and high school textbooks just hit the highlights."

"But what happens to the people who don't take those courses?" I disinfected Grandma's bed rail with a fierce vengeance. "And what happens to the lowlights?"

"Guess they stay dim until somebody like your grandmother writes about them." Dad came to stand next to me, and together, we watched Grandma sleep. Her breathing was slow and even. Her face looked calm, but her fingers worried at the edge of her sheet. Her hands had gotten so thin. I wanted to reach out and stroke them, but I didn't want to wake her.

"If you really want to go to Square Books instead of camp, I'm fine with it," Dad said, "as long as you keep talking to us, and telling us if something bothers you too much."

"I'll keep talking," I said.

Dad gave a little grunt and narrowed one eye at me. Then he said, "Fred Harper called. He wants to go with you tomorrow. Indri's mom gave the go-ahead for her, too."

He put his arm around my shoulder and hugged me to him, and I let him, even though I was completely icked out by the thought of Dr. Harper showing up at Square Books. I couldn't shake off the shivers from that look on his face when I thought he was going to try to grab the key. But if I told Dad I didn't want Dr. Harper to come, he'd start asking questions, or maybe call off the whole Square Books field trip.

I let myself lean into Dad a little more. From far off in the distance, thunder rumbled. I didn't know if it was heat lightning, or a storm coming in. I didn't much like storms. I turned my face in to Dad's shirt. He smelled like cologne and shower soap. When I looked up at him, he was still staring at Grandma.

"What happened to her the night of the Meredith riot?" I asked him.

Dad frowned, and his eyes lost some focus. I got worried that he wouldn't answer me, but after a time, he said, "I honestly don't know all that much, and you know how she was about talking about the worst part of the '60s. I do know she went to campus with Avadelle to meet Dr. Harper and pick up books for the classes she was teaching in Abbeville, because Black schools didn't get much money for anything, and he put back classroom supplies and books for her. On her way to his office, she got caught in the riot. She ended up falling into one of the steam tunnels, one close to the Lyceum. Hurt her pretty bad."

"Why didn't she go to the hospital here?"

Dad went stiff. His lips pulled tight, and his eyes closed. Then he said, "Baby girl, hospitals around here weren't integrated yet. That didn't happen until the late '60s. We didn't have access to specialized medical care. I always figured maybe her back or neck got injured, since she had to go to Chicago to get it treated."

"Chicago is so far away. Jeez." I turned my face back in to his rough shirt and tried to imagine a world where an injured woman couldn't walk into a hospital and get help just because she was Black.

"I was only eight years old," Dad said. "We were living over near Sardis Lake, and your great-grandmother, she was in really bad health. Cancer killed her less than three years after Mama came home to look after her. Then I had an aunt go down from diabetes, and Mama saw to her too. We didn't have much medical care back then, with segregation like it was. Except for getting shots, I didn't really see doctors until I joined the Army."

"All those people to take care of—is that why Grandma never left Oxford, even though it was bad?"

"Oxford wasn't as bad as some places, after the campus integrated." Dad let out a long breath that sounded like a tired sigh. "And yes, our family was here. Back then, folks took care of their own."

I turned back to Grandma. "We're taking care of our own now."

He kissed the side of my head. "You're right. Now give your grandmother a hug and take the trash out. It's getting toward bedtime."

When I pressed my lips to Grandma's forehead, her skin felt silky and cool, and it smelled like shea butter and coconut. She smiled without opening her eyes, and her lips puckered. She whispered something, and it sounded a lot like *Oops*.

I took the trash to the cans outside, then brushed my teeth and stood in my bathroom, working lemony-scented argan oil into my scalp and hair, all the way to the tips, like Mom and Grandma taught me. As I rubbed my hair, I shut my eyes and listened to the house go late-night around me. Mom and Dad switched off their television and put on music, and faint strains of Mary J. Blige's *No More Drama* bumped down the hallway. My muscles relaxed as I thought about my parents dancing together in their big bedroom. They liked to do that some nights. Hearing their music and knowing they were smiling at each other as they moved made me feel safe, like everything in the whole world was happy and fine.

Music was still playing as I wrapped my hair and snuggled down in my bed. I picked up a book I had been reading, one about werewolves and witches fighting a big war, but when I tried to get into it, the magic felt all wrong. Or just not real.

Disappointed, I put the book down, shut off my lamp, and tried to go to sleep. My thoughts wandered over the day, from Mac to Dr. Harper's, to Ventress Hall with its stained glass, and eating lunch in the Grove, and—

And Mac.

Anger flared through me, but it burned out fast. He wanted to go to Square Books when Indri and I did. Was that what I wanted?

I reached for my phone to text him, then put it down. No. Mac was a jerk. Plus, Dad would kill me. Forget Dad. Indri would kill me, and she'd probably make it hurt a lot worse.

But he asked to go, and he asked nice.

I picked up the phone again. And I put it down again. For a while, I just lay there in my bed, staring at the ceiling. It would be great if *the right thing to do* would announce itself in neon letters across the plaster, wouldn't it? I shut my eyes, opened them, and glared at the uncooperative white paint. Sometimes, it just felt like the whole universe was messing with me.

I snatched up the phone and sent Mac a quick message about Square Books but told him it was probably better if he didn't go. Then I shut the phone off so he couldn't text me back and set off the Jerk Alert, or start a conversation I'd have to confess to Indri, or make anything more complicated than it already was.

Then I turned off my light and went back to staring at the shadowed ceiling. Some time later, the world faded away from me—until I snapped awake in the darkness. My hands danced against my throat, and I grabbed for—what? Nothing. Nothing was there against my skin, but I thought I was choking. I coughed and coughed and sat up, my eyes wide, staring around at the nothingness in my room. Starlight. The soft whirr of my parents' bedroom table fan. The thump of my heart. Nothing was here. I wasn't choking. I was fine.

A bad dream. No, a nightmare. I just couldn't remember it, or I didn't want to. I thought about going to my parents' room and climbing into bed with them, but I didn't want to be a baby. Still, the longer I sat there trying to remember what had scared me in my sleep, the more I didn't want to be alone. Finally, I got up and slipped across the hall to Grandma's room, and sat down in the chair beside her bed. The soft yellow glow of her nightlight played across her sheets, almost like candle flame dancing in the darkness, and I realized it was raining lightly against her open window. Drops pattered on the sill, and a few tapped on the floor.

When I touched her hand, she was warm, and her chest rose and fell, rose and fell, the rhythm of it as comforting to me as my parents' music had been earlier. Her pulse was eighty. Perfectly normal.

"Sooner or later," I whispered to her, "we're all gonna be okay. Right?"

No response.

"I know you tried to write your ghost story, Grandma. Your time line, it's pretty amazing, even if you never got to the Avadelle part."

She didn't react, but I liked to think she heard me when I talked to her, even if she seemed to be sleeping. "I still don't know what the key unlocks, but I think Dr. Harper does."

No reaction.

Then I told her about seeing Mac, and how he hadn't acted a total butthead, and how Indri said she needed a shower to wash off contact-cooties from being that close to Worm Dung, and how I texted him our Square Books plans even though I knew Dad and Indri wouldn't like him showing up, so at least I told him it would be a bad idea for him to do that.

No response at all. That was fine. It was nice to explain it all to somebody who wouldn't yell at me over being happy that Mac had been nice. Grandma probably wouldn't have yelled, even before she got sick. Frowned, maybe. But her frowns used to be pretty epic.

"I don't know why you and Avadelle stopped being friends," I said, toying with her fingers. "And I don't know what you want me to do with the key."

"It's past time," Grandma said. "You got to open it. I got to—I need—"

The sound of her voice startled me so badly I dropped her hand on the sheets and looked at her face. Her eyes were closed. Had she really just said that? The words had been whispery and slurred, but clear enough to understand.

"Open what?" I stared right at Grandma's lips to see if they moved. "What does the key unlock, Grandma?"

Nothing. Just slow, soft breathing.

I kept watching Grandma's mouth but took her hand in mine again, trying not to let the disappointment and frustration grind at me. "I know you got hurt in the Meredith riot. Dad said you had to go to Chicago because the hospitals here wouldn't treat you since you were Black."

In the shadowy light, I saw a tear slide down Grandma's face and hit the pillowcase. "Ava," she said. Her mouth moved. I was sure of it. And then, "Why?"

Nothing else.

I stopped talking, because I so didn't want to make her cry. No more tears appeared, and her breathing went back to even, like she had fallen asleep. I kept tracing my fingertips along her skeletal hands, glad they were still so warm, even if they were soft and fragile.

Dad found me there later, when he came in for one of the night checks. Instead of fussing at me for not being in bed, he picked up another chair from around the desk, brought it over to the bed, sat down beside me, and put his arm around my shoulders.

"You upset, Dani?"

"No." I leaned against him.

"You telling the truth?"

"Yes."

He yawned and gazed at Grandma with me. "I noticed you didn't call Indri after dinner tonight. You two have words or something?"

"Nah. She had another Skype call with her dad tonight. They were trying for around eight our time, but it's whenever he gets to the front of the line and gets his turn."

Dad's profile looked huge and funny in the near darkness as he turned toward me and asked, "How long can they talk?"

"Half an hour, maybe. He can get back in line after that, but it takes hours to get another turn."

"Huh." His attention shifted back to Grandma. "That didn't start until after I retired. I would have liked to talk to you and your mother when I was deployed, but I probably wouldn't have had the patience for all that waiting-in-line mess."

"Yeah."

I didn't tell him about Grandma talking. We all knew she did it now and then, but it seemed private, the conversation she and I had before Dad came into the room. I wondered if he had his own private talks with her when Mom and I were gone for the day. I hoped he did.

The two of us watched Grandma breathe in, breathe out, breathe in, breathe out. She seemed peaceful and easy now.

13

A Smart Person Would Have Bolted

Excerpt from *Night on Fire* (1969),
by Avadelle Richardson, page 316

Am I your friend, CiCi, or am I not?

Of all the . . . what was I supposed to say to that? What was the truth? I dug around inside myself, sweat forming at the back of my neck. "Yes. I rate you as a friend, Leslie."

Her tense shoulders relaxed. Then she sat down at one of the classroom desks. "So what am I supposed to do when I'm sorry isn't enough?"

And here we were, back to why I had trouble moving past the Kream Kup situation. A crushing weariness took me. "Do you know who Billie Holiday is?"

Sitting at that desk, Leslie looked like a ninth grader trying not to laugh at her teacher. "Well, yeah.

Only the most famous jazz singer ever."

"Which of her songs are your favorites?"

"God Bless the Child," she said. "Oh, and Summertime, and Ain't Nobody's Business."

"Those are ones everybody knows. Did you ever hear Strange Fruit?"

She shook her head. "No."

"Well, I'm no Lady Day, but Strange Fruit goes like this." I cleared my throat and closed my eyes. My hand moved to my gut, and I squeezed the dickens out of my dusting rag as I pulled up the deep tones and made myself form the gritty words that almost shut down the Café Society club in Greenwich Village in 1939, the first time Billie Holiday sang them.

Southern trees bear a strange fruit,
Blood on the leaves and blood at the root . . .

I opened my eyes to take a breath, and all I could see was Leslie's horrified expression. I sang the rest of the verses, only two more, but each worse than the last, poetically describing the pastoral Southern scene, what a hanged person looks like, fruit for the crows to pluck . . . a strange and bitter crop.

When I finished, Leslie stared at me. Waiting. I wasn't sure what she wanted me to say.

"That's why you got to be more careful," I

whispered, my throat raw from the song. "Enough of us are gonna die as it is."

Leslie nodded. Then she put her face in her hands, and she cried.

DAD TOTALLY SURPRISED ME WEDNESDAY morning by having a sitter for Grandma, and taking Indri and me to Courthouse Square himself instead of having Mom drop us off. He said Dr. Harper would meet us there, and I managed not to tell him I'd just as soon Dr. Harper stay far, far away from me. If Dad was along, nothing bad could happen.

Indri and I sat in the backseat of Dad's black Mustang convertible, with the top down and Fink's "Hush Now" blaring from the radio. Damp morning air tingled against our faces. Everything smelled like grass and dirt and concrete, so soon after last night's rain, and Indri kept grinning as the wind whipped her ponytail in big circles. We had on nearly matching blouses, pink like a lot of the flowers we passed. I felt like spring and summer all at the same time, and I grinned too. Dad drove the slow loop around Courthouse Square looking for a parking spot, I hugged my pack with Grandma's writing and the key.

We passed the courthouse and the tall statue of a Confederate soldier gazing off in the distance. Then we drove past city hall on the right, with its familiar bench holding the bronze statue of William Faulkner. He sat on one end, in the same cross-legged pose I had seen all my life, smoking his eternal pipe and staring out across the square. On the other end of the bench sat Avadelle Richardson, dressed in a pink jogging suit, wearing her fedora hat that exactly matched the one on the statue, holding her eagle-head cane, and looking crankier than ever.

Spring-summer-pink popped like a balloon inside me, and I blinked my eyes fast, hoping she was a hallucination. A soft groan from the seat beside me let me know that Indri had seen her too.

Indri leaned forward to my ear and whispered, "What's *she* doing here?"

I almost said I had no idea, but that would have been a lie, so I just gave a little shrug.

Indri groaned again. "You didn't. You really, really didn't. Dr. Harper—and now *her,* too?"

"Sshh. Dad'll hear you." I started to sweat even though it wasn't hot. I mumbled to her about how Dr. Harper called Dad and planned to show up, and about what I texted to Mac. Then, too loud, I said, "How was your Skype call with your dad last night?"

Indri's evil look went way past epic, but she gave Dad a sideways glance and answered with, "Good! He thinks he might get to come home over Thanksgiving."

Real emotion chased away her annoyance, and she actually grinned. Meanwhile, I was thinking, *Thanksgiving. Wow.* That was like months from now, but she looked so excited. I smiled for her and tried to look excited back, but I couldn't imagine being away from my mom or dad for months and months and months, with just Skype connecting us.

"I'm glad your dad might get to be here for some of the holidays," I said as my dad parked.

Indri's smile got pretty huge. I decided she was a lot stronger than me. The whole warrior thing, it must seep down from soldiers to their kids—but maybe it only worked when the soldiers weren't retired. I mean, my dad had been career military before I could really remember. How did I get to be such a weenie?

"Come on, ladies," Dad said. "Ms. Manchester doesn't have all day."

We got out of the car, and Dad led us through the crosswalk to the entrance of 160 Courthouse Square, the two-story brick building with a balcony that most everyone in Oxford and outside of Oxford knew about: Square Books.

Dad held open the glass door and we walked into a world that smelled like old books, older wood, and really new books too. Right near the door, tables heaped in copies of bestsellers took up most of the space. Wooden shelves along each wall bent under decades of other books, and through it all wound the unmistakable aroma of brewing coffee from the little coffee bar upstairs. Indri drifted immediately to one of the tables that seemed to have a blue cover theme, and Dad instantly got distracted by a pile of green gardening encyclopedias.

I shouldered my pack as my eyes got pulled to gallery art,

then to shelves full of mysteries, then to the stairs, and . . .

Um, oops.

Mac Richardson leaned against the bannister about ten feet in front of me, wearing a yellow T-shirt with a guitar on the front and jeans with holes in both knees. He gave me a nod, but then his gaze flicked to Indri, and on to my father, and back to me with narrowed eyes.

You didn't say anything about your dad bringing you, that look said.

I tried to be stern with my answering expression, going all, *Hey, I didn't have to text you about coming here, did I?*

But I couldn't quite move, so I just formed an ice barrier of total freak-out between Dad and Indri and Mac. A smart person would have bolted out the front door.

Weenie, weenie, weenie.

Indri came up beside me. I didn't have to look at her to know she was glaring. As for Dad—no. I just couldn't even turn around to see what he was doing.

"Don't look for sympathy from me," Indri said in a deadly quiet voice.

"It'll be okay," I whispered back. "Don't make a thing out of it."

"There is something seriously wrong with you," she said.

A big hand closed on my shoulder. "Mackinnon," Dad said loud enough to be heard through the whole store. "This is a surprise."

Mac had the good sense to keep looking uncomfortable,

177

but he managed to straighten up and nod to my father. "I had to bring my grandmother to the Square for her morning walk and communion with the bard, and I knew you'd be here to see my Aunt Naomi about the Meredith riot."

"You knew—" Dad started, but Indri cut him off with—

"Communion with the bard?" She folded her arms. "What, she worships William Faulkner? Wasn't he a mean old drunk?"

I closed my eyes for a second, but at least Indri left off the *too* on that sentence.

Mac didn't take the bait. "GG says Mr. Faulkner liked his whiskey and mint juleps, just like her." His lopsided grin was cute. "I thought maybe I could help y'all figure out what happened the night of the riot, since GG won't tell anybody."

"I see," Dad said.

My head got a double-cold sensation, like Dad might be staring freeze-lasers into my skull. A thousand excuses and explanations popped into my brain, but before I could fumble around with any of them, Ms. Manchester appeared at the top of the steps.

Dr. Harper was standing right behind her.

Indri and I both jumped at the sight of the professor, but he was dressed in khaki slacks with a tweed jacket, and his white hair had gone back to unkempt. The unlit pipe in his teeth finished his transformation back to nice-old-guy, but I couldn't help staring straight at his face, waiting for that *other* professor to make an appearance. The angry one, with the edge of something like hunger.

"Morning!" Ms. Manchester waved down to us, and I had an insane urge to run up the stairs and hug her, but I didn't want to get that close to Dr. Harper. Instead, I waved back as she spotted Mac. "And hello, nephew mine. Where's Mom?"

"Out by the statue." Mac jogged up the steps and gave his aunt a hug. "You know, searching for inspiration, or whatever it is she does on that bench."

"What she does on that bench is scare the town with her grouchy face," Ms. Manchester said, her tone matter-of-fact.

"Well, yeah." Mac grinned again, and I fixed my eyes on my feet as I climbed the steps to avoid noticing he was cute this time.

Dad and Indri followed along behind me, not helping my shivery insides with their cold silence. Jeez. It wasn't like Mac robbed gas stations for a living. Maybe I should have hated Mac for disrespecting our friendship, but I just didn't anymore.

As for Dr. Harper, maybe he was having a bad day yesterday. *Or maybe he's going to drag you into a dark alley and club you in the head to steal that key.* Yeah. That little fear spoke itself in Indri's voice.

I almost walked right into Ms. Manchester, who had stopped at one of the coffee bar tables. She pulled two of the tables together, then gestured to Mac to bring the high-backed wooden chairs closer.

I took the spot at the end of the table, with Dad on one side and Ms. Manchester on the other. I was thinking about the locker scene with Mac. Maybe, just maybe, if Mac and I kept talking and being peaceful, I'd get to ask him the real reason he wanted to stop being friends.

"Baby girl," Dad said, annoyed. "This is your show, remember?"

"What?" I snapped my gaze away from Mac and gaped at Dad, then slowly, slowly remembered why we had come. "Ms. Manchester, you know my grandmother's not well."

Ms. Manchester nodded, and her smile faltered. Her eyes drifted to my father, and filled with sympathy.

"She's been getting agitated this last week or so, and saying stuff that I think is related to Avadelle—to your mom, and to whatever happened between them. Dr. Harper told us that most feud scholars believe the fight started over *Night on Fire*, and something your mom did or didn't say in her novel. But Dr. Harper also said the fight could have started before that, and their friendship seemed more troubled right after the riot. So, I'd like to understand more about the night James Meredith came to Ole Miss."

Ms. Manchester didn't answer right away, so I added, "We know Grandma got hurt during the riot." I pointed to Dr. Harper, who was sitting beside her. "He also told us about that. We're hoping you know something more than the rest of us."

She stayed quiet, but she got up, went over to a stack of books beside a shelf, took off the top one, and came back. When she put it on the table, I realized it was a bound document, not a book—and by the title, it was the paper she had written about the Meredith riot. She opened the paper, pulled a pencil from behind her ear, and tapped the first paragraph. "I'll answer what I can, but a little context will help."

"Oh, here we go with the context again," Indri said, sounding miserable. Across the table from her, Dr. Harper laughed, and she closed her mouth.

Ms. Manchester tapped the bound document in front of her. "James Meredith first applied to Ole Miss in 1961. Let's trace history from that point forward."

14

UNDER ATTACK FROM EVERYWHERE

———

**Excerpt from *Night on Fire* (1969),
by Avadelle Richardson, page 361**

*Early on Saturday Morning, July 7, 1962, I woke
to somebody pounding on my front door. My heart
jumped straight to my throat, and I near about fell
out of bed. Rain pattered on the tin roof as I pulled
on my robe and slippers. It might be the police. The
classes, helping with voter registration—I was going
to jail.*

*Aunt Jessie and Abram and I hit the living room at
the same time. Mama had stayed in bed, in too much
pain to move. I grabbed my boy and pushed him at
Aunt Jessie. "Take him to the kitchen. If it's the police,
you go out back with him, and you keep going, and
you don't stop until you get three states north, you
hear me?"*

Aunt Jessie set her mouth and nodded. She took hold of my son's hand, and she towed him out of that room, leaving me to face the door alone.

Bang. Bang. Bang.

I didn't hear anybody hollering for me to open up, but then, that's how they did sometimes, sneaky-like and mean, so you couldn't be ready or run. I straightened myself, tied my robe, and made my feet walk.

Hand shaking, I gripped the handle and pulled open the door, my eyes blinking so fast, my skin and bones already waiting to be grabbed and tackled and beaten. Instead, I found Leslie standing in the rain like a half-drowned puppy, bawling her eyes out.

I snatched hold of her and pulled her into my house, slamming the door quick behind her. "Are you out of your mind showing up here in daylight?"

"He had a heart attack, CiCi." She sobbed, then covered her mouth. "It was a heart attack."

"What are you even talking about?"

Leslie lowered her hand, but her eyes were barely focused. Her words sounded like so much crazy rambling. "At Byhalia. At the sanatorium where he goes, you know, after a run of drinking—Wright's? I think that's the name of it."

Noises behind me let me know that Aunt Jessie had realized I wasn't being arrested. She and Abram

183

eased up beside me to face Leslie, and Aunt Jessie put a hand on my elbow.

Understanding began to dawn. I stepped back from Leslie, my breath leaving me like I'd been punched. My world got darker and sadder, and I would have cried if life had left me with any tears at all. "Oh. Oh, good Lord."

Leslie nodded and sobbed again. "He's gone, CiCi. William Faulkner died yesterday."

"BY 1961," MS. MANCHESTER SAID, "Southerners felt like they were under attack from everywhere because people were insisting that the races get mixed and treated equally. James Meredith applied to Ole Miss, and his application was denied due to his race. On September 10, 1962, the United States Fifth Circuit Court of Appeals ordered the University of Mississippi to enroll James Meredith, effective immediately. Three days later, Governor Ross Barnett got on television and radio and stated, 'We must either submit to the unlawful dictates of the federal government or stand up like men and tell them never!'"

"Sounds like he wanted people in Mississippi to riot." Mac frowned. "Telling people to do violent things—that's not legal, is it?"

"What a nutjob," Indri said, sitting back in her chair.

Dad quit rubbing his head long enough to pat Indri's arm. "That's how people talk when they're scared."

"That's how people talk when they're huge idiots and want to make people panic and grab guns and start shooting," Indri fired right back, making Dad smile at her, even though his eyes were half closed.

He held up his hand to block some of the light coming in through the windows. "You have a hippie's heart, little girl," he said to Indri. "I knew I liked you for a reason."

"Thanks." She smiled back at him. "I think."

Ms. Manchester pointed to her paper, to another underlined section. "The situation at Ole Miss with James Meredith turned into a flashpoint for the push for integration. On September 29, President John F. Kennedy issued a proclamation calling on the governing authorities and the people of the State of Mississippi to 'cease and desist' their obstruction to Meredith's registration, and to 'disperse and retire peaceably forthwith.'"

I had seen videos of President Kennedy before, and I thought about that stern, solemn face, and his weird Yankee accent, and imagined him saying *cease* and *disperse* and *forthwith*.

Ms. Manchester relaxed in her chair and put both of her hands on the table, on either side of the paper she had written. "The next day, James Meredith arrived at the University of Mississippi, and a riot erupted."

"That's insane," Mac muttered. My father glanced at him, and Mac moved slightly to the left, giving Dad plenty of space as his aunt kept talking.

"One group of marshals took Meredith to safety in a

residence hall while another group faced the mob," Ms. Manchester used a different voice than the one she used to tell us ghost stories. No drama. No flashlight. But I shivered anyway, because this was scarier than her spooky tales.

Dr. Harper cleared his throat. His face sagged with a huge frown, and his voice was too quiet when he said, "I knew there was trouble, that there would be much, much more, but honestly, I was deep into working on an article and didn't expect the worst to happen until school actually began." He paused, keeping his eyes on his hands. "I remember sitting in my Bondurant office, smelling fire, smelling tear gas. When I looked at the clock, it was around nine p.m., and that's the moment I understood I was in trouble, that the campus was in complete turmoil—and that Ruth might be at risk when she came to get the books I had collected for her elementary school class. It was far too late to warn her, since we had no cell phones. Gunfire erupted, seemingly from everywhere. I remember stuffing towels around my doors and windows and huddling on the floor until morning. I prayed very hard for your grandmother's safety."

"Ruth and my mother had been working at your grandmother's school," Ms. Manchester said. "Like Dr. Harper, they expected the big showdown to happen the next day. By the time they reached campus, the Lyceum was under siege. A mix of students and citizens and Klan members and paramilitary groups had taken control of the Circle, and they raised the Confederate flag on the university's flagpole.

Groups of fighters roamed the campus, making trouble and attacking people."

"I can't imagine that," Indri said. "I mean, I know the campus like my own backyard. I've been to the Lyceum a zillion times. I knew there was a riot because of that statue of James Meredith, but I just can't see a real military attack happening right out there on the grass."

Ms. Manchester studied her. "That's one of the reasons I made it the focus of my paper, to try to get a better understanding of what happened, and how. That night, the badly outnumbered marshals fired tear gas, but the mob fought back with rocks and Molotov cocktails and attempted to drive cars, a fire engine, even a bulldozer into the marshals' position at the Lyceum. By eleven p.m., most of the students had withdrawn, leaving Ku Klux Klan groups shooting at the marshals. More marshals came to reinforce the first group, but the Lyceum had become a field hospital. Hundreds of injured marshals were holed up inside with some journalists and medical folks, just trying to stay alive."

She stopped to let us absorb all of that. My dad got up, went to the coffee bar, and poured himself a cup. When he came back to the tables, he tried to pay Ms. Manchester for it, but she waved him off. After Dad sat back down, his face as grim as when he tried to watch war movies, Dr. Harper told us the rest.

"I had my radio on by then," Dr. Harper said. "President Kennedy called in the National Guard, and when that wasn't

187

enough, he sent in the United States Army. They started arriving in Oxford by air around one in the morning. By the next morning, two people were dead, a French reporter and a jukebox repairman. Over one hundred sixty federal marshals were injured, along with about one hundred forty other people."

Not in our history books, I thought. *Not in our history books, not in our history books*. I knew that the riot happened, but I didn't know the names of the two dead people. I didn't know the names of the three hundred hurt people—except for one, Ruth Beans—and this stuff happened right *here*, where I lived.

"On October 1, 1962," Ms. Manchester said, "James Meredith officially matriculated into the University of Mississippi. By the next day, twenty-three thousand troops occupied Oxford to keep order, and Mr. Meredith had to be escorted by federal marshals until he graduated in 1963. There's a lot more to the details, like secret deals made and broken by the governor, and the fact that Ross Barnett's own son had to face down his father to do his duty as a national guardsman during that crisis."

Indri held up her hand. "Wait. Twenty-three thousand troops? Here?"

"I have photos." Ms. Manchester pushed back from the table and went to the stack of books. When she came back, she had a folder full of black-and-white pictures. When she spread them out, the scenes looked like something straight out of World War II—jeep after jeep, transport after transport, packed with rifle-toting Army soldiers, rolling through streets I recognized. In one photo, gas-mask-wearing soldiers with their round helmets marched ten across, for as far as I could see. In another, troop transports crammed the football field and the area all around it.

"If that happened today," Indri whispered, "I would freak out."

"The Posse Comitatus Act—that's a federal law—limits when regular military troops can be deployed on U.S. soil, even to keep order," Dr. Harper said. "So it's rare. Thank God."

Ms. Manchester gathered up her photos and faced me, holding the stack in both hands. "The bottom line is, Ruth and my mother unknowingly drove into the middle of an armed insurrection during a time when the highway patrol wasn't restricting access to the Ole Miss campus. From what I can piece together from what Mother has told me, and from what she wrote in *Night on Fire*, she and Ruth made it to the Circle and got stopped by the mob and the tear gas. They got out and tried to get past the Lyceum to Dr. Harper's office. The mob went after Ruth, and Mom stood up to them and tricked them into backing off. They got separated, and Ruth wound up injured. Mother thought she might have fallen in a steam tunnel."

My chest ached at the thought of Grandma hurt in the steam tunnels, lying down there in the dark and calling out for somebody to rescue her, and realizing nobody would come.

The screams from the steam tunnels. Just like that ghost story.

Wait. Didn't that start in the 1960s?

I didn't have the book with me, but I was sure that's when the screaming-in-tunnels tale first got told. Had people heard my grandmother screaming and turned it into a story?

No way. No way!

The thought made me a little sick, and I wondered about the family of the guy who died in the car wreck, the ghost that was supposed to be haunting Saint Anthony Hall. They probably got ill every time they saw anything about *that* story.

All of a sudden, I didn't want to read any more about ghosts that might have been real people. Witches and werewolves and vampires, those were probably still fun enough in the right book, but ghosts—no. I was done with ghosts. Real-life death and pain just didn't seem that entertaining.

But there was one thing I was beginning to realize I did need to read, and more than just the excerpts I'd seen on websites about the feud. *Night on Fire*. Wonderful. I could almost feel the boredom and misery clawing at my brain, and I didn't even have a copy yet.

"I'm going to get more coffee," Dad announced, and he got up without waiting for an answer. Talking about this was bothering him, I could tell. Ms. Manchester went with him, and Mac got up and scooted down the stairs, I assumed to make sure Avadelle Richardson wasn't in a fistfight with the William Faulkner statue, or some innocent tourist.

That left Indri and me alone at the table with Dr. Harper.

When I glanced at him, he was staring straight at me, and my heart did a tap dance in my chest. Indri got a bad case of lemur eyes, and both of us were just about to shove back from our spots and go over to the counter with Dad and Ms. Manchester when Dr. Harper held up both hands, palms out.

"Girls," he whispered. "Please wait. I owe you an apology."

We didn't get up, but neither of us relaxed. Indri's gaze darted from Dr. Harper to Ms. Manchester and Dad, like she was judging the number of steps to the coffee pot and safety. I found myself meeting Dr. Harper's eyes, sort of mad, sort of scared, but also curious. When I nodded, he spoke, low and quiet.

"Just after your grandmother was diagnosed with Alzheimer's, she brought me a lockbox and asked me to keep it safe for her, until she passed away." He pulled off his glasses and gave them an inspection like he was checking for smudges, but I figured he just didn't want to see our faces as he dropped that little bit of dynamite into our brains. Indri twitched in her chair, and I leaned forward in mine.

A lockbox. A lockbox! That key—yes. It would be perfect for something like that. My thoughts rushed ahead so quickly that I barely heard what Dr. Harper said next.

"She told me that once she was gone, I should give it to you, Dani. That you'd have a key to open it, and I could help you decide what to do with what she had left inside."

"So, the key I have goes to that lockbox?" I asked, so excited I wanted to get straight up and run back to his office.

191

"I suspect so, yes. Needless to say, I wanted very much to see what she had hidden in that box." He got one of his huge, sad frowns. "I'll admit the thoughts of income from publishing papers and books solving the feud mystery weighed on my mind. I felt very greedy."

"Well, let's go over there and open the box!" Indri whispered, so loud it was almost like talking.

"I'd love to," Dr. Harper said, putting his glasses back on, "but she took back the box."

"What?" Indri and I asked at the same time.

"About a year ago," Dr. Harper said, "just before your family started keeping her mostly at home, she showed up late one evening, when I was working. She demanded that I return the box. Went on about people stealing from her and conspiracies and disrespect. She said she was going to give her story to history and let the ghosts keep it for Dani. When I tried to talk her out of it, she slapped me."

Give her story to history. Let the ghosts keep it. . . . I'd heard that before, from my grandmother's own lips. My mouth sagged open, and heat rushed to my face. "She—what? She hit you? Oh, I'm sorry. I—wow."

He waved me off. "I knew it was the disease, not her. In the end, it was her box, so I returned it to her."

"But," Indri said, sounding shocked and lost, "where did she take it?"

Dr. Harper lifted his shoulders and let them drop, looking totally beaten. "I have no idea. I locked my door when she left, because I didn't want to be yelled at or slapped again. She stayed in the building for some time, then I saw her walking off into the dark, in the direction of the Lyceum. She had something in her hands, probably the box. When I saw her all alone like that, I got worried that she would get lost or struck by a car, so I ran after her. I caught up with her on the steps of the grand old building—but alas, no box. She couldn't even speak coherently about it when I asked her."

The noise in my head was unbelievable. My thoughts pinged from glass soldiers to the thousand spots between Ventress Hall and the Lyceum where my grandmother could have hidden the box. "Have you looked for it, Dr. Harper?"

"Indeed I have. I've done a fair search of Ventress, and walked the route she took—all to no avail." He shrugged again, and looked even sadder.

Indri seemed like she was deep in concentration. "Why did Avadelle visit you yesterday?"

Dr. Harper fidgeted in his seat, and for a second, I worried that he might go back to being that other guy, the greedy one who scared us both. After a few more fidgets, he seemed to decide that he was definitely and fully on our side in this little fight, and he said, "Avadelle wanted to know if Ruth had talked to me about the night of the riot, or about anything. She asked me if Ruth had left me any of her writing, and more specifi-cally, if she and I had discussed *Night on Fire*."

I managed not to imitate his fidgeting, but it was hard. I kept trying to take whole, relaxed breaths, but that was hard too. "What did you tell her?" I finally asked him, when I thought I could trust myself not to be too loud.

"The truth as it stands now," he said, his eyes wide and his expression earnest. "That I have nothing of Ruth's."

"Did you tell her about what we showed you?" Indri asked. She glanced over at my father and Ms. Manchester, making sure they were still away from the table and not paying attention to us. "Did you tell her about the key?"

"Absolutely not. We have an agreement." He shook his head. "I'm certain Avadelle has gotten concerned about something being discovered about that night—I just don't know what."

"Dani, we need to—"

And that was when we heard the first *thump*.

I slowly registered the sound, like a rubbery bump against wood, and my heart stuttered.

Thump!

It was the rubber tip of a cane hitting wooden steps.

"Maaan," Mac muttered as he appeared at the top step, moving backward and fast, like he was fleeing something carnivorous. "She's got fifteen minutes left on her morning communion. Why'd she have to come in here?"

Thump.

Thump!

I grabbed the stack of papers from the coffee table and worked them into my backpack, pronto. The zipper kept jumping away from my fingertips.

"Oh dear," Dr. Harper said, loud enough to get Dad and Ms. Manchester's attention.

I finally got my pack closed as Avadelle crested the stairs. Dad came to stand behind me, still squinting from his headache, while Ms. Manchester and Mac stopped behind Indri. For some reason I couldn't explain, we all looked guilty, like we'd been caught at something.

Avadelle took a few steps toward us, cane bumping hard on the floor, and then stopped.

I felt like the principal had just walked into my class and found me texting instead of doing my work. My attention snapped to her face, or her cheeks and mouth, which was all I could see under her Faulkner fedora. Her wrinkled skin wasn't red, like I expected. It was pasty white and covered in sweat. Her mouth was twisted, and her expression was all thunder and rage, but under that, something else—

Fear.

No.

Terror.

Had she heard us talking before she started up the stairs?

I found it hard to breathe. But we weren't doing anything wrong, and she couldn't stop me from hunting for clues about what happened to my grandmother the night of the Meredith riot. She wasn't *my* grandmother, no, and she wasn't even nice to me—but I hated thinking about anybody old getting embarrassed or upset, for any reason.

Whether or not she had been eavesdropping, Avadelle

seemed to realize we had been talking about something related to her, because she focused on her daughter and said, "What's going on here, Naomi?"

"The girls had questions about the Meredith riot," Ms. Manchester said. "They're learning about the town's history."

"Town's history, my eye!" Avadelle screeched, holding her position between us and the stairs. She pointed at me. "That one's digging up bones about the feud. She'll have the paparazzi down on us again, and the clamour won't ever end."

I realized she had us blocked in, unless we wanted to bail over the second-floor railing. Mac leaned in that direction, like he was considering the option.

"Please calm down," Ms. Manchester said as she got up. "We're just trying to help Ruth—"

Avadelle cut her off, still pointing at me. "Leave the past be, you wretched heathen!"

Heathen? I didn't know whether to yell back or laugh. My cheeks got hot. I stood, and Indri scrambled out of her chair. Carefully, hoping Avadelle didn't focus on it too much, I picked up my pack and slid it onto my shoulder. My thoughts sped up, dashing from point to point on Grandma's time line, and bouncing between all the questions I had.

"Did it ever occur to you that Ruth's not in her right mind anymore?" Avadelle reached out to a display table on her right and shoved all the books on the floor. "All of you, stay out of her business, and stay out of mine!"

"That's enough," Dad said. "It's nearly time for the store to open. Dani, Indri, come on. Let's go on outside."

"You made a mess, Mother." Ms. Manchester sighed. "Mac, give me a hand with the books."

Avadelle's lips trembled, but she didn't yell anything else. Mac followed his aunt closer to his grandmother to pick up the books, but I could tell he didn't want to go. Indri moved behind me and seemed to get smaller, like she was trying to be invisible.

"Answer one question and I'll stop looking into what happened the night of the Meredith riot." The words left me in a rush, and I almost clamped my fingers over my own mouth, I surprised myself so much.

Dad and Indri didn't make a peep, and Mac and Ms. Manchester paused in mid-display repair, obviously surprised too. Avadelle tilted her head back to study me under the brim of her hat. A second ticked by, and then another.

Avadelle snorted. "No. I don't believe you. I'm not telling you a thing."

"Whatever. I'm going to the library and I'll read your book, and everything Ms. Manchester gave us, and anything I can find that my grandmother wrote about that night. I'll talk to her any time she's able to talk, and I'll visit any place that might give me a clue, and I'm going to figure out what happened. So if you want me to stop, why don't you just tell me yourself? What happened the night of the Meredith riot that you don't want anybody to know about?"

I balled up my fists at my sides, waiting for the next explosion, but Avadelle just stood there staring at me. She went even paler. All the anger and meanness seemed to drain right out of her, and I realized her hands were shaking.

She pulled her cane toward her body and pressed the eagle head into her chest. "Read my book," she said, then choked off. "Ruth's articles . . ." She sputtered again. "They don't—it's not . . . well, do it. Go to the library, then. Read whatever you want. Just go!"

Then she burst into tears.

Before anybody could start talking, she wheeled around, barely balanced, and lurched toward the stairs. If Mac hadn't dropped the display books he was holding, lunged forward, and grabbed her arm to steady her, Avadelle Richardson, Oxford, Mississippi's, most famous living author, would have fallen headfirst down the Square Books stairs and broken her neck.

15

LOOK AT THIS MESS

Excerpt from *Night on Fire* (1969),
by Avadelle Richardson, page 386

On September 13, 1962, my class crowded around a little black-and-white TV set in my classroom. Ed Simmons had brought it, and we all agreed to meet at the school and watch together. Leslie had her hand on the foil and rabbit ears to keep the connection. Her eyes looked about as wide as the moon.

The grainy face of Governor Ross Barnett stared back at us, solemn as a funeral director. This man, who was a member of the white supremacist Citizen's Council. This man, who said Black people lived in Mississippi in such number because we loved segregation, and claimed that God was the original segregationist, never intending for the races to mix. Just the sight of him made me clench my fists.

His glasses shined in the studio lights. Reception blinked in and out as he rambled on, saying, "We must either submit to the unlawful dictates of the federal government or stand up like men and tell them no. . . . There is no case in history where the Caucasian race has survived social integration. We will not drink from the cup of genocide."

"He's calling for a riot rather than let James Meredith be admitted," Leslie said.

Aunt Jessie stood. "People are gonna get dead over this, maybe a lot of them."

"It's worth it," Leslie countered.

Aunt Jessie pointed a finger right at her nose. "You won't be the one they lynch, little girl, so you just watch your mouth."

I'M GOING TO THE LIBRARY and I'll read your stupid book, and everything Ms. Manchester gave us, and anything I can find that my grandmother wrote about that night. . . .

Yeah. Wasn't that a lot of big talk?

An hour after Dad dropped Indri, Mac, Dr. Harper, and me off at Ole Miss's J.D. Williams Library, I realized just how big a boast I had made. Avadelle's reaction and near-suicide-by-stairs had surprised Dad and Ms. Manchester, so Ms. Manchester dismissed Mac from babysitting and took her mother home. Dad agreed to let us stay with Dr. Harper without asking too many questions, but the way he eyed me,

I was pretty sure he was getting suspicious that something was up—something he didn't totally understand. That made me feel bad, since I still hadn't told him about the key, or how much Grandma wrote to me, or what that key might open. He seemed to be in so much pain from that headache. I couldn't help but wonder if I had caused it.

Mac stuck with Dr. Harper, Indri, and me. We didn't talk much to him, but we didn't take potshots, either. As soon as Dad was out of earshot, we had filled him in on the key and the lockbox, and what Grandma had written before she got too confused to keep going. He had volunteered to help us without any hesitation, even though we might find out something that made his life babysitting his grandmother harder. "I'd rather know," he said. "That way, stuff can't sneak up on me—and maybe I can figure out what else to keep her away from so she won't freak out again."

"Here." Indri snapped me out of my increasing guilt trip about Dad and Mac having a hard time when she dumped about twenty books in my lap. They hit my knees and thighs and tumbled onto the tile floor, where I was sitting outside Dr. Harper's library carrel. His spot wasn't in the nice, blue-carpeted upstairs part with bright lights, wooden partitions, desks, computers, and Starbucks. Of course not.

Dr. Harper's secret hideout was down where everything smelled like paint and old water. Pipes ran across the ceiling and crowded floor-to-ceiling metal shelves held dusty volumes of just about anything nobody ever wanted to study.

Dim lights flickered every now and then, and the pipes gave off bumps and groans that echoed all across the cavernous space. The librarians rarely came to this crossroads of Creepy and Nowhere, which was probably a good thing, because they might have killed us over the mess. Technically, Indri, Mac, and I weren't supposed to be here without our parents, but I figured Dr. Harper had to count for something.

Mac sat on the floor beside me, silently working his way through the books his aunt had loaned us, making notes on a legal pad Dr. Harper had given him. He seemed to be creating his own time line about the riot, but also writing down random facts that caught his attention.

Dr. Harper sat inside his carrel at a little desk, looking up stuff on his iPad, studying articles my grandmother wrote, and making his own notes. Indri had collected Avadelle's books, and I was now buried in a stack of all the library's copies of *Night on Fire*, because Indri was, by nature, overly thorough. "I thought you might like one better than the other," she said as she plopped down beside me. "Besides, there are different editions. I don't know if that matters."

She started thumbing through Avadelle's other works—about a dozen novels and ten collections of short stories. We had pads to take notes too.

The first hardback copy of *Night on Fire* I picked up looked shiny and new. It had a plastic protector, but the publisher's cover had a gold label on the bottom that said, *50th Anniversary Edition*. The picture on the front showed two women, one Black and one White, running through flames and looking terrified. I opened the book, turned past the card catalogue pocket with the check-out card, and read the dedication.

"For everyone who suffered, and everyone who suffers."

Did she mean my grandmother? Somebody else? I wrote the line on my pad, along with those questions. The book was thick, maybe five hundred pages or more.

I read fast, but how was I ever going to get through all that mess, especially if it was boring? Dr. Harper said there were hundreds of papers and even a few books analyzing the novel, but he insisted I should read the actual text because I might see something new, since much of it related to my grandmother, and I'd have a different context.

The first line of the book was pretty simple.

"It was hot."

Really?

All those prizes and awards, and the book started with three words about the weather? I frowned. I guess I expected all kinds of flowery sentences, tightly packed, telling some boring, rambling story with lots of metaphors. But the next lines were, *"It was too hot to live, and too hot to die, but Death drove to Mississippi anyway. In fact, the old monster squealed into town on bald tires, and I think I saw him grinning as he tossed a flaming bottle on the grass and blew up the world."*

"Mom calls *me* dramatic," I mumbled to myself.

Drrraaaaammmmmaaa got entered into my notes next, along with a frowning circle and two lines underneath that was supposed to be a skull and crossbones to represent Death.

Mac muttered something about the riot being crazy, then said to Indri, "Bob Dylan wrote a song called "Oxford Town." One of the verses says, *Guns and clubs followed him down/ All because his face was brown.*"

"Put it in the notes," Indri told him, then leaned her head back on the wall, eyes closed. "Avadelle's so sarcastic about everything. Her short stories—they're like listening to her talk, only lots meaner. I didn't think that was possible."

Mac snickered. "Dr. Harper said to look for themes, or mentions of the riot, or mentions of giving something to history."

"Shhh," Dr. Harper said from inside his carrel. "This is a library."

"It probably has a thousand ghosts," Indri whispered. As if obeying her whim, the lights flickered, and a pipe pinged as water rushed over our heads.

Mac made a face. "Somebody probably flushed somewhere. Ew."

I put down the shiny new copy of *Night on Fire* and checked out some of the older ones. The pictures and type on the covers looked different. One had a shadowy building like the Lyceum with flames all around it. Another showed a crowd carrying signs emerging from smoke and fire. One had no picture at all, just the old-fashioned heavy library binding

I remembered from books Mom used to bring home to study. I opened each edition and looked at the first few pages. Some had yellow highlighting where people had ignored library rules about writing in books. The fourth one had a typed note about who donated it. I made myself read all the way through the first chapter.

"Main charcacters are CiCi Robinson and Leslie Marks," I scrawled on my pad. *"CiCi is a Black school teacher in Holly Springs."* Under that, I wrote, *"Grandma was a schoolteacher, but over in Abbeville."* CiCi had some stuff in common with Grandma, like being obsessed with classic books and book quotes, and keeping herself very, very neat and fixed up in public. Avadelle didn't mention her smelling good, though. Leslie Marks was Jewish and from up North, not born in Oxford or anything, like Avadelle. Plus, Avadelle described Leslie as "a tall thing with a big smile," and "her thinking was all daisies and sunshine."

Ha. Definitely NOT Avadelle-like.

"Interesting," Dr. Harper said in a very quiet and library-like voice. "Ruth never mentioned the riot in her articles or papers. Not once. She touched on just about every major event in this state, especially pertaining to racial unrest—but never that crucial moment. Why did I never notice before?"

"I don't think Avadelle ever wrote about the riot again either," Indri said, shifting her pile of books around and picking up another novel. "All of these stories tell about other places and times."

"They're not in any of the pictures I've seen so far," Mac said, "and the books don't list Ruth Beans as one of the injured, either."

Their voices faded away from me as I read Avadelle's story, seeing 1960s Oxford line by line, description by description. Some of the stores and businesses Avadelle mentioned were still in town, like Neilson's—"the South's oldest store" since 1839. Other sites were long gone. Still, I could imagine myself walking around the places she discussed, because Oxford had always been my home. I bet Dad actually did walk around a lot of the spots.

My eyes drifted to my fingers, brown against the white pages. *Guns and clubs followed him down/All because his face was brown. . . .*

Then again, maybe Dad didn't walk around a lot of them. When Dad was twelve like me, where was he allowed to go? Where would have been too dangerous, full of those guns and clubs? How did he even begin to figure that out, or live through it? I couldn't quit looking at my fingers, trying to imagine that time, that world, so much like mine, and yet so different.

What would it have been like, not to be allowed near a library, or a public restroom, or a water fountain, just because of how I looked?

Dad's face floated in my mind, eyes squinted, rubbing the sides of his head to make his headache go away, like he did in Square Books. It couldn't be any fun, remembering bad times like the ones in Avadelle's book. No wonder he didn't want to talk about civil rights or his childhood much. I wouldn't either.

I closed the copy of *Night on Fire* I was reading and put it down. Slowly, trying to shake off a growing sadness I couldn't explain, I rifled through the rest of the copies Indri had dumped on top of me. When I opened the one with the library binding, I saw it had the original publication date. A typed note on the card catalogue page read, "Donated by Ruth Beans."

My whole body went motionless. I stared at those typed words, surprise nearly making me dizzy. When I turned to the dedication page, just under the part about suffering, my grandmother's handwriting waited for me.

Ruth Beans was here.

When she first told me about the key, she said something like that. *I was there. You get that stuff out of my bag, you hear me? Give it to history. . . . I was there. . . . Get the key.*
Ruth Beans was here.

Like something a little kid would write. But what did she mean? Where was *here*? In Oxford? In the library? In the book? She had dated it September 2, 1969—the day after the book was released. I showed the inscription to Indri, then to Mac. They both read the line quietly, then looked up at me, obviously as clueless as I was. When I took it to Dr. Harper, he nodded. "I suspect that's the version you need to read."

I frowned at him. "But why did she write that?"

"I have no idea," he said.

Hours passed as I sat just outside Dr. Harper's carrel door, submerged in *Night on Fire*. Some parts of some chapters seemed boring, so I skimmed, but mostly I read, and the chapters seem to go faster and faster. I sort of heard Indri and Mac talking sometimes, and Dr. Harper, but I didn't pay any attention to what they said. At some point, Dr. Harper asked me to show him Grandma's key. In a fog of darkness, fire, and people yelling horrible things all because a man with brown skin wanted to go to college, I slipped the key out of my pocket and held it out for him to compare against a picture on his iPad.

It was a lockbox, with a key.

He nodded. "Etsy is a lifesaver. That's definitely the key to the box I saw." Barely paying attention, I lowered the key, moving it gently between my fingers as I absorbed more of the short, speedy chapters.

By page three hundred ninety-three, the moment of the riot was drawing closer, and I could feel the dread of it in my belly.

When Leslie said, "If we're going to campus, we'd best hurry," I wanted to scream *NO* and get her attention, but . . .

Leslie put her hand on the mailers I was sealing at my teacher's desk. "Tomorrow, all hell's gonna break loose." She hesitated as I scooted my stack of envelopes

to the side and got to my feet. "Or you could stay and
keep working, and I could go without you."

"Why?" I gave her a frown. "Because you're White
and won't anybody bother you?"

She sighed.

I crossed my arms, wondering why it made me
mad that she offered. She was right. Nobody would
notice her at Ole Miss, and they might notice me.

"Yes, because I'm White and nobody will bother
me," she said. "Even if people are already making
trouble, I can go in and come back out without get-
ting involved."

That made me laugh. "You can't even buy ice
cream without running your mouth and putting us
all at risk for getting arrested."

They were so different, CiCi and Leslie, but here they
were, friends, doing dangerous things together. That fasci-
nated me. As for looking at the South before civil rights, that
horrified me. What it was like for CiCi and her family made
me want to cry. People treated other people so badly. Ole
Miss—*my* Ole Miss—my town, caught up in so much rage
and hatred—so scary.

"I don't like the looks of this." I gripped the wheel
of my old Chevrolet. Traffic snarled around us as
we inched into the Circle—way too many cars and

trucks. Was that a bus? The roads were lined with troopers, and those marked cars looked to be packed with uniforms.

They sat in their vehicles and ignored the stopped traffic and the bystanders.

Leslie sat in the backseat, hair up and fooling with her nails like some shallow, rich White woman. We had to keep up a maid-and-lady show to make it okay for us to be in the same car together.

"Are those students gathering on the sidewalk?" she asked.

"Some of them," I muttered. But some were way too old to be college kids. And some had on military uniforms, but they didn't look regular. More patched together, or like retired officers putting their colors back on for one last fight.

Everyone I looked at wore grim expressions. Those closest showed slit-eyed, clench-jawed anger. I could almost taste their bitter rage on the evening breeze. And then—

Oh, God help me, those are white hoods and sheets.

"Why are so many people on campus now?" I heard fear in Leslie's voice, which gave me the screaming willies, because Leslie usually didn't have enough sense to be scared when she should have been.

"Those men over there have badges," she went on,

talking too fast. "The federal marshals are already here. And there are boys with guns in those trees beside them."

She pointed.

Something popped. Again. Pop, pop, pop!

And then Leslie screamed.

"CiCi, they're shooting at the marshals!"

"Look at this mess." The voice cut into my consciousness, making me jump. Dr. Harper jumped almost as high as I did. Indri and Mac started scrambling around outside the carrel, and a few seconds later, Ms. Donalvan, one of the head librarians, filled up the carrel door, glaring at Dr. Harper.

"Fred, what on earth are you letting these children do? They have piles of books spread everywhere—and you—look at you with those newspaper and journal binders! You know the limit is three, not three thousand!"

"I'm sorry, Jessica." He gave her his best bumbling professor smile. "We're working on a joint project, you see, and—"

"What you're working on is a suspension of your carrel privileges." Ms. Donalvan wasn't much taller than Dr. Harper, but she seemed to tower over the little space. She had to be about seventy, but like my grandmother, she didn't have a single wrinkle, just crow's feet at the corners of both eyes. She smoothed her hands against the sides of her head, patting down the dark hair she wore in a tight bun. She was dressed in black pants and a black shirt. Red colored both of her cheeks, and her mouth made a straight line across her face, just like Mom's did when she was about to commit kid-i-cide over something I'd done.

To Mac, Ms. Donalvan said, "Is that a pack of peanuts? I *know* you are not eating in my library stacks."

"Um" was the best Mac could do. I couldn't see him, but I heard the crinkle as he scooped up his peanuts.

My stomach growled in spite of the ninja librarian scolding all of us. I gripped *Night on Fire*, my grandmother's copy of *Night on Fire*, desperate to see what happened next to CiCi Robinson, Leslie Marks, and Ole Miss.

Ms. Donalvan wasn't having any of it. She pointed at the stacks of books spread around the carrel. "Put those on the cart against the far wall, right now. For future reference, you may have three books out of the stacks at any one time, and no more than five in a carrel."

"These are my aunt's books," Mac said, pulling most of his stack toward his legs. "They're from the store. Here, see? They don't have cards to check out."

Ms. Donalvan gave him a suspicious look and bent to inspect his pile. While she was busy, Dr. Harper quickly picked up the newspapers he had brought into the carrel, scooped up the journals, and started out with them. I closed *Night on Fire*, tucked it under my arm, got up, and helped Indri carry books to the cart Ms. Donalvan had indicated. It didn't take long to fill it.

"Didn't know there were limits, sorry," Indri managed as we went back for another load.

Ms. Donalvan closed the last book in Mac's stack. "Dr. Harper knew," she grumbled as he returned to gather more journals. "He brought you all in here, so as far as I'm concerned, this is his responsibility."

"No worries, Jessica." He kept trying to sound friendly instead of so completely busted. "I'll take care of it. See? Almost done."

She followed him as he carried the rest of his journals back to the periodicals section, scolding as she went about courtesy privileges, suspending his carrel agreement for three days until he reviewed policies, why limits were necessary, and how professors, of all people, should respect library rules.

"I'm cleaning that carrel myself," she told him. "If I find any more food, or any damaged materials, we'll be talking, Fred Harper."

"So sorry," he kept repeating.

We barely got out of that basement in one piece. It was all Dr. Harper could do to convince her to let him check out Grandma's copy of *Night on Fire*.

16

ANSWERS LEADING TO MORE QUESTIONS

Excerpt from *Night on Fire* (1969),
by Avadelle Richardson, page 403

We threw ourselves on the floorboards. I tasted dirt
and my own sweat.

"What do we do?" Leslie shrilled from the back.

"Hush!"

Rat-tat. Rat-tat! Pop! Pop! *It sounded like fire-
works. People started shrieking. Horns blared.
Somebody smashed into us from behind. The car
lurched forward and crushed into the bumper ahead
of us.*

*I banged my head on the glove box. Pain shot across
my forehead and Leslie started to whimper. The car
squealed as the other vehicle moved and towed ours
with it. The impact had smashed the metal of the
bumpers together.*

Trapped!

We wouldn't be driving away from Ole Miss tonight. My heart thundered in my chest, and all I could think about was my boy, my son, my poor, poor little boy about to be without a mother because his mother was a fool.

Outside, the yelling and hollering and popping and chants and slurs and cars revving blended into a mind-numbing roar. Somebody shot out campus lights one at a time, and with each bang, the world got darker.

The car rocked back and forth as people knocked against it. Somebody tried the passenger handle, but the door didn't open. It was only a matter of time before that door did get yanked wide, and Leslie and I would get dragged into the middle of a full-on riot.

"We got to get out of here," I shouted to Leslie. "Make for the Lyceum and get behind it; try to get to Jim's office!"

"We'll be killed if we go out there!" She sounded like the child she was now, and I cursed myself for being a fool twice over. When I died on this campus tonight, I'd orphan my son and leave this helpless bit of good intentions to her fate. What kind of a person was I?

A rock smashed against the back windshield, and I let out a shriek right along with Leslie. That seemed to decide things for her. I felt the car shimmy as she leaped toward the door. I pushed myself up and grabbed hold of the passenger handle.

We spilled onto the pavement together on our hands and knees.

Clouds billowed around us, thick and white and burning. Tear gas. I coughed and wheezed. My eyes watered and started to swell. A hand fumbled against mine, and I grabbed Leslie's fingers. We huddled against the car, helping each other pull our shirt necks up around our mouths and noses.

When we got to our feet, tears streaming, a single spotlight illuminated the Circle flag—only it wasn't the stars and bars of the United States, or even Mississippi's standard. A starred blue X stood out against a red background as the Confederate flag flapped wildly above the rising clouds of gas.

"Move," I told Leslie, and we ran into the clouds and the crowd, heads down, holding hands to stay together.

Bottles and bricks sailed past us. A rock clipped Leslie's forearm. She cried out but kept running. The night turned into dark prisms as I squinted to see through my gas-induced flood of tears, mixed with real tears. I gasped out sobs, so terrified I couldn't take a whole breath, tainted or not.

People jostled against us. Students. Uniforms.

Suits. White T-shirts and jeans. People wrapped in Confederate flags. We ran and we ran and we ran. Bullets pinged off the Lyceum bricks as we ducked to the side, half-falling, half-scrambling toward the bushes and the back of the building.

We pelted around the back corner and I steered toward Bondurant and Jim Devon's office. A minute, maybe two, and we'd be clear—

Leslie stopped dead and jerked my arm so hard my shoulder wrenched. Off balance, I spun into her and we went face-to-face, me swearing from the pain.

"What are you doing?" I yelled, but clamped my mouth shut at her flat, frozen look.

All of a sudden, I didn't want to see what had made her pull us up short. I didn't want to. I didn't want to.

Slowly, keeping my arms flat against my body, ignoring my throbbing shoulder and my pounding head and my thumping heart and my swollen eyes and wheezing breath, I turned.

A line of men and boys faced us, holding bats and clubs and rifles and long, swinging socks crammed with God-only-knew-what.

One of them, a bearded old-timer wearing jeans and a Confederate-flag T-shirt, stepped forward and leveled his shotgun at my chest. He stared at us for a few seconds, then just at me.

"Well, well, well," he said, deep-South accent heavy enough to make those words two syllables each. He spit tobacco juice to his left without shifting the rifle. "Boys, just look here at what we caught ourselves tonight."

WHEN I GOT HOME, MOM and Dad didn't seem to know we were all persona non grata in the library system for seventy-two hours, so I wasn't grounded. Yet. In fact, my parents seemed to be impressed that I was finally reading *Night on Fire*. Or maybe they were shocked stupid. It was hard to tell.

After we fed Grandma, I hugged them and went to bed early, without even taking off my clothes. I just wanted to read.

When Leslie stepped in front of me, I was so surprised I almost fell down. I tried to grab the fool girl and pull her back, but she wouldn't budge. Before I could stop her, she held up both hands.

"We don't want any trouble," Leslie said, doing a fair job of a cultured Southern accent.

"What you want don't matter, girl." The man with the shotgun kept his aim steady even though he'd have to shoot Leslie to get at me. "You got trouble, right here and right now, comin' onto this campus with the likes of that filth behind you." He spat again, then drawled a string of racial slurs that made my stomach heave.

Leslie didn't give ground. "I'll thank you to watch your language," she said, smooth as any high-dollar society lady, with just the right touch of cold Southern politeness. And then, somehow, she lied better than I ever had in my entire life. "We didn't know there would be so much happening tonight. This woman is my maid, and I need her help to carry the books Dr. Devon bought for my Sunday School class."

A few of the boys behind the gunman shifted uncomfortably and glanced at each other. One of them spoke up to the man with the rifle, saying, "Look here, Curtis—"

"Shut up," Curtis growled.

I shook all over, waiting for the shotgun blast.

"Sarah Jane," Leslie said to me, reaching back and grabbing my wrist even as she pulled that made-up name straight out of the air. "Come on with me. We're going to Bondurant right this minute. This is no place for ladies, and I need to wash my face before that horrid gas ruins my complexion."

Curtis gaped at her. "You seriously think I'm lettin' you pass by me, woman?"

"Oh, you won't shoot me, Curtis." Leslie walked toward him, dragging me along behind her. "Because if you did, one of these fine young men would tell my husband and the police your name." She stuck out her chin as she drew almost even with the barrel of *his rifle. "In Oxford, people respect ladies with God's work to do."*

As we passed the dumbfounded Curtis, Leslie pulled me around her so I was in front, and she stayed between me and any aimed guns. "This violence isn't God's work, gentlemen," she called back over her shoulder, her accent falling away just enough to scare me into next week. "I can't believe you'd tear down our beautiful campus like this. You should be ashamed of yourselves!"

It was later, around midnight, when I finally closed *Night on Fire*. My notepad was pretty empty because I hadn't stopped to take notes. Notes just didn't seem that important when people were getting shot at and firebombed on the Ole Miss campus.

I was so relieved that they got away. Did Avadelle really do that for my grandmother? And if they escaped the mob like that, how did my grandmother get hurt? Answers leading to more questions—so frustrating!

I knew Mac still had books to read, and Dr. Harper was going over Grandma's articles again, and Indri had planned to research Avadelle's short stories online, using her mom's library account. Had they found something I didn't know?

And before we got jumped by the librarian, Dr. Harper had been looking up lockboxes to be sure the key really did go to the one he saw, and—

Oh.

Oh no.

Sweat broke across the back of my neck as I jumped all the way out of my bed. My heart hammered as I crammed my hands in my jeans pockets.

They were empty.

"No," I said out loud. I ran to the chair where I'd dropped my pack, grabbed it, unzipped the big pocket and the front pocket and fished around.

Nothing.

I dumped the pack on the bed and examined everything. Grandma's envelope was there, but it held only papers.

I squeezed my eyes shut.

I couldn't have been that stupid. I couldn't have been! I checked my pockets again, and the pack, and my covers, and all around the room, even though I knew the truth.

No key.

I didn't have Grandma's key, because in all the confusion, I'd left it on the floor of the library carrel.

17

BECAUSE IT'S MINE

———

**Excerpt from *Night on Fire* (1969),
by Avadelle Richardson, page 420**

*"Was it worth it, what happened to get James
Meredith into Ole Miss?" Leslie asked me the next
day at my school, which had been turned into a
makeshift hospital for all the Black people hurt in
the unrest in town. We had beatings, whippings,
knife wounds, and gunshots to deal with—and none
of these folks were even on campus when they ran
into trouble.*

*I touched the two stitches over my right eye, feeling each bruise and scrape from the riot as I reached
for bandages to work on a man's cut arm.*

*"It was worth it," I said, and I tried to sound sure
of myself, even as my traitor mind whispered,* Was it?
Will it make any difference?

WHEN YOU REALLY SCREW SOMETHING up for someone, it's so hard to face that person. This stays true even if it's the morning after the worst night of your life, and the person has Alzheimer's disease and doesn't even open her eyes when you check her pulse and her breathing, then apologize sixty thousand times for maybe sort of losing her precious key and maybe sort of destroying the only chance for her to find peace about a fight with her best friend before she dies.

It stays true even when you're convincing your skeptical mom and grumpy post-migraine dad that you really, really do need one more day away from Creative Arts Camp to work with an old professor researching history they don't really want you reading about, even if that's just a cover story. Never mind what happens when you call your best friend and have to admit YOU LOST THE FLIPPING KEY TO EVERYTHING IN THE UNIVERSE.

Your ex–other best friend, Worm Dung, who really deserves to get his name back now, might surprise you. He might stay calm and tell you he'll meet you on the steps of Ventress Hall, and to stop worrying. He might promise that since his Aunt Naomi is looking after his crazy GG, he'll help you get the key back, because you have to get it back. That's the only allowable outcome. Period.

No matter what happens, no matter what you have to do— You. Will. Find. That. Key.

"I'm not certain this is the best idea," Indri said as the three of us crowded toward the library door. She rubbed her elbows for the umpteenth time like she might be cold, which wasn't even possible, because like *Night on Fire* said about Oxford, *It was hot*.

"Ms. Donalvan might kill us on sight," Mac said. He had on jeans and a sleeveless black tank with a white guitar on it, and unlike me, he wasn't sweating. "I mean, she suspended Dr. Harper's library privileges for three days because of us. Left him babbling about bearding the lioness in her own den and stuff."

"Bearded—what?" Indri gave him one of her looks as she shoved up the sleeves on her purple blouse. "What does that even mean?"

"Ms. Donalvan said she was going to clean the carrel herself though," I reminded them. "She probably found the key."

"We'll get it back for you," Mac said, sounding confident.

"What, now you're Dani's big hero?" Indri muttered. "Just a few weeks ago, you were blowing her off forever, remember?"

Mac didn't say a word back to her, but I saw his head droop a little. He wouldn't look at me, and all of a sudden, I couldn't look at him, either.

We got to the front doors of the library, and Mac pulled one open and held it for Indri and me, old-school gentleman-style. I thanked him. Indri just glared.

We found the ninja librarian herself at the main desk. She wore all black again, pants and big shirt. All she needed was a cape, and she would have looked just like an evil wizard in one my favorite fantasy books. My teeth actually rattled together as we stepped back to give her room.

"What, may I ask, do you three want *now*?" Her glare fell on Mac first, then Indri, and finally rested on me.

Were her dark eyes glittering like a snake?

I shuddered, then had a sudden, wild thought that she could sense my grandmother's copy of *Night on Fire* in my backpack, and that if I moved or spoke, she'd leap forward and snatch it straight through the fabric.

"Um," I said.

"Err" was all Indri could manage.

Mac, standing straight and tall with a big, friendly grin, said, "Hello, Ms. Donalvan. We seem to have lost a key in Dr. Harper's carrel yesterday, and we were hoping you found it."

Indri gaped in his general direction. I pasted a polite smile on my face and tried to ignore the sweat trickling down my back.

Ms. Donalvan shifted the full force of her evil wizardly attention to Mac. "A key."

"Yes, ma'am," Mac said, way too bright and happy.

"If I did find such a thing in a professor's workspace," she said, her tone a cross between a purr and a growl, "why would I give it to you?"

"Because it's mine," I meant to say forcefully, but in a friendly tone. It ended up sounding like a mouse whisper, but my words were loud enough to bring that glittering gaze back to my face.

Ms. Donalvan studied me so intently I wondered if she might be searching for freckles even though I didn't have any. Slowly, way too slowly, she folded her arms, all the while keeping her stare right on my face. Finally, she said, "Interesting."

What?

But—

"Excuse me?" Indri's question popped out, then she covered her mouth, turning lemur-eyes above her fingers.

"I said that was interesting, you claiming ownership of the key." Ms. Donalvan leaned toward me. "That's not what Dr. Harper said when I phoned him this morning."

Excitement competed with hope in my chest, but dread also made an appearance. "So . . . you found the key? And you called Dr. Harper?"

Ms. Donalvan nodded, like she might be dealing with first graders incapable of understanding her complex grammar, or maybe fraudulent delinquents making a bid for jail time. She still scared me to death, but also, she was starting to tick me off.

"The key belongs to Dani," Indri said, politely, but with just a touch of ice. "Her grandmother gave it to her."

"We'd just like to get it back," Mac added, all sweetness and light.

Ms. Donalvan glared at me for another few seconds, then shifted her focus to Mac. "Well, then. I suggest you speak to Dr. Harper, since he picked it up from me about an hour ago."

Mac and Indri immediately looked at me like I'd have something to say, but I didn't. My brain fogged up and the world got spinny.

Dr. Harper apologized to us at Square Books. Wasn't he a good guy again? Why would a good guy come pick up the key without saying a word to us? I couldn't help thinking about that look he got the first time I talked about the key. What if—what if he still had Grandma's lockbox?

If that whole "she took it back" speech had been full of it, then he might be opening the box right this very second.

"But it's mine," I whispered again.

Ms. Donalvan seemed to have had enough. "Out you go," she pointed at the main door. "I don't expect to see you unsupervised until you're old enough to come here alone—and without peanuts, Mr. Richardson."

I didn't move, not until Indri got my hand on one side, and Mac on the other. The two of them marched me out the library door.

"It's probably lost forever," I mumbled as the door closed behind us. "*How* could I have let this happen? I can't believe Dr. Harper just took my key."

"We'll go back to Ventress," Mac said, blinking against the really bright morning sun. "We'll talk to him."

Indri dusted off her hands, like she was glad to be shed of the library and Ms. Donalvan, and any need to be polite to anybody. "You bet we will. Right now. Come on."

———

By the time we got to the old turreted building with the Civil War stained glass, I felt all jumpy. "What if Dr. Harper's really crazy?" I asked. "Psycho or something. If he is, he'll just lie about having the key."

"We'll make him tell the truth," Mac said. "Pretty simple. Ms. Donalvan gave the key to him, so he's got it, and he's going to give it to us."

Indri stopped with her hand on the door to Ventress Hall. "And if he refuses—what then? You gonna knock some old guy over the head and search his stuff?"

Mac shrugged, like that wasn't completely out of the range of possibilities.

"Whatever," Indri snarled, then opened the door and stomped inside. I followed behind her, and Mac brought up the rear.

I held my head perfectly still as we went up the steps, refusing to pay any attention to the stained glass windows and the eerie, dead soldiers watching us.

"Isn't the tower here supposed to be haunted?" Mac asked as we made it to the second floor.

"Yes," Indri said. "But Dani thinks it's ugly."

I sighed. "It *is* ugly. All that graffiti."

"All that history," she countered.

The three of us turned toward Dr. Harper's alcove. His office doors were pulled shut, but not completely closed. My steps slowed on the patterned rug even as Indri and Mac clattered along on the hardwood beside me.

"Wait," I said. They stopped, then glanced at me, and I

swallowed hard. "What are we going to do? I mean, how are we going to bring this up?"

"How about, 'Good morning,'" Indri suggested. "'Give us the key, right now.'"

"That might not work," Mac said. "We should think about bargaining. What do we have that he wants?"

I thought about the papers in my backpack, what my grandmother had written to me. I almost said something about them, then decided against it. Indri didn't say anything either. Dr. Harper knew we had the papers. If he wanted to try to get them, he would.

"It's your key, Dani," Indri said. "He can't deny it, especially not with all of us right there in his face."

I eyed the partly closed doors and thought about the hungry look he had gotten when he realized I might have the answers he'd been looking for—that everyone had been looking for—the explanation for the Magnolia Feud. That, plus how sincere he had seemed when he apologized to us at Square Books. I didn't really know what he'd be capable of denying, or doing. My breathing got rough and shallow as we started forward again.

Mac reached the doors first, and he knocked on one of them. I decided to hold my breath rather than sound like a wheezing rhinoceros.

No answer.

Indri knocked next, and said, "Dr. Harper? We need to speak to you."

Still no answer.

Letting out one gaspy rhinoceros puff, I leaned forward and pushed one of the doors open. Sunlight streamed through his big windows and glared off the hardwood floors. Dust drifted lazily in front of his massive bookcases. The chair at his big wooden desk was empty, and his pipe and magnifying glass lay unattended. The air smelled a bit like pipe smoke. *Somebody* might not have been following campus no-smoking rules.

"The doctor is not in," Indri said in her coolest, most controlled voice even though she had lemur eyes happening in a big way. "Is that a good thing or a bad thing?"

Mac turned toward us for a few seconds, then pushed the door wide and strode into the office like he had been invited. With no comment at all, he started looking through the things on the table, shifting books and papers, peeking underneath them like the key would suddenly pop out and shout *hello*.

"Uh, Mac," I said. "You can't do that."

"Why not?" Mac kept moving stuff around. "He left the doors open. And he took your key."

When Indri and I didn't move, he shrugged and kept right on hunting around, as if to say, *Hey, somebody's got to do something.*

"Get over yourself, Richardson," Indri grumbled. She glanced over her shoulder, then eased into the office too. Once inside, she zeroed in on Dr. Harper's desk and started searching around his stacks of books.

This is wrong, I said in my head, but not out loud, because truth be told. I was glad they were searching for the key. If I could only breathe and swallow and make my heart beat right, I'd search with them.

My knees got a little wobbly. I finally made myself move forward, putting my hand on one of the doors to steady myself. "Okay," I said. Then one more time. "Okay." I pulled the door shut behind me without letting it latch.

Mac grimaced. "He's got way too much stuff in this room. It's like a fire hazard or something."

Indri scooted a statue sideways on the desk, then lifted it, checking underneath. "The key could be anywhere. I wonder if he has a safe."

That got me moving, and I scurried over to the edge of the desk, got down on my knees, and started opening drawers. In the biggest bottom drawer, I found hanging files, which turned out to be papers and grades for his current students. I closed that one and went to the next, and found a stack of letters, apparently from his wife before she died. Those, I didn't read, or even touch, except to pick them up and make sure the key wasn't hidden underneath them.

In the top right-hand drawer, I found fresh pipe tobacco, cherry-scented. I took a deep breath, enjoying the smell, but hacked and coughed when Indri slapped me on the back.

"Ssshhh!" she whispered. "I hear something."

I clamped my teeth on my tongue, held my breath, and listened.

Yes. Murmurs coming from the hall near the door.

I got to my feet.

Mac stepped away from the table.

Indri got up, grabbed my arm, and towed me around the desk next to Mac. We all saw Dr. Harper's coat closet at the same time, and as if we had planned it all along, we bolted for the hiding place.

18

FOND OF SCARY STORIES

———

**Excerpt from *Night on Fire* (1969),
by Avadelle Richardson, page 441**

*"Are you leaving Oxford now?" Leslie asked as we sat
in my classroom, which was finally only a classroom
again. She wouldn't stop with the questions, even two
weeks after the Meredith riot.*

*I shook my head, but I didn't say anything sharp
to her for asking—because I had considered it. I spent
almost a week studying Abram's face, hour after hour,
sometimes all night long. I had thought about taking
him out of Mississippi. I had thought about sending
him away to our cousins in Chicago.*

*But like me, my baby was born on Mississippi
soil. He had roots in this state, deep into the bedrock.
What would he become if I cut him loose from Mama*

and Aunt Jessie and me, from everyone and everything he had ever known and loved?

"This is my home," I told Leslie. "It's our home, my
boy's and mine. If we leave, they win. It's like giving up,
and my parents didn't raise me to give up, not ever."

Leslie rubbed the spot on her arm where she'd had
stitches from her rock cut. The doctor at the local hospital took them out for her yesterday.

"You'd stay alive if you left," she said.

I sighed. "And what meaning would my life have
then?"

THE CLOSET LIGHT POPPED ON when we opened it, but as
soon as we stuffed ourselves into the tiny space and closed
the door, it turned off.

Blacker than night. Blacker than a black hole. I couldn't
see a thing. All I could smell was cherry tobacco. A sweater
tickled my left ear. I felt Indri lean away from the door and
press into me. I leaned back, and realized I was resting against
Mac's chest.

His hands touched my shoulders.

A creak and a clank outside made me jump, and his fingers squeezed my arms as if to say, *It's okay. It's going to be
all right.*

Had Dr. Harper come back? Who was with him?

My brain did stupid things, like imagining him opening Grandma's lockbox with my key, and finding something

amazing and world-changing, and calling up reporters and bloggers. I felt totally frozen by fear, even with Mac trying to make me feel better.

"Dani?" Indri whispered.

I flinched, feeling guilty over Mac touching me, even though it was a tiny closet—or maybe it was the fact that he was touching me and I didn't mind so much.

"What?" I got out around the catch in my throat.

"What now?" she asked, no louder than a breath.

I had no idea. My ears strained against the muffling wood and sweaters and coats in the closet, trying to pick out voices. Dr. Harper was out there, all right. And somebody else. A woman. Maybe a couple of women, and another guy.

"Breathe," Mac said.

And I tried to.

I really, really did.

Think, I told myself.

If we stayed in the closet, we weren't any closer to getting the key. But if we popped out now, we'd look completely guilty of busting into Dr. Harper's office when he wasn't around. Which, of course, we had done, but—oh, never mind. Maybe he'd go away again, and take his friends with him.

Yeah, right. Maybe in a few hours. I already had to go to the bathroom.

"We probably should go talk to him," Mac murmured. "It's not like we've got a lot of choices."

"I'm fine here," Indri whispered back.

". . . See them?" came a woman's voice.

My heart did a huge flip as I recognized the speaker.

"Ohmigod, Dani, it's your mom," Indri whispered a little too loudly.

"They said they were coming to see you. . . ." Mom sounded annoyed. Maybe worried. Bad combination.

I leaned harder into Mac, and he let me. Indri leaned into me. "We're so dead," she whispered.

"It'll be okay," Mac said into my ear. "We'll get the key."

His breath felt so warm against my ear. I knew he was trying to help. I wished he would say something like, *You know what? I'm sorry I was a jerk the last day of school*, or, *Maybe I really do like you.*

He opened his mouth again and said, "We probably should go out there."

I blinked fast with disappointment, and somewhere down inside, I finally accepted that I was never going to get an apology from him. That just made the awful morning *so* much better. Not.

"I have to go to the bathroom," Indri said, making my bladder weigh one hundred more pounds, instantly.

Outside the closet, the voices got quiet.

Then, a very, very, very, very loud Mom voice said, "Danielle Marie Beans."

I went rock-still. All of us did. For a long, breathless moment, I stared hard into the darkness, like I could see through the closet door.

"Come out of that closet," my mother instructed. "Right. Now."

Indri moved before I could form a thought, throwing open the closet door.

Light blasted against my eyes, and I clamped them shut as Indri scrambled up, saying, "Bathroom, sorry, bathroom," and just like that, she was gone and out the door.

I opened one eye.

My mother stood just outside the closet, arms folded tighter than any ninja librarian, glaring directly at me and Mac. Next to her stood Dr. Harper, and Indri's mom, and my dad.

"What. On earth. Are you doing in that closet?" Mom said. Not even a question, really. I didn't know how to answer, or even if she wanted me to. I just opened my other eye and crawled out.

"Bathroom," I squeaked, following Indri. I was allowed to escape just long enough to take care of my business. But then I had to walk back into that office.

Indri stood between my mom and hers looking like a lemur caught by poachers. She didn't try to speak or move or anything.

Mac stood near the now-closed closet, hands in his pockets, trying to appear relaxed but looking way nervous instead, especially since my dad's attention was fixed on him.

"Explain," Mom said. "Immediately."

I couldn't hear much besides the *pound-pound-pound* of

my pulse in my ears. I couldn't see much more than Mom's frown, Dad's scowl, Ms. Wilson's concerned expression, and Indri's wide eyes. As for Dr. Harper, he looked . . . miserable. And confused. And worried.

I'll be grounded for the rest of my days, Indri's expression said. *I'll never be allowed to use my phone again. Ever.*

"It's my fault," I said to Mom. "We went to the library this morning to look for, um, a book we lost. It was my idea." I glanced at Ms. Wilson. "Honest. And then when we did finally come here, Dr. Harper was out, and we let ourselves in to look for the book. All my idea."

"I don't doubt that this was your doing," Mom said.

"Indri isn't five years old, Cella," Ms. Wilson said. "She could have refused to do what she knew was wrong."

Indri seemed to shrink as her mother spoke.

Mom didn't even acknowledge what her best friend said. Instead, she gestured to the messy piles we had moved and disturbed. "You came into Dr. Harper's office while he wasn't here."

"You went through his things?" Dad asked—me, specifically. His expression mixed sad with angry, making me feel twice as guilty.

"I—uh, this is likely my fault," Dr. Harper said, making all eyes swing to him.

Whoa. I stared at him, waiting for him to sell us out completely, and tell my parents and Indri's mom about the key. He had his nice-guy face on, but I knew better than to trust that.

"We were working on some research related to the Meredith riot and the Magnolia Feud," he said. He pulled off his glasses, cleaned a spot, and put them back on, all the while letting his smile get bigger. "Yesterday, at the library, we had to stop too early. I suspect the children needed one of the volumes I checked out, to pick up where we left off."

My mouth came open. So did Indri's. I couldn't see Mac behind me, but I heard him give a little sniff of surprise.

"Isn't that right?" Dr. Harper said, and I realized he was talking to me.

"Uh, yes. Actually."

"There were also some articles," Indri said, but trailed into nothing when her mom glared at her.

My parents had matching we're-suspicious looks. Mom's left eyebrow lifted. "Mackinnon?" she said.

"Yes, ma'am." He came to stand beside me, very, very close, but not touching. "We couldn't get past Ms. Donalvan since we didn't have IDs or an adult with us, so we came back here. When Dr. Harper wasn't in his office, we thought it would be okay to get started without him—but we couldn't find our notes from yesterday."

Mom's eyes narrowed. "And the closet?"

Mac ran right out of steam with that one. Indri had gone total lemur eyes. This one was up to me. And I had nothing. Nada. Zero. Zip.

Mom started to turn pink, which meant maaaaaaaad.

Really, really mad. The gears in my brain froze solid, and not a thought would turn.

Dr. Harper coughed. "Well, now. I can explain that one too."

Once more, all the attention in the room shifted to him.

"Our girls here, they're fond of scary stories, and you know the legends surrounding this building." His smile seemed so natural, and he even winked at me. "No doubt they thought we were a bunch of ghosts come to scare them silly. Right, Dani?"

All I could do was grin like an idiot and shrug, gesturing toward the turret. "Lots of ghosts here, yeah."

Indri nodded like a bobble-head doll. Mac stayed all cool and relaxed until I wanted to punch him in the shoulder.

Mom regarded Dr. Harper for a few seconds, obviously still very suspicious, but she didn't challenge his explanation. "What were you trying to research this morning, Dani?"

When I didn't answer fast enough, she asked Indri, who squiggled and opened her mouth, then closed it again as she gave me a desperate look.

Mom looked at Mac. "Mackinnon, what were you trying to figure out?"

Mac leaned away from me and put his hand on a stack of books on Dr. Harper's table. "We, ah—you know. We were trying to see if Ms. Beans ever spoke to anyone about the night of the Meredith riot before *Night on Fire* came out. Since, you know, that's when both my GG and Ms. Beans stopped discussing what really happened."

"What's fact and what's fiction," I said, just above a whisper. "It's hard to figure out where to draw the line."

"Yes it is," Mom said, sounding confused, and finally, finally, just a little bit convinced.

After a few heartbeats, Dad said, "So, we're supposed to believe this was all just research, and that you and Dr. Harper got wires crossed, which is why you came to campus to see him and he came to our house to see you?"

My eyes went wide. When I looked at Dr. Harper, he gave me a very, very cautious smile, as if to say, *Take care now. Tread lightly.*

"Yes, sir," I said, and wanted to kick myself for the lie.

Time passed. Silence sat in the book-lined office with us as Mom and Dad and Ms. Wilson took turns studying our faces.

"I think you've been enough trouble to Dr. Harper today," Mom said. She rubbed the bridge of her nose. Another few seconds went by, then she made a motion with both hands, like shooing a fly. "Mackinnon, go on with Marcus. He'll take you home."

"Yes, ma'am," he said. He stood up straight, then walked over to Dr. Harper and extended his hand. Dr. Harper hesitated. Mac wiggled his fingers, then touched the tips together and turned his wrist like he was opening a door. Dr. Harper still looked perplexed. He put his hand in his pocket, then finally seemed to realize Mac was offering to shake. He took Mac's hand firmly, and he smiled like he'd never made the mistake.

"Thanks, sir," Mac said. Then Mac turned to Indri. He put out his hand to shake again. "Sorry, about, you know. Everything. School and stuff."

Her eyebrows lifted. So did mine. Why was he doing this now, of all times? Had he totally lost his mind?

Indri shook with him, but her expression screamed, *This is stupid!* She had to be reconsidering whether or not she should just kill him, but all she said was "Uh-huh."

Mac came over to me next.

In spite of his weird, wrong timing, I felt something. Maybe nerves. Maybe relief. Definitely frustration. I couldn't sort it all out.

He put out his right hand again. "Sorry, Dani. You were right, at school, I mean. I should have made my own decisions, and I wish I hadn't hurt your feelings."

His eyes flicked from his hand to mine, and he seemed pretty desperate for me to shake on his apology.

I had wanted this so much, for weeks now. Just not here. Not now. Not like this. It felt completely wrong. I didn't believe him. I sort of wanted to smack him. Okay, I *really* wanted to smack him. But I couldn't. I had to make nice, or we'd all be in that much more trouble.

Whatever.

Stomach starting to churn, I reached out and shook his hand—

And something cool and metal pressed into my palm.

My eyes widened. Mac's gaze bored into mine, and he

seemed to be willing me to understand, to not react, to be very, very quiet and just keep shaking, even as I patched together that Dr. Harper really was a good guy, that he had gone to my house to bring me the key as soon as Ms. Donalvan had given it to him, and that he had just passed the key to Mac without ever giving the secret away.

I kept shaking Mac's hand.

The corners of Mac's mouth tugged upward as he let go. His left eye closed quick in a wink, then opened as he looked up at Mom and Dad and nodded his thanks.

When Mac pulled his hand away from mine, I closed my fist tightly around my grandmother's key.

19

TIRED OF GHOSTS AND SECRETS AND PRETENDING

―――

**Excerpt from *Night on Fire* (1969),
by Avadelle Richardson, page 453**

*"Are you leaving Oxford now?" I asked Leslie on the
third week after the riot, because she'd gone quiet on
me for days, and I had started to wonder.*

*She looked up from the mailers she was working
on at the student desk closest to the front of my classroom. "No. I'm not leaving."*

*"You answered me too quick." I sat back in my own
chair, pushing at the registration cards I had stacked
in front of me. "Think about it, Leslie. Mississippi
isn't your home. This isn't your fight."*

*"You're wrong," she said, as sure as I'd ever heard
her sound. "It's everyone's fight, CiCi—even if they
don't know it yet."*

―――

INDRI AND I SAT NEXT to Grandma's bed on Wednesday evening, two weeks after the Great Closet Disaster, watching her sleep. Grandma hadn't said a word since I got in trouble, but she wasn't sweating. Her pulse was eighty. Her breathing was even. Death really was being mean to her, wasn't it? Coming too late, and letting her linger like this, with her body working and her mind so far away.

"Sooner or later, Grandma, we're all gonna be okay." I said it like always, but I wasn't sure I meant it, even though there had been an itsy-bitsy, teeny-tiny crack in *grounded forever*.

Dad and Mom and Ms. Wilson had decided to let Indri and me spend some time together outside of camp—where we hadn't even been allowed to sit with each other. Some very supervised time, at one house or the other. Something about moping/depression/driving them crazy with chatter— whatever. At least we could see each other some, and maybe sit with each other at camp again, even though we still didn't have phones, and probably wouldn't again until we were thirty and married (this was Mom's estimate).

Grandma shifted in her bed, and Indri flinched from surprise. Then she asked for the tenth time that hour, "Do you think Mac ever got in any trouble?"

"No way to know," I said. Again. "Haven't spoken to him since it happened, 'cause I'm not allowed to speak to anybody but my family, and now you."

Silence.

Indri picked at her yellow blouse, then the dark ends of her

245

loose hair. For the twentieth time, she said, "I feel bad about how we didn't trust Dr. Harper, and all the, um, stories we told."

I didn't say anything. I felt awful about that part too. But not about getting the key back. Part of me wanted to yell at Indri for asking the same stuff over and over, but I couldn't, because I was just too glad to be talking to her in some way other than hand signals and tossed notes at camp. Plus, even though I was watching Grandma, from the corner of my eye I could see Indri fidgeting in her chair. She seemed absolutely miserable, way more than she should have been, especially since we had a chance at getting some of our lives back.

"What's wrong?" I asked her.

She fidgeted some more, then shrugged, then looked away from me. "I just feel bad about everything."

"I've seen you feel bad about a lot of stuff," I said. "But you don't usually have that awful look on your face."

The look got awful-er.

And all of a sudden, panic gripped my insides, and I knew, just knew, she was going to tell me she didn't want to be friends anymore. The closet thing, it had been too much. She probably thought I wasn't good for her, or that I didn't care how much trouble I had caused her.

This is it, my inner worrywart insisted. *The scene at Dr. Harper's office was the thing too awful and huge to fix by saying I'm sorry.*

Tears ran down my face, but just before I started sobbing, Indri said, "Do you think God's going to get even with me?"

"Huh?"

"Get even." She rubbed both her eyes, and her tears came right out. "God. Do you think He'll get even with me for me doing something bad?"

"No! I mean, I don't—um, I guess I don't—well, you know I kind of sit on the fence about God." I watched her, and saw more tears sliding down her face, so I added, "But if I did believe totally in a God, I wouldn't see God like that. All mean and vengeful."

When Indri kept crying, I gathered up both of her hands in mine, squeezing them and waiting for her to tell me why she was so upset.

"I always promise to be good," she said, gulping air between bouts of sniffles. "I tell God I'll be as good as I can be, and to pay me back for that, He'll keep letting my dad be safe and lucky. It's a deal, see? But I didn't keep my part of it."

"And you think—oh, wow. No. Come on now." I scooted my chair closer to hers and hugged her. She pushed her face into my shoulder and cried really hard.

"God definitely wouldn't be like that," I said, hoping I was telling her the truth. "He's not going to hurt your dad because you made a mistake."

"If I can just be good enough," she babbled. "Strong enough. I have to be. All the time, or something awful's going to happen to him."

I squeezed her harder. "No way. That's not how it works.

Your dad'll be home for the holidays, just like you said."

Please, God, be there, somewhere over my head, floating up in Heaven. Please, God, don't let me be lying.

Indri kept crying and I kept holding on to her. When she finally sat up and pulled her fingers out of mine, she used Grandma's sheet to wipe her face, and said, "Sorry."

"Don't be sorry. I don't blame you for being scared about your dad."

She dropped the tear-stained sheet and nodded. Then she seemed to zone out, and I closed my mouth. Too much talking about her dad now. *Roger that*, as my dad would say. Time to hush unless she brought it up again.

I opened my mouth to ask her if she needed me to get her a damp cloth to wash her face, but what came out was "Do you—do you ever think about not being friends with me anymore?"

Indri gaped at me. "Uh, no? Where did that come from?"

"Because, Mac—I didn't see that coming," I finally cried, and it felt sort of good, not fighting the tears. "And I've been thinking a whole lot about what makes friends friends, and what makes them stop being friends, and *Night on Fire* was so amazing, but Grandma and Avadelle stopped being friends." I tried to stop and breathe, but I couldn't do it, and the tears and words just kept coming. "And it's hard to sort out what's my circus and what's my monkeys, and how the truth isn't always the truth, and what makes people be people, and when they're really gone, and what ghost stories really mean, and why people wouldn't make up if they really cared about each other, and I guess I worry."

"You think too much, that's what you do." Indri pulled up Grandma's damp sheet and wiped my face. "Circuses? Monkeys?" She wiped my nose, too. "Never mind. Dani, you're my best friend. You'll always be my best friend."

"Ava," my grandmother rasped, rough but clear enough to make us both jump. Indri almost yanked the sheet straight off her bed. We looked at Grandma, then we glanced at each other, and back at her.

"Ava," she said again, and she started to cry too.

Indri stood and leaned over my grandmother and just put her head on Grandma's belly and hugged her. I snuggled my face to Grandma's, and I held her too. "It's okay," I whispered. "We're all gonna be okay, Grandma. I mean it."

I traced her tears with my fingers, wiping them gently from the dusky wrinkles on her face.

"She said *Ava*," Indri murmured. "No question."

"I know."

"I think maybe she wants to see her," Indri said.

"I've been wondering about that too."

"Maybe we should ask Avadelle to come."

And two weeks ago, I would have called that a stupid idea. But now . . .

Now the three of us just stayed there, cuddled together, until Grandma stopped crying and started snoring. I sat up, I checked her pulse and watched her breathe.

As Indri settled back into her own chair, my focus shifted back to her. Maybe watching that stuff so carefully like I did with Grandma really wasn't so different from Indri trying to do all the right things to bring her father home, or people telling ghost stories about stuff that scared them to death. Just something to do, to pretend we could do *something* to make a difference.

My stomach tied itself in knots, and I shoved all that thinking straight out of my head. That is, until Indri asked, "Do you think you'll be sitting next to Ms. Beans when she passes—you know, like we're sitting right now?"

I bit at my bottom lip and tried to think about witches or fairies or sprites or vampires or even ghosts. Anything but what it was going to feel like to watch my grandmother breathe for the very last time. I had to clear my throat before I spoke. "I don't know. The hospice nurses say lots of folks die really early in the morning, when everyone else is sleeping. It's almost like they don't want to be any trouble to the people they love."

"Mmm." Indri fiddled with her hair, smoothing it behind her ears. "Well, if you have the choice and it doesn't sneak up on everybody, do you *want* to be sitting here when she goes?"

Oh God. I blinked really fast so brand-new tears wouldn't leave my eyes and make Indri feel like she was bringing her dad bad luck again. "No. Yes. I don't want her to be alone."

The front door opened and closed downstairs, and I almost yelled with relief, because that was probably Ms. Wilson, come to gather up Indri and head to their house. After a few seconds, we heard voices, male and female both, and Indri went the color of Grandma's linens. I felt the blood leave my own face too, and I grabbed Indri's arm because I knew what she was thinking.

"Look at me," I demanded. "No, I mean it."

I waited for Indri's huge eyes to fix on mine, then said, "That is *not* your mom with a chaplain and some soldier coming to tell you something's happened to your father. It's just my dad talking to your mom."

Indri got up from her chair, pulling me with her. I didn't even have a chance to make sure Grandma was all tucked in before Indri bolted for the bedroom door. I followed her, heart pounding and pounding and pounding, willing the voices downstairs to be Dad and Ms. Wilson, or Mom and some friends from work, or buddies of Dad's.

We ran down the stairs together, and almost smacked straight into Dad and Ms. Wilson as they came up to meet us.

The two of us stopped so fast and stared so hard that Dad folded his arms and looked suspicious. "What? You two *already* up to stuff?"

"No," Indri and I both said at the same time, which didn't help anything.

Indri threw herself at her mom and hugged her hard. Ms. Wilson, who looked like a taller version of Indri, but even more colorful with her purple and gold sari, hugged Indri to

251

her hip, looking confused. "Well, okay," she said. "Hello, little one. I thought this visit would make you happy."

"It did." Indri pulled away from her mom and forced her face into some semblance of normal. She even worked up a decent smile, which impressed me. "Can we do it again soon? Or sit together at camp?"

"We'll see," Ms. Wilson said.

I raised my eyebrows at Dad, who shrugged and said, "I'll talk it over with your mother, but probably not until tomorrow. She's working an extra two hours tonight, playing catch-up from teaching that class."

Ms. Wilson made a sad sound. "She really is the best friend ever, for helping out at the university. I wish I could help her like she's helping us."

"Even trade," Dad said. "We needed the extra income for Mama's supplies." He walked Indri and Ms. Wilson down the stairs and toward the front door, his hand on Ms. Wilson's shoulder. "We appreciate it a lot, you helping Cella get that opportunity."

Right before they went outside, Indri turned and waved at me. "Don't think too much," she instructed.

I waved to her and mouthed, *Best Friends Forever*.

She nodded, and Dad closed the door behind them. Then he turned to me and raised one eyebrow. "What on earth was all that about, when you came down the stairs?"

I sat on the bottom step and gazed up at him. "Indri told me she was scared her dad would get killed because she did something bad. When her mom came and we heard y'all talking, we thought it might be—you know. The chaplain and those guys in dress uniforms that come with him."

Dad sat on the floor across from me, his back against the stone wall of the entryway as he looked at me. "That's pretty heavy, kid."

"I know."

He closed his eyes and rubbed the sides of head. "I'm glad I retired so you don't have to worry about that."

"Me too."

When Dad focused on me again, I noticed his eyes were bloodshot. "What did you tell Indri?"

"That no God I could imagine would punish her dad for mistakes she made."

"Good job." He gave me a quick grin, and his next words rumbled low in his chest, the way he sounded when he was being serious and playful at the same time. "So, while you're being straightforward, want to tell me what that whole office and closet scene was about? Because I didn't believe anything you all said about it. Not even for a second."

I took in a breath. Let it out. People always talked about moms having radar for lies and eyes in the back of their heads and stuff. Well, those people never met my dad. In our family, he was the one who seemed to know everything.

A dozen reasons to avoid the truth blinked through my brain, but I didn't pay much attention to them. After hiding in a closet and almost peeing on myself and getting busted and being trapped in our old house for days and days except for camp, and having such a heavy conversation with Indri, I was tired of ghosts and secrets and pretending.

"A key," I said. "We needed to find a key that I lost."

Dad gazed at me, waiting, and I took another deep, deep breath. Then I spilled it all, about Grandma's writing about how she would tell me about the feud but then getting too confused to finish, about the key that was too big for a diary and too small for a door, and the lockbox Grandma took back from Dr. Harper, how she made it disappear, and how I lost the key at the library and thought Dr. Harper might have taken it for himself, and Grandma whispering Avadelle's name earlier, and how it felt to read *Night on Fire*.

"I mean, the book was good," I said, having to work not to think about the story and the images. "Really good. I guess I see why she won awards, even if I kind of hate admitting that. But I know it's not all true, especially the part about what happened to Avadelle and Grandma the night of the Meredith riot."

Dad looked totally stunned about everything I had just told him, but he stayed completely Dad-like, his face stern. "*Night on Fire*, it's fiction, baby girl. Well, those bits about Mama's history, those are spot-on. And maybe some about the friendship itself and how it grew. But all that research you and your friends have done, when it comes down to it, we still don't know anything at all about what was in Mama's heart and mind—or her life—the night of the riot. We don't know what upset her, and what divided Avadelle and Mama so deeply." He shook his head, then chuckled. "A key for a box you don't even have. All that at Ventress—for that key? I never would have figured that out, not in a hundred million years."

"I'm sorry about not telling you." I pulled the key out of my pocket and held it up, letting our entryway light play off the gold edges.

Dad studied it, but he didn't try to take it away from me. He didn't even ask to hold it. "Sooner or later, I want to read what Mama wrote. All of it. Okay?"

"Okay," I said. "And yes, *Night on Fire*'s fiction, but there's truth in it, and fiction, but I think there are lies, too. Lies, or something else Avadelle wants to keep to herself."

Dad started to argue with me, but I put the key back in my pocket, then raised one finger. "First, we know Grandma and Avadelle didn't get clean away like the two characters in the book. Grandma got hurt—and that ghost story about screams in the steam tunnels around the Lyceum, it's probably related to that night." I raised a second finger. "Their friendship ended when *Night on Fire* came out." Third finger. "The way Avadelle acted at Square Books—there's definitely something she doesn't want anyone to know. Something Grandma's ready to tell. Something she *needs* to tell. She keeps trying to say it, so hard. I think—I think she might need Avadelle."

Dad leaned his head back against the rock wall and closed his eyes. He seemed to be thinking. "I just can't see any good coming out of this, Dani."

I didn't want to hear that. I didn't want to lay everything out for him and have him say it didn't matter. It did. My Grandma's tears and misery counted. Her pain, that was important. The fact she wanted me to find out what happened, that meant a ton to me too. Anger flashed all over me, but I knew I wasn't mad at Dad. Not really.

Weird. I had no idea what or who I was actually mad at.

My fingers curled against the wooden step beneath me, and I pushed myself to my feet. I crossed the wood and tile floor and sat down by Dad, my leg resting against his. Everything inside me kept jumbling up until my own feelings didn't make any sense at all.

"The copy of *Night on Fire* I read, it was Grandma's," I said, fishing for anything I might have forgotten that would help Dad understand how much we needed to figure this out. "She donated it to the library, I guess. Her name was in it, anyway, and an inscription. It said, 'Ruth Beans was here.'"

Dad turned his head in my direction and opened on eye. "Seriously? That's what she inscribed?"

I leaned in to him. He smelled like garden sweat and spearmint, too, a little. And pineapple, and lemon, from all the different types of mints I knew he had been trimming. "I thought it was strange, like what a little kid might write."

"Nah." Dad opened his other eye and gave me a sad smile. "It's a soldier thing. In wartime, Kilroy—remember him? Bald sketch with just the top of his head and a nose? That little guy got to be a thing in World War II, when your grandmother was a kid. Now, when soldiers are deployed or campaigning, it's tradition to graffiti him up somewhere. *Kilroy was here.*" He shrugged. "Guess it's a way to say, *Remember me, I was real, I fought here. . . .*" He stopped for a second, then added, "You know how she liked William Faulkner. Well, Faulkner said, 'What matters is at the end of life, when you're about to pass into oblivion, that you've at least scratched "Kilroy was here," on the last wall of the universe.'"

Suddenly, Grandma's inscription made all kinds of sense. *Ruth Beans was here.* Her mark on the universe.

"I wasn't even old enough to enlist in World War Two," Dad said. "But Mama, she was fighting her very own war, I guess, even that far back, and every year after." He glanced up the stairs. "But this one she's fighting now, she's losing it. Soon, I think."

He closed his eyes again, and rubbed his head. "Sorry. Headache again. I think my allergies are getting worse."

"Want me to get you some aspirin?"

"Thanks, I'll get some when I get up." Still with his eyes closed, looking way more tired than I wanted him to be, Dad asked, "What exactly are you wanting to do about this key, baby girl? Spell it out for me."

Hope fluttered up in my chest, and the shiver in my throat made it hard to talk. "I want to go look for the steam tunnel entrance where you think Grandma fell, in case she put the box in the tunnel. I also want to search between the Lyceum and Ventress." I swallowed, working not to talk too much too fast and make him quit listening. "I mean, if she gave me the key, the box has to be somewhere, right?"

For a few seconds, Dad didn't speak. His eyes came open, and he seemed to stare in the general direction of Grandma's room. Finally, he said, "I don't even know where that steam tunnel entrance is—or if it's even still there, after they relandscaped the Circle. And what if you find it—or find that lockbox? What if that box holds some deep dark terrible truth about the riot or about *Night on Fire* that blows Avadelle's novel all to hell and back? Will we be turning that over to the press so they swarm us and the Richardsons and tear Avadelle and her people all apart?"

"Well . . . um." I hadn't thought that far ahead. Just about finding the secret. "No. I guess I'll bring it to you, and we'll figure out what should happen, and what Grandma needs."

Dad made eye contact with me then. He shifted one of his arms, and put it gently around my shoulders, pulling me to him. I leaned in and rested against his chest, not caring about the dried dirt that flaked off on my face and fingers.

"Mama's peaceful enough now, baby girl. She barely talks at all, and whatever agitation she had, it's not much now. I think for everybody's sake, this big hunt for answers needs to stop. Avadelle might have had the right of it, that digging up bones doesn't do anything but make angry ghosts."

I wanted to argue, but what could I say? At that moment, when he was so tired and hugging me, and Mom was struggling to work late, and Grandma was sleeping, and the house was so quiet, I almost agreed with him. Almost.

"How about we make a little deal?" Dad gave me an extra squeeze. "You let this go so I can be sure you won't do any more craziness like going places you don't tell us and hiding in Dr. Harper's closet, and I'll talk to your mom. We'll see about easing up on the grounding, step by step. See how it goes?"

I sighed but didn't agree.

"Come on," Dad urged. "You can get yourself busy with camp projects and reading, and helping me take care of Mama. That's enough activity for anybody, baby girl."

"It is," I agreed.

Dad seemed to think I was taking his deal, because he said. "Good. Now, let's get Mama taken care of, and get you ready for bed before Cella comes home and calls me a slacker."

"Okay," I said, already feeling guilty, and wondering if I really should leave everything alone, like Dad thought I would, and sort of promising myself I'd do just that. "Does this mean I get my phone back?"

"I said we'd make a deal, Dani, not call down miracles from heaven."

Oh well. It was worth a try.

20

RUTH BEANS WAS HERE

**Excerpt from *Night on Fire* (1969),
by Avadelle Richardson, page 462**

After people die—especially those who weren't soldiers and accidentally stumbled into the battle—
everyone questions why we fought. I know I did. So
did Leslie. But that didn't stop us.

"Jim Crow isn't just a bunch of laws," Leslie told
the new class full of White kids even younger than
her. Despite the riot—maybe even because of it—
those kids meant to head into Hell itself, to help with
voter registration in Mississippi.

"It's an entire system of oppression designed to
keep White people in charge and Black people kneel-
ing on the ground." She glanced at me, a little nervous, since this was the first time she had taken the

lead. I gave her a smile. She smiled back. Then she talked for near about an hour.

Right about the time the whole group looked flattened, Leslie finished with, "I decline to accept the end of man . . . I refuse to accept this. I believe that man will not merely endure: he will prevail." The kids perked up at those hopeful words, and they listened that much harder.

The lines were from William Faulkner's Nobel Prize banquet speech. He gave it in Stockholm in 1950. My aunt Jessie could call him a shiftless drifter all she wanted, but to me, William Faulkner was a visionary. He saw the Civil Rights Movement coming decades before it happened, and that always made me wonder how much everyone saw coming.

Then again, most people don't notice that single, heart-stopping moment when rage and fear turn human and dig in for war.

LATE-DAY HEAT SHIMMERED OFF THE cross-walked pavement in front of Ventress Hall, turning the scene into an oil painting in the bright afternoon sun. Indri sat at the base of the Confederate Monument, a splash of pink shirt and faded jeans across the white marble of its chess-piece base. Above her, the confederate soldier stared down University Avenue, hand to his forehead to block the light, his rifle clutched close to his side. Behind her shoulders, the statue's inscription read *To Our Confederate Dead, 1861–1865, Albert Sidney Johnston Chapter 379 U.D.C.*

Indri seemed to be imitating the soldier, holding her hand to her forehead and squinting across the redbrick walkway and road that separated us from the rounded turret end of Ventress. She had a sketchpad open on her lap, trying to get the curves and angles just right. I sat beside her with a notebook open on my lap. I had drawn a picture too, but mine was of the route between Ventress Hall and the Lyceum. The Circle, the treed area behind Indri and the statue and me, was laid out like an uneven wagon wheel with twelve spokes. My grandmother could have buried the box with her hands just about anywhere in that area—but she would have had to stuff it in the ground pretty quick, since Dr. Harper followed her to the Lyceum soon after she left Ventress.

She could have stuffed the box into something else, or under something too. Or left it lying on the sidewalk, and somebody threw it away, or took it home and tossed it in a garage, or—

I didn't want to think about those possibilities.

My sketch had a few X's and O's in spots, reminding me of one of Mom's body diagrams. The marks were spots I thought might make for good box-hiding between where Dr. Harper last saw Grandma and the Lyceum. I marked little trees with soft dirt and pine shavings all around them, a bench, flowerbeds, and added a question mark because I didn't know if the old steam tunnel entrance where Dad thought Grandma had gotten injured still existed.

I planned on starting with the trees—but after camp, after Indri left, so I wouldn't drag her into my breaking the deal with Dad that I sort of didn't make, or get her in trouble for poking around the Circle.

"Don't look now," Indri muttered. "Jerk alert. And he has the Wicked Witch of Oxford with him." She lowered her head to keep sketching, but I couldn't stop myself from craning my neck until I spotted Mac and Avadelle moving down the sidewalk away from us, heading toward the Grove. Avadelle had on something loud and purple, along with her usual fedora. Mac was just in jeans and a T-shirt, like always.

My hand moved to my pocket for the phone I didn't have. Indri didn't have hers either, and neither of us had been able to check e-mail or messages since we were grounded. No way to know if Mac was trying to communicate with me or not. No way to get him any info, either.

I blew out a breath.

Yay for a little freedom, but the whole situation still sucked.

"Guess he's not in that much trouble," Indri said without looking up from her sketch, which was turning out really good. I could pick out the spire at Ventress, and all the main angles of the old building. "Though I guess escorting Avadelle around town could be its own form of punishment."

"No kidding." I tried to go back to my own sketch of the Circle, but my eyes kept drifting up, following Mac and

Avadelle until they disappeared into the Grove. A few minutes later, Ms. Yarbrough came over and inspected our work. Indri's sketch earned an enthusiastic, "Excellent first effort!"

As for mine . . .

"That looks a bit like a treasure map, Dani." Ms. Yarbrough managed a sort-of smile. "Were you trying to draw the building?"

That had been the assignment, but I hadn't bothered. Stick people, stick houses, stick buildings—yeah, I wouldn't have gotten very far. I shrugged one shoulder. "I didn't figure I could do it justice, so I was working on the greenery."

Sort of the truth, right?

And it earned me another sort-of smile. "I see." Ms. Yarbrough didn't comment on my notes with the question marks and cross-outs. "Well, ladies, camp's at an end for today. I'll take you back to the Grove with everyone else to get picked up—except for you, Ms. Beans. You're a walker today, and I believe it's closer for you to head out from here."

"Yes, ma'am." I closed my notebook and tucked my pencil behind my ear. Then I gave Indri a quick hug.

"Maybe we'll get our phones back soon?" Her smudged fingers smeared black pencil dust on my arms as she let me go. "For the weekend at least?"

"I hope so," I told her.

She walked off with Ms. Yarbrough, giving me a few extra waves every few steps, until they passed Ventress Hall and shifted into the Grove's trees. I waved back every time, until

I couldn't see her anymore. Then I glanced down the long sidewalk that ran along beside University Avenue, and knew my father was expecting me to head down it, toward home. *Trusting* me to do that.

Instead, I turned back to the Circle and started toward the Lyceum.

Mom was working late like she had to do every night now. Dad would be gardening until sunset and looking after Grandma, and oblivious to the outside world. So I figured I had almost two hours before Dad would notice I wasn't home yet and come looking for me.

Using the grid I'd drawn, I hurried down the widest wagon-wheel spoke of the Circle, the main sidewalk that would take me to the center flagpole. A few paces down that spoke, I turned right onto the grass and headed to the first little tree. I tried to pretend I was Grandma the night she took the box back from Dr. Harper, in a hurry, maybe confused and thinking somebody was watching me or wanting to steal my precious lockbox. I got close to the little tree, dropped to my knees, set my notebook aside, and pushed my hands into the sun-heated dirt and shavings around its base. Above my head, tiny leaves fluttered, casting shadows across the ground in front of me as I dug.

As I watched my hands plunge into the red mulch and crumbly brown dirt, I couldn't help remembering the black-and-white photos Ms. Manchester had shown us, the ones from the Meredith riot. If I had been in this exact spot that afternoon, I would have seen carloads and busloads of folks driving onto campus. I would have seen angry people and scared people and curious people. I would have seen furious people with guns and baseball bats, determined to stop progress because they thought change would ruin their lives or end their world or—something.

That kind of hate and violence didn't compute. My heart bumped hard as my fingers moved against pebbles and roots. I wiggled my fingers and pushed my hands deeper, as deep as I figured Grandma could have done the night she fled Ventress hall with her lockbox.

Had the same thing happened to her the night she took the box back? Was she remembering the riot the night when she hid her treasures? Sometimes, for people with Alzheimer's disease, the past could seem like yesterday, or even right now. I hated to think of how scared she might have been—both when she got hurt in the riot, then later, when her disease could have made her relive every minute of that pain.

I went all around the soft dirt area of the first tree, but I didn't find anything. I didn't find anything under the second tree, either, so I moved to the next, and the next, until I'd poked around all the little trees in that first section of wagon wheel. Each time I gave up on an area, I patted the dirt back down and smoothed out the shavings, then drew a line through the tree on my sketched grid.

People passed by me as I dug, but nobody said anything. So I just kept digging. Fifteen more minutes, then fifteen more. About half an hour later, digging behind the second bench I had marked on my grid, I had managed to collect a green toy soldier with a chewed-off leg, a golf ball, three acorns, and a quarter. I also had about a pound of dirt crammed under my fingernails and caked all over my jeans, and sweat trickled down both sides of my face.

I sat against the back of the bench, picked some of the dirt out from under my thumbnail with my teeth, and spit it off to the side.

"Hey!" somebody yelled. "Ew!"

And I closed my eyes, because I knew that voice.

"Truce, okay?" Mac said. "No more spitting."

I opened one eye and looked up at him. He stood between me and a bunch of trees and Ventress Hall, with late-afternoon sunlight streaming all around him like a halo. The bright light made his shirt and jeans look almost neon.

I shaded my eyes. "You don't sparkle in the sunlight. Your vampire powers must be fading."

"I vaaannnt to feeed," he said with a horrible Dracula accent. "For zee sparklies to come back, you know?"

I didn't even bother with groaning. I was pretty sure people on the other side of University Avenue could see my eye-roll.

Mac eased out of the sun's glare, and sat down in front of me near the bench. His gaze moved from my dirty clothes to my dirty hands, and finally to my face. "Do I want to know why you're digging up the Circle?"

"Do I want to know where Avadelle is?" I wiped more dirt off my hands, then off my jeans. "Is she about to swoop down on me like a fedora-wearing bat and hit me with her cane?"

Mac laughed. "No. My aunt picked her up ten minutes ago."

"Thank goodness." I wiped sweat off my cheek, then realized I had probably smeared dirt all the way to my chin. "Not up for bats and canes right now. I'm trying to find Grandma's lockbox. I thought she might have buried it somewhere in the Circle the night she took it from Dr. Harper, since it disappeared from her hands between Ventress and the Lyceum."

Mac glanced around. "There's, um, a lot of ground to dig up, if you're planning to search everywhere in this wagon wheel. You know that, right?"

"I thought I'd try to find the old steam tunnel entrance Ms. Manchester and Dad told us about, if it's still here, and check out the spots with loose dirt, the ones that would have been the same a year ago. You know, the little trees and benches. Maybe the flowerbeds." Why did I always seem to be filthy, or in trouble, or sweating down the back of my neck when Mac showed up? Why did I even care? I wished I didn't care.

"You're not serious about those flowerbeds," he said. "They'll never let you paw around in the tulips. Even if you come back at night, the lights will rat you out and security'll be all, *Miss, we need your parents' names*."

I banged my head on the back of the bench. "That box has to be here somewhere. Dr. Harper said she left Ventress with it, and she didn't have it by the time she got to the Lyceum."

Mac studied me with his eyebrows raised, letting his gaze drift around to the different trash cans and sidewalks.

"No." I held up one dirt-crusted palm. "I know what you're thinking, but I refuse to believe Grandma threw that box in the trash, or that some stranger picked it up, and now they're sitting on it somewhere with no idea what they've got."

"Okay," he said, and he stopped giving me the you're-goofy look. Just like that. Wow. I had forgotten Mac could be easy to get along with, like Indri. "I've tried to call you," he added, "to see how you were. Your phone's been off for days."

"Yeah, still grounded." I picked up my notebook and stood, and Mac stood with me, and he followed me as I walked around the bench to stand on the main wagon spoke side-walk, staring toward the Lyceum and the big flower beds he said I'd never be able to explore. "But thank you for getting the key back for me. That was amazing."

"I owed you," he said. "But I would have done it anyway."

I stopped walking, suddenly feeling nervous. Mac stopped too. Together, we looked at the Lyceum's six huge white columns, the ones that most everyone in the South recognized in pictures. Somewhere, sprinklers had come on, and water made a gentle whooshing sound, turning the air damp. The scents of grass and dirt and trees and fresh tulips mingled with hot concrete and asphalt.

It should have been relaxing. And yet . . . "You owing me—you mean, because you blew me off the last day of school?" I squeezed the binding of my notebook hard, and didn't look at Mac.

"Yeah." His voice seemed too quiet.

My brain shifted into high gear and full speed. So, he *was* apologizing. Sort of. Well, he did at Mom's office, and he gave me my key back like a peace offering. Did hurting my feelings the last day at school add up to something Mac couldn't fix by saying he was sorry?

Guess that was up to me.

Setting sunlight glared off each one of the fourteen windows behind the Lyceum's columns, yellow and pink and searing white, making my eyes tear up from the brightness. That had to be it, because I so wouldn't go all misty over Mac apologizing and wanting to be friends again, right?

"So all that stuff you said when you shook my hand and gave me the key at Mom's office, did you mean it?"

Silence.

My jaw started to hurt. I realized I was grinding my teeth, so I stopped, but I kept squeezing my notebook and staring at the bright, bright windowpanes behind the Lyceum's columns.

"My parents threatened to take away my guitar and music lessons," Mac said. "They told me they'd break up my band if I stayed friends with you. It was so stupid, but they said we'd end up being some national news story because of our

270

grandmothers, and the reporters would never leave us alone. I got scared about the music stuff. I'm really, really sorry. You meant a lot to me. You mean a lot to me, but my music—" He stopped. Kicked at something on the ground next to my foot. "Just, sorry, this is coming out all wrong."

I let myself blink, but even with my eyes closed, outlines of the bright windows stayed etched on my eyelids. "I get that. Your music's important."

Mac kicked the ground again. "I didn't know how to say *no* to them, even when I knew they were wrong, and I really wanted to."

I thought about Mom at work, assuming I was already home, and Dad out in his garden, trusting me to show up when I said I would. "I get that part too," I said.

Then we both stopped talking for a few seconds, or maybe a few minutes. My eyes roved the Lyceum, from the clock at the top to its big columns to the windows to the redbrick face to the five marble steps leading to its white doors with the golden handles.

Mac pointed to one of the columns near the top, then to a spot over the Lyceum's main door. "Supposed to be bullet holes in those places," he said. "Some from the Civil War and some from the Meredith riot."

"I still can't believe it happened here," I told him. "I mean, I can. It's just that everything feels so different now."

"My folks got grumpy when I tried to ask them about it," Mac said. "Dad griped about how the South, and Ole Miss

271

especially, never gets to move on from the past. Everybody still sees us as a bunch of psycho racist rednecks."

I shrugged one shoulder, and the side of my hand brushed Mac's arm. All of a sudden, the evening seemed very, very warm. Almost stuffy. I wanted to step away from him, but at the same time, I didn't. Confusing.

"Well, there *are* a lot of psycho racist rednecks around here," I reminded him.

He groaned. "There are psycho racist rednecks everywhere. Indri's dad probably even meets guys like that all the way over in Afghanistan."

I stared at the columns, then the flowerbeds, then all the big, old trees lining the sidewalks. Words from *Night on Fire* came to life, just like those photo images from Ms. Manchester's books. Tear gas clouds covering the exact spot where we sat, drifting over dozens of exhausted-looking men wearing gas masks and carrying rifles. It was hard to imagine, but that's what Avadelle and my grandmother drove into. By the time Grandma got out of her car, rioters had taken the Circle and raised the Confederate flag, right where the center flagpole was now. They were trying to run over the marshals or break into the Lyceum driving trucks and bulldozers.

Was Grandma scared? Probably terrified. The thought made my teeth clench again—but I knew Grandma. She came to get books for the kids she was teaching, so she would have gone straight on with her plans, determined to finish what she intended to do.

"My grandmother wanted to get to Dr. Harper's office," I said, finally opening my eyes all the way again, and pointing back behind the Lyceum. "And I think Avadelle would have helped her. With where his office was in 1962, they would have had to cut to the left of where we're standing."

Mac stared in the direction I was pointing. "If all the tear gas was here in the middle where the marshals were," he said, "she probably would have pulled to the curb and stayed as far to the side as she could without getting off the road and risking getting caught between buildings."

He led the way to the curb at the edge of the Circle, and we turned around, taking in the view as she would have seen it.

"All of this was mostly grass then, right?" Mac asked.

"Yeah." I inched forward, like I might be Grandma, head down, face covered to keep the drifting gas out of my eyes and nose. *Why didn't you just get back in your car and run away? Stubborn woman.*

Yep, Oops, I imagined her answering. *Just like you, with no earthly business being out here when you're still half in trouble and supposed to be home.*

"In the videos, people were running around a lot," Mac said. He started jogging back and forth and pretending to throw air-Molotov cocktails at the Lyceum. He looked seriously ridiculous, but I couldn't find it in me to laugh.

On Mac's second pass, he bumped into me. I stumbled to the right, dropped my notebook, and I almost stepped on metal bars set right into the ground. The steam tunnel grate.

It was about three feet across and four feet long, rusty but solid, and held down by a thick chain and padlock.

I stared at it for a few seconds, then sank down beside it on my knees. This was the right spot. The steam tunnel entrance my dad mentioned. It had to be.

Mac knelt beside me, put my notebook on the ground next to my leg, and then fiddled with the big chain. "That opening is pretty small. Not big enough for a person to fall through, really, is it?"

"A person could fit on purpose if they tried," I said. "If it was unlocked and open and stuff. Mom was right. There's no way the marshals moved Meredith through these smaller steam tunnels to get him to classes, like some people think. It would have been too tight a fit."

It was weird, how many times I'd been to Ole Miss, and the Circle, and even the Lyceum, and I'd never noticed this little grate, sitting over in the grass by itself, with its chain and lock. I didn't know it mattered.

I leaned forward and peered into the darkness beneath the bars. It seemed to go on forever, bottomless and black. If this were one of my fantasy books, it could be a portal to some other universe—but this was real life. Likely nothing was at the bottom besides concrete, dead leaves, and rank, stagnant water.

"There's a ladder," Mac said, showing me the metal rungs at the side. "Makes it even more of a tight fit."

"There's no way Grandma fell down this tunnel by

accident," I said. "That's for sure. If she went to the bottom, it was on purpose, and probably on that ladder."

My mind danced around the thought like the hundreds of fireflies beginning to play in the dusky air around us. Wink, wink, wink—I could sort of see the truth, but I didn't think I wanted to. Not really.

Mac settled on his knees beside me. "Could there be some other tunnel entrance?"

"This is the one closest to the Lyceum, like in the ghost story I read. People said they heard screaming coming from just out front. Dad and your aunt think it was this one too. Besides, the nearest other entrance is nowhere close to where they would have walked to get to Dr. Harper's office."

"Maybe there were different entrances in 1962?" he suggested. "I know the websites say nothing was padlocked back then."

"Mac, Grandma was a Black woman who walked into a race riot. Even though Avadelle was with her, that would have gone badly. In *Night on Fire*, some of the rioters saw them and caught them—that's probably true."

"In the book, GG tells them off, and the two characters run away."

"But not in real life," I picked at the grate. It moved on its hinges, just a little. "In real life, Grandma ended up down at the bottom of this steam tunnel entrance, hurt. Maybe the rioters pushed her down there. Or she went down to keep them from hurting her worse."

I suddenly was too aware of the tanned whiteness of Mac's skin, and my browner tone. Fifty years ago, one of us might have been arrested, just for talking to the other one.

Mac rattled the chain keeping the grate closed. "It's rusty," he said. "I can pull it a little—here." He stuffed his free hand in his pocket and pulled out a keychain with a little flashlight on the end. "Use this. It's bright enough."

Grunting, he shifted the chain, and I was able to move the grate just enough to make space for my arm. I pushed the little flashlight through and switched it on, illuminating the ladder and the stone walls at the top. Dirt and mold clung to the rocks in places, but I was surprised how clean it seemed.

Bit by bit, I moved the light down the ladder, pressing my face into the flaking metal of the grate, peering through divides in the lattice. I tried to imagine my grandmother climbing down, down . . .

The beam played off a rusted, snapped metal rung.

"There's a broken step," I said. "Maybe that's what made her fall."

Mac grunted again, and I realized he was leaning all the way back, holding the chain so I could keep the grate shifted to the side. If he let go, the grate would probably smoosh my arm off. I flicked the beam down to the bottom of the entrance, and saw the yawning circle of the actual steam tunnel. Spiderwebs covered it, and leaves were all over the bottom, like I had thought there would be.

Did Grandma fall into leaves like that?

I turned the beam to the walls—and almost immediately, I saw it. Scrawled writing, only it was more like etching, rock on rock, words cut into the stone by some other bit of stone, just above the tunnel floor, as if somebody had done it from a prone position. My heart thundered as I read the words, and tears filled up my eyes almost immediately.

"Dani," Mac said. "What is it? Do you see something?"

"Yeah." My voice sounded choked. "There are words on the wall. 'Ruth Beans was here.'"

I pulled my arm out of the grate so Mac could let go of the chain, and I sat up and handed him his keys. Then I choked up even more.

Mac rubbed his hands like they might be cramping from holding the chain. "So, definitely the spot—but no lockbox?"

I didn't move.

Mac switched on his flashlight again, and leaned toward the grate to look for himself. He had his back to University Circle, so he couldn't see the cars moving, or the black mustang parked in the spot nearest to us, or Dr. Harper getting out of the passenger side, moving slowly around the car.

Mac also couldn't see my father, grim-faced and glaring, seeming to take up half the sky as he stalked toward us.

21

LET THE GHOSTS KEEP IT FOR YOU

**Excerpt from *Night on Fire* (1969),
by Avadelle Richardson, page 471**

*My father always said snow falls in the South like an
unwelcome guest, that it comes in those secret hours,
when darkness begs for dawn. He told me a frozen
Mississippi moon could turn cold enough to hide the
devil's own heat.*

*"All that preaching on Satan your mama's church
does," my father warned, "you mark my words, CiCi.
They'll call Old Scratch's name so many times he'll
show up right here in town, cloven hooves and all."*

*When Oxford nearly burned for the second time,
I knew my father had been right. Even God wouldn't
have been able to sort sinner from saint the night
James Meredith came to Ole Miss.*

FROM A NOTE, STUCK TO my door:

Since I'm not getting through to you out loud, I thought I might try writing. Honey, why won't you let this go?

        —Dad

I wrote one back:

I don't like making you angry, Dad. I don't like making Mom angry. I really, really hate disappointing you. I don't want to disappoint Grandma, either. I know you and Mom and most people think she's already gone, and maybe she is, but I don't believe that, way down in my heart. I think some piece of her's still with us, for as long as she breathes. Grandma asked me to do something for her. It's probably the last thing she'll ever get to ask me to do, so how can I just let that go?

        —Dani

When Dr. Harper drove you home with
your father night before last, he told you
he couldn't in good conscience help you
anymore, since we didn't approve. Indri's
mother is planning on keeping her home from
camp now. Mac got in trouble last night with
campus security and his folks for searching
tulip beds with his dad's metal detector.
The Richardsons came by to ask us if we
could get you to stop whatever you've doing,
because Avadelle's having chest pains. Is
this what you want? To hurt people?

—Mom

I don't want to hurt anybody, not ever.
I don't understand how looking into
something that happened so long ago
can be such a huge problem. And Mac?
A metal detector? Wow. That's seriously
awesome. Did he find anything?

—Dani

Mac didn't find anything with that
stupid machine, unless you want
to count sprinkler lines, pipes, and

280

a gardening trowel somebody left
buried on the south end. Do you
like that boy, Dani? Is it time
for us to have . . . the talk?
About boys and girls?

        -Dad

Nobody does that anymore, Dad. The
Internet and books take care of it as
soon as most of us are able to read. And
I like Mac as a friend. I don't know if
I like him for more. Do I have to know
right now?

        -Dani

You absolutely do not have to know until
you're ready. I'll take care of this with
your father.

        -Mom

I'm reading this too, you know, Cella.
        -Dad

I took down all the notes and threw them away so my parents would stop using them to try to "communicate better."

I sat in Grandma's room, beside her bed, watching her sleep and trying to write about whether I liked Mac or not, or come up with ideas about where to look next for the lockbox without getting grounded longer, getting arrested by campus security, getting my friends in trouble, or giving the Wicked Witch of Oxford a heart attack.

"This is complicated," I told Grandma as I tore out yet another page of false starts and pitched it in the trash near her bed. "I don't have a single clue where you put that lockbox. *I gave it to history. I let the ghosts keep it for you.* Okay. What does that even mean?"

And should I even keep trying to figure it out?

I wasn't allowed at camp, per Mom. I wasn't allowed out of the house, per Dad. I had no phone, no computer time, nothing but my books and a notebook, and hanging around with Dad and Grandma. Dad talked plenty enough, about squash and lettuce and aphids and soil mixtures. Grandma hadn't said a word in days.

After a while, I gave up and walked over to her open window and looked outside. Dad was in his garden like always, picking produce and digging in the dirt. He didn't look up, even when I willed him to. He just gardened on, oblivious to all my staring and wishing.

I wasn't sure what I wanted. Maybe for him to glance up and grin and wave, like I was still his baby girl. He hadn't called me that since he picked me up on campus. Just *Dani*, and a few times, *honey*. Mom was still mostly using all of my names, every time she said anything to me out loud.

"Grandma," I said, "are you sure we're all gonna be okay? Lately, I've really started doubting it."

When I turned toward her, her eyes were closed, but I thought she might have been smiling. I went back to her bed and gave her a kiss. Her skin felt warm against my lips, and for a while, I kept my head on her pillow, breathing in the scent of baby oil and freshly washed cotton. When I sat back, I realized Mom had taped two pictures over Grandma's bed. A couple of weeks back, in Creative Arts Camp, we studied flowers around campus, and tried to draw them. Indri's Dutch crocus looked like something off the cover of *National Geographic*. It fluttered on the wall in the slight, hot breeze. Next to her masterpiece, my version of the flower looked like a blue and purple deformed ghoul-goblet.

Grandma didn't seem to mind. To her, everything I created turned to solid gold.

I put my face back on the pillow, pressing my cheek into her hair, and I cried. More than anything, I wanted her to wake up and just be okay. I wanted everything to calm down and get easy again. Why did nothing feel easy? Would life ever be easy again?

There, with my eyes closed tight, my thoughts kept going back to one word. *Ghostology*. The study of ghost lore. *I let the ghosts keep it for you*. That's what Grandma told me about the lockbox. And when she took it away from Dr. Harper, she headed to the Lyceum. Except for the steam tunnel scream story, which was probably about Grandma the night of the Meredith riot when she got hurt, the Lyceum's ghostology was mostly about the Civil War, about people seeing the spirits of Confederate soldiers who passed away there after the Battle of Shiloh. My mind flashed on the creepy window at Ventress Hall, and the bizarre stained glass eyes of dead soldiers in gray uniforms. I shivered. The whole Civil War thing on campus, all the statues, and that stained glass, and the turret where soldiers and students scribbled on the walls, and—

And then my eyes popped open. I lifted my head. My hand dropped to my jeans pocket, where I traced the familiar outline of the key.

Of course.

How could I—wow. All that digging. The metal detector. All the searching. Every bit of that had been completely stupid.

Ruth Beans was here.

"I gave it to history," I said out loud, feeling lightheaded. "I let the ghosts keep it for you. I think I got it. I think I understand."

I gave Grandma another kiss, and I walked back to her open bedroom window. The pieces of what I needed to do clicked into place in my head, almost like a map, as neat and perfect as any picture Indri might draw. Part of me wondered if I should feel excited, or worried, or all pulled in half by how furious my parents would be and how much trouble I'd get in *this* time, but I didn't feel any of that.

Mostly, I felt relief. And a little peace. And some easy. Finally, a little bit of easy.

For a long time, I watched Dad digging in the dirt below. Sunset turned everything in the garden bright shades of yellow and red and green, and Dad seemed like an unstoppable nature spirit from one of my fantasy books. He finally sensed me watching and stood, propping himself on his hoe. He pulled his blue bandana off his head and mopped his face and neck. After a few seconds he lifted it and waved it at me.

"I love you, baby girl," he said loud enough for me to hear over faraway traffic and the cranking up of crickets and frogs and a few cicadas.

I waved back at him. "I love you too, Dad."

A little after ten o'clock, when I was sure both my parents would be asleep, I got up and stripped off my pajamas, pulled on jeans and a T-shirt, stuffed Grandma's key into my pocket, and put on my sneakers. I eased into my parents' room without worrying about waking them up, because they both slept like big, snoring rocks. Saying a silent apology for being such a rotten kid, I went back to the hallway and pulled out my phone I had swiped back from Mom's bedside table and charged while Dad was still outside. I flicked the sound switch to *mute*, then turned it on. As fast as I could, I texted Indri and Mac.

I know where the lockbox is.

I gave them the location, and told them I was headed over

to get it, and I'd let them know what I found inside. Then I went downstairs, took a flashlight out of the kitchen junk drawer, and as quietly as I could, let myself out into the hot night. When I got to the sidewalk that ran beside the long strip of University Avenue between my house and campus, guilt finally tickled the back of my mind, but I tried to ignore it. In the white glow of streetlights, I watched my feet move, and saw my shadow drifting along. I felt like a wraith, passing between one life and the next. The sensation almost made me wobbly.

Traffic whizzed back and forth, even this late, and at crosswalks, I had to wait for the light before I could walk. When the light turned, and I crossed the last street and got to campus, excitement made me move a little faster, even though I was huffing from walking fast.

Off in the distance, I saw taillights moving around the Circle, near the front of the brightly lit Lyceum columns. I crossed to the right-hand sidewalk when traffic permitted, and focused on the old, looming, castle-like building.

Ventress Hall rose into the darkness against a backdrop of spooky-looking trees, surreal with its yellow ground lighting casting shadows across the rounded tops of its windows. Most of the panes were dark, but as I had hoped, the upstairs window where Dr. Harper worked still glowed white. Since he was in his office, the street-level door would be unlocked.

I moved quickly up the few steps in front of the building, and opened the door. The top hinge creaked, making me wince. I stood for a second, holding the door and listening to see if Dr. Harper would come out of his office. When he didn't, I slipped inside and gently closed the door.

The downstairs offices were locked up tight, but a single light showed me the carpeted stairs that led to the stained glass window with the beautifully created but bloodied University Grays looking down from above. Outside lights blazed, making the soldiers' eyes seem glow-y and demonic. Silence pressed in on me, and the sound of my own heartbeat seemed way too loud. I didn't want to switch on the flashlight for comfort, because I knew it might look odd if it bounced off windows, and would bring campus security in to check on the building. I told my feet to move, but most of me did not want to go up those stairs.

I took a step. Breathed. Counted to ten, then twenty. I did not look at the soldiers again, or their demon eyes. Another step. Another. My blood rushed so hard I could feel it pulsing in my throat. If ghosts were real, they were here in this building, right now, watching me. I felt that deep in my skin, in my bones and fingers and toes. One step at a time, I climbed, forcing myself to think about Grandma, and how straight she would have stood, how she would have marched past this window without so much as a glance.

When I finally had the window at my back, I climbed even faster, on to the second floor near Dr. Harper's door— but that wasn't where I was going. Instead, I turned in to a big office and faced a desk, empty at this hour, but standing guard nonetheless. Behind that desk was a different kind of door, closed and polished on the outside, but I knew on the other side it was dusty and spider-webbed. I couldn't quite believe I was here at night, and I was about to open it, much less cross into the otherworld it seemed to hold back. Nobody got to go up there anymore. Most people only ever got to peek behind the door, with the dean's permission, and the person at the desk guarding the space during business hours.

I gave it to history. I let the ghosts keep it for you. I should have realized what Grandma meant when she first said that, even if it was in Alzheimer's code. Where was the most haunted place on campus? Where were the real ghosts, if ghosts existed?

Here. Right here in Ventress Hall, up in the turret, where the ghosts had been signing their names for years.

My stomach clenched, and my chest tightened. I didn't know whether to think about ghosts, or Grandma the night she took her lockbox away from Dr. Harper. He thought he saw her leaving Ventress with the box—but he also said he stayed locked in his office for a while, until he saw her out his window. She had time.

I made myself cross the empty office. My sneakers squeaked against the wood floors, and I held my breath, not wanting to make a single noise to alert Dr. Harper I was in the building—or wake up the ghosts, because for sure, I was digging up some serious bones now.

I put my hand on the door handle.

The metal seemed cool. Too cold, really, for the heat. My teeth chattered. Ventress Hall had been renovated, restored, then renovated and fixed up again when it flooded because of those broken pipes a few years back. Only one part of the building got left untouched. The turret.

I pulled open the door and shut my eyes for a count of three.

When no ghost blasted out to possess me, I peeked at the narrow, dark entryway. Then I switched on the flashlight and stepped into the turret. When I put my foot on the first step, the wood gave an ominous snap and groan, making me hold my breath all over again as I started up.

The narrow stairs seemed to be covered in dust and plaster, and I didn't have a rail to steady myself as they turned and twisted. I grabbed the smooth wooden pole in the center, and let my flashlight play on the damaged plaster. Names and dates and doodles passed by, so many it was like looking at one of Dr. Harper's "context" lessons. Here, 1949. A little farther up, 1972, 1983, 1969. Sketches of hearts with initials, squares, geometrical designs, an eyeball or two, tons of squiggles I couldn't identify—Indri had been right when she told me I had no artistic sensibilities. It had seemed like so much scribble when I had seen it before, but now, I wondered about every single name and date and drawing. Who were these people? Where had they come from? What happened to them?

And most of all, had my grandma scrawled her name somewhere in this mess, in big letters or tiny ones? A sinking sensation almost made me stop climbing and sit down. It could take me longer to search these walls than to dig up the entire Circle, tulip beds and all. I climbed a few more steps, running the flashlight left and right to be sure the box wasn't just sitting out, or tucked somewhere obvious. No sign of it, or of Grandma's handwriting. Each step took me around and higher. My fingers pressed into the wooden pole, and I didn't look behind me or down through the opening, afraid the view would freak me out completely. The space seemed to get more narrow inch by inch, and the graffiti swept along, never stopping, layer upon layer of people and time and messages, none of them what I wanted to see.

About three steps from the very top, another step gave a loud creak, making me wince—and stop. The wood had actually shifted under my foot, like it might be loose. I gripped the center pole and turned the flashlight down to my sneaker, gently rocking the stair board back and forth. It definitely moved.

I eased back down a few steps, until I could lean over and give the almost triangular board a tug. It slid to the side, showing me a dark space underneath, like a hidden drawer.

Lying in that dark space was a box, exactly like the one Dr. Harper described. Surprise made me move the flashlight to the wall, and that's when I saw it, in shaky but distinctive pen-scratched letters.

Ruth Beans was here.

22

The Riot Was Real

––––––

Excerpt from *Night on Fire* (1969),
by Avadelle Richardson, Epilogue

In 1962, Martin Luther King and John F. Kennedy walked this earth like gods. Medgar Evers and Malcolm X cast mighty, mighty shadows as the world's eyes stared unblinking into America's second Civil War. Images of lunch counter battlefields flushed the face of a shamed nation only just beginning to realize the full might of television news.

Children fell in front of their wide, disbelieving gaze, skin stripped by firehoses. Enraged police dogs chewed on little arms and little legs. Tiny hands covered tiny faces and grown men in uniforms beat them with fists and clubs. Horses rode down unarmed men and women in the street. Politicians in suits spewed hatred and called for armed insurrection rather than peaceful change and equality. Bullets and tear gas formed their own language.

Mother country raged, and father world frowned. The time had come.

The bloody bastard South was in for our own righteous beating, and we knew it. Somewhere in our hearts, we all knew it, just as surely as any guilty child sent to cut his own switch.

But that didn't stop us from fighting.

Nothing could stop the Movement—not even the bullets that would leave our gods dead at our feet.

FOR A LONG TIME, I couldn't breathe. I couldn't think or move. When I did finally reach down to gather the box, it felt like swimming in a dream. The dusty, cool turret air shimmered in the flashlight beam as I picked up the metal container. Something rattled inside.

The entire world seemed to move completely away from me, leaving me totally alone in the turret with nothing at all but the flashlight, the key, and the box. I set the lockbox on the step below the open space, pulled Grandma's key out of my pocket, and sat beside the box. Using the flashlight like a guiding beam, I slid the key into the lock. Perfect fit. It opened with a single turn, and the rusty hinges ground as I lifted the box's lid and shined my light inside it.

A stack of books lay against the back wall of the box, thin with yellowed covers. I carefully thumbed through them. They looked like accounting ledgers. I picked one up. It said *Boots* in curly writing, then in bold print *Scribbling Diary, 65th Year of Publication, British Manufacture Throughout, Three days on a page*. Below that, it was stamped with a great big *1961*.

Right above that date, my grandmother had written her name on the book. When I opened it, I found pages with squares on them, and lots of tiny writing in the squares. Each page had dates, and tons and tons of entries. Grandma had recorded her life, almost step by step. Tweeting before Twitter existed? Too awesome.

My finger traced down the page I had open, and I found, "Tougaloo. Nine students at the library, arrested. Ava can't shut up, raging about arresting people for trying to read." Unbelievable. Just like in *Night on Fire*, and all the stuff Ms. Manchester told us. Grandma had written about it as it happened.

Outside the turret, the building grunted and groaned a few times, but I didn't even jump. My brain tried to tell me somebody was walking around downstairs, maybe even near the turret door, but I ignored that, along with a few spooky thumps. *Too late now, ghosts. I've got the books*.

I put down 1961 and grabbed 1962. Immediately, I paged over to September, to the end of the month.

Sunday, Sept 30, 5:17 pm

Books! Fred has three boxes. Science and
literature. Ava driving. Meredith due to
arrive tomorrow. Life looks up! Maybe we'll
catch a glimpse of history.

Sunday, Sept 30, 6:30 pm

Campus so congested. Police everywhere. Ava
thinks there will be trouble tonight, even
sooner than we thought. She's probably right.

Sunday, Sept 30, 7:00 pm

Never seen anything like this. Took half
an hour to make half a mile. Police cars
everywhere. Going behind the Lyceum and
taking the quick path to Fred's office when
we can find a place to park.

Sunday, Sept 30, 7:30 pm

Something very wrong. Police pulling out,

moving away from campus. Crowd looks out of control. We're trying to leave but can't move an inch.

I looked up. So, they didn't get out of the car? Hmm. Really different from *Night on Fire*, then. I frowned and turned the page. The next day's dates were blotted out by a blackish-brown stain.

Blood?

I almost dropped the book. The word *RIOT* glared up at me from beneath the stain. From outside the turret, seemingly closer, I heard shuffles and thumps. My eyes narrowed. That didn't sound like ghosts. It sounded like a person moving around.

A person coming closer.

Dr. Harper?

My heart danced against my ribs, and I had a sudden memory of that look on his face when I thought he was going to take the key from me.

Footsteps—definite footsteps—echoed in the office below the turret, near the door. The door I had left standing open. I gripped the book and flashlight tight but switched off the light as I stood.

The door bumped the wall as someone opened it.

I started to climb, put my foot in the open step, and fell backward on my butt, hard. If I hadn't bumped against the center pole, I would have fallen head first, all the way down to the bottom. Breath rushed out of me, half from the fall, half from terror. The flashlight went flying out of my hand. It banged down the stairs and smashed on the wood floor below. I heard it clatter into pieces, and I clutched the book tight to my chest.

"I know you're up there," came a scratchy voice. Thumping and bumping made me want to scream, but before I could even move, a flashlight beam, twice as big and strong as mine had been, blazed up the circle of steps and nailed me right in the face. "I saw the message on Mackinnon's phone. It's in the study where it got taken up from him over that metal detector fiasco. Idiot thing kept buzzing on the desk where I was writing, and I couldn't make it stop. I came here to make sure you didn't break your fool neck, running around this building in the dark. I owe Ruth Beans that much."

I didn't say a word. I just sat there and held Grandma's 1962 book, blinded by that flashlight, with my butt hurting like I'd taken a good, swift kick in the pants.

"I owe her a lot more than that." Avadelle Richardson sighed. Then she asked, "You okay from that fall?"

Her grumbly tone made me think she was kind of hoping I wasn't okay at all.

I wanted to hide the books back in the step, but my stupid foot was still stuffed into the space, and anyway, Avadelle would see any move I made. I blinked and blinked, trying to get used to the harsh light, and as I saw a bit more, I realized that her lumpy, fedora-crowned shadow filled up my only escape route behind that flashlight beam, unless I did want to plunge to my death down the middle of the twisty staircase.

The beam moved from my face to my hands, to the volume I was holding.

"So," she said, "you found her old journals. I thought you might be getting close to hunting down her hiding place. I never could."

My lips stayed pressed together and my heart kept right on hammering as Avadelle diverted her flashlight beam to the wall and leaned on her cane, her shoulder pressed against some of the stairwell's cracking plaster. "Time was, Ruth wrote every word of her life, right up until we got pulled out of that car in the Circle."

"Pulled out?" My voice sounded choked, but curiosity jerked the words out of my throat. "You didn't get out of the car on purpose—to go get Grandma's books?"

"Of course not." Avadelle's loud grumbling seemed to echo in the small space. "Do you think we were total fools? It was stupid enough, going to campus that night. We knew it was historic, Meredith coming. Maybe we just wanted to be a part of it."

"I only got to the bloodstain and the word *riot*," I admitted. "But I'm going to read the rest unless you take the book away from me."

Avadelle shined the light into her own face, probably so I could see her glaring at me. "I know you think I'm a monster, but I don't hit little girls, even nosy, insufferable brats like you."

I almost said *thank you*, then thought better of it. Instead, I worked my foot out of the open stair and pushed the board back into place, in case I really did have to make a run for it.

"I won't take Ruth's journals away from you," Avadelle said. "But since you found them, it's just as well that I tell you what that one says, later, months later, when Ruth was able to write again."

That shocked me back into stillness, so I sat and rubbed my scraped ankle, holding the journal and waiting.

Avadelle moved the flashlight beam to the floor, and her dark shape shifted in the stairwell as she leaned harder on the wall, like she needed the support. "Her journal says the rioters broke our car windows and pulled us out into the middle of all that mess in the Circle. My arm got cut, and I bled in Ruth's book, but she wouldn't put it down, and she wouldn't give it up even when they pushed us and taunted us and tried to take it. We ran, but they caught us."

Her voice trailed off. "Lord, but there were so many of them, and not all students. People I'd never seen in my life."

She sounded sad, and scared, and when she went quiet, I almost couldn't stand it. "In *Night on Fire*, you talked to them," I said. "You made them think you were an Oxford town lady on campus by accident, and you shamed them into letting you go."

"I know what that book says, girl," Avadelle snarled. "I wrote the godforsaken thing, didn't I?"

"So, you didn't talk to the rioters?"

Avadelle laughed, but it sounded angry and almost hopeless. "Oh, I talked to them all right. I babbled on about running a charitable errand, and how we had just come to get books for children, and didn't mean any harm. I told them my family was rich and could make a lot of trouble for them." She stopped. Sniffed. Her arm moved in the semidarkness, like she was wiping her face. "I thought they'd let us go. Such a little idiot, I was."

I waited, and I waited some more, but she went quiet, and I tried to figure out the best question to ask. My fingers twitched against Grandma's journal, and if Avadelle meant it about not hitting kids, I could get up and push past her and read it for myself. It didn't seem like the right thing to do, though.

"They let *me* go," she whispered all of a sudden, then dropped into silence again.

I worked on that statement, trying to make sense of it, to understand, and—

Oh.

"You," I said, and I went cold inside. "They only let you go, not Grandma."

"And God save my soul, *I went*," Avadelle whispered.

I reached one hand out to the center pole and steadied myself. "You left Grandma with the mob."

"They beat her," Avadelle talked right over me, as if I wasn't even there. "They left Ruth lying on the ground, clutching that book you're holding. They left her for dead, mind you—and she probably would have been killed if she hadn't crawled down into that steam tunnel. I don't know if the fall broke her back, or the beating. She was down there nearly all night before somebody heard her screaming and they pulled her out."

I tried to absorb everything she was saying, but I didn't want to believe it. I had wanted to know so badly, but this—this, how could I even begin—

"But in *Night on Fire*—"

"That was a *book*, girl! A novel. The riot was real."

I swallowed a few times and tried to keep my voice steady as I asked my next question. "So . . . Grandma stopped being friends with you because in the book, you made yourself a hero, but in real life you ran away and left her to get beat up and nearly die?"

Silence. Total. Not a creak or a groan or a breath.

And then another laugh from Avadelle broke the quiet into pieces. "No. That's the worst part, don't you see? She forgave that. Ruth said anybody with half a brain would have run—should have run—just like I did. I won't say we were as close after that, but we tried a while longer."

"Then what was it that stopped the friendship?"

Avadelle pulled off her fedora and shined the flashlight into it, like answers might be swimming around in all her head sweat. Some time later, she said, "After she got hurt, Ruth started writing the story of what happened to her that night. A nonfiction piece, for magazine publication, or maybe as the start of an academic paper. I launched off writing a novel instead. Fiction. I never could do truth like Ruth did, at least not on paper."

"Did she know you were writing the novel?"

"Yes, and no. I didn't show her the work, and she didn't show me hers. We just talked about what we were doing, now and again. I got finished and sent my manuscript off to New York for consideration and didn't even have to wait a month to hear from an editor."

Now I felt confused. "It made her mad that you—what? Got your novel published before her articles?"

Avadelle kept studying that hat like it had answers. Her voice got whisper-quiet. "Ruth was furious that I wrote *Night on Fire* through her eyes—and changed my role in it to the hero, like you said."

"Wait—that—I mean, so? I mean, I get the part about her being mad that you made yourself a hero. But people write stuff through other people's eyes all the time."

"Writing that book was Ruth's dream. But back then, as a Black woman from Mississippi, Ruth never would have gotten a novel published." Avadelle put her fedora back on and shifted the flashlight beam to my feet, like she might be checking my ankle to see if I had gotten hurt when I fell. "Nobody would have even read the manuscript. I took her experiences and everything she went through, and I used it for my own. Appropriation. You know that word?"

I gazed down at my ankle, at the small trickle of blood running into my shoe. Just a scratch. "I don't, no. Sorry."

As I said that, I cringed and waited for her to call me stupid. Instead, she said, "I stole Ruth's story. That's the short and long of it. Because a White woman told it instead of a Black woman, the book got published, and the world listened. That's what Ruth couldn't abide. It festered inside her, until she pretty well couldn't stand the sight of me." She paused, and her voice dropped lower. "Ruth never even tried to write her own novel about the riot, or anything else. She just got busy with her scholarly work, and told her truths with nonfiction."

She must have taken my confused silence for judgment, because the next thing she said was, "Before you ask, we did try to talk it through. Some days, some weeks even, we'd do all right, but then something else would happen. A good review. A bestseller list. An award. Ruth watched me living her dream at her expense, and I didn't even have the gumption to own up to it in interviews and articles."

Avadelle let out a wheezy breath, and coughed. "I tried to sign over half the profits to her, but she refused. Said she wouldn't take food from my babies' mouths when they were innocents in the whole mess, and she could make her own way in life for her and hers, thank you very much. That seemed to break it, finally. Everything I did from that point, it just seemed to make things worse between us."

"I get that," I said, thinking about my tiny little hard times with Mac, and with my parents. Nothing up against what Avadelle and Grandma went through, at the hands of others, and between themselves, but I understood how once

302

something started heading south, it picked up speed on its own.

"Why haven't you tried to explain that to the press, to anybody, since you got older?" I kept my eyes fixed on Avadelle's shadow, alert for any sudden movements. "Is it the being-a-coward part that stops you?"

"No. My family's scared to death it'll hurt my income, but that's not why either. I don't try to explain because Ruth asked me to let it be. That, and half the world still wouldn't understand. They might think Ruth had the wrong of it, and I know she didn't. She loved me even though I was young and stupid and a coward. It was the thieving of her story and her dreams that she couldn't get past."

"I think she wants to see you," I said. "She's said your name over and over, and sometimes, she cries when she does it."

Avadelle went so still I wasn't sure she was still breathing. She stood like part of that turret wall, the flashlight focused on her fedora. The longer she stayed frozen, the more I worried she was about to really melt down, maybe fall out or finally come at me and throw me straight out a window.

"I think—I think Grandma forgives you," I said. "Maybe that's what she wants to tell you."

Of all things, Avadelle chuckled. "Ruth doesn't forgive me. She probably wants me to come by to slap me bug-eyed when I try to sit by her bedside. But that's okay. She doesn't owe me forgiveness. She knows I care about her anyway, just like she cares about me no matter how many rotten things I've done."

All of a sudden, a big clamor broke out below us. Doors knocking open. Voices. Feet running up the steps. I heard Dr. Harper come out of his office and start calling out to whoever had come in.

Avadelle called out next, a wavering, almost tentative, "Hello?"

"Dani!" Mac called.

Indri said, "Oh, thank God."

"Well, that's it," I told Avadelle. "I'm fried toast. If my friends are here, they've come to say good-bye before my parents kill me and bury me in Dad's garden."

Avadelle gave a grunt that might have been a laugh. "Just hope nobody called the police. When it's me, people always call the police. They arrest me just for fun these days."

It sounded like an entire herd of horses had gotten loose in Ventress Hall. Dr. Harper got to us first, and he flicked on the lights in the stairwell. When I could see again after getting used to the glare, I didn't like the look on his flushed face. His wide eyes and open mouth made my heart beat funny, and I glanced from him to Avadelle, then to Mac and Indri, who crowded into the door behind him.

They both looked awful and sad and scared. I stood, clutching Grandma's book, just as Ms. Wilson pushed into the stairwell. She ran up the steps past Avadelle and dropped to her knees in front of me. My fingers felt numb against the journal.

Ms. Wilson put her hands on my cheeks, making me look

into her tear-streaked face. I tried to breathe, couldn't, and felt dizzy. The white plaster walls and all the graffiti and ghosts of the past seemed to revolve in a slow, sick arc, blurring the whole world.

"Honey, I've got to get you over to the hospital," Ms. Wilson said. "Your father's had a stroke."

23

FOR THE VERY LAST TIME

———

MY FIRST THOUGHT AS MS. Wilson hustled me into the intensive care room was, *That's not my father.*

And then louder in my head. *THAT'S NOT MY DAD!*

The ride over to the hospital spun through my memory like a Ferris wheel cut loose to roll away from a fair.

Stoplights, blinkers.

Ms. Wilson staying within the speed limit but holding the steering wheel so tight her arms didn't move.

Was Indri right? Does God get mad and punish you when you don't keep your deals? Did all the stupid stuff I've ever done cancel out Dad's luck and health?

Indri and Mac in the backseat, saying nothing at all.

Headlights from the car behind, Dr. Harper following us, with Avadelle riding shotgun.

Each time we went under a streetlight, I saw flickers of Indri's tears and guilty expression. *It's not my dad*, her eyes had told me. *I'm so sorry, but it's not my dad.*

Indri and Mac didn't come into the intensive care unit with us. They stayed outside the door with Dr. Harper and Avadelle while Ms. Wilson and I went inside.

It's not Dad. My brain repeated what I had seen in Indri's expression on the drive over.

My father was strong, with wooly hair and a woolier beard and big eyes and a bigger smile and so much energy he made rooms vibrate. He wore jeans and bandanas, and he smelled like gardens and spices.

This man in the white hospital gown lying on the big blue air mattress, he was motionless except for the rise and fall of his chest every time the machine next to his bed pumped and clicked. The stench of alcohol and rubber wrinkled my nose as I studied the big tube taped in his mouth, and the white squares taped to his head, and IV lines running into his arms. All his hair had been shaved, and his beard, too.

This bald, flat man couldn't be my father. He seemed too small, and way too weak. Only, that was my mother, crying and kissing the man's bald head, all along the awful-looking line of staples and bandages that started at his scalp and disappeared into the pillow. At the very top of his head, a metal probe stuck out of a wad of tape, like some horrible antenna.

"I should pull that out," I said, and my voice sounded dry and cracked and like somebody else was talking. "It's got to hurt."

I walked forward, but Ms. Wilson held me back. I tried to pull away and she held on harder. Mom seemed to notice me then, and she let go of *not Dad not Dad not Dad* the man in the bed and came around to my side of the bed.

"Dani," she whispered, but I wouldn't look at her.

Ms. Wilson kept a tight grip on both my arms. My eyes had moved to the monitor hanging above the man's bed. His blood pressure was sixty over thirty. Too low. His pulse—I didn't have to take it to see it switch from thirty to twenty then shoot to one hundred and drop back to forty again. The machine showed all that to me every few seconds. His lips had a bluish color, and the machine breathing for him meant he probably couldn't breathe right on his own.

A man in green scrubs came into the room, and I looked at him long enough to note the stethoscope and surgical mask hanging around his neck. He was bald too, but nobody had stapled a zipper into his head.

"Is this his daughter?" the man in scrubs asked.

"Yes," my mother said in a voice too tiny to belong to a grown-up. "Dani, this is Dr. Albert."

I glanced at him again, but my eyes went straight back to the man in the bed, and I couldn't help mentally tracing the nose, the jawline, then looking down at his hands. Strong hands that dug and pulled and held and hugged and patted and weeded. Dirt crusted under every single fingernail—*that's excellent dirt, baby girl, I made it myself*—and I knew they'd never be clean, and I knew Dad didn't want them to be clean, because—*it's good dirt, Dani, and it means I'm working hard*—that was garden dirt under his nails.

"Dad," I whispered, and pain spiked so deep into my chest and belly that I opened my mouth and yelled without making any sound and stopped feeling like I was even wearing my own skin.

The real me floated up to the ceiling and looked down on the crowded room, where Mom held my dad's shaved face in her hands and Ms. Wilson held my arms and the doctor said, "Dani, your father suffered a massive bleed on his brain. We tried to take the blood out, but there was too much, and it was too late."

"We were asleep," Mom said. "He started moving. Flailing in the bed . . . I thought it was a nightmare. . . ."

Ms. Wilson let go of me and went over to Mom. Mom leaned in to Ms. Wilson and closed her eyes. I couldn't close mine. All I could do was stare at Dad from the ceiling *it is him oh God that's my father that's my dad* as the doctor came up with things like, *catastrophic* and *no chance for meaningful recovery* and explained how the bottom part of my father's brain got crushed from all the weight on top and it was probably due to his blood pressure and maybe genetics and how he didn't get good health care growing up and his age and possibly dehydration from working in the sun all day and everything faded in and out because none of that mattered *because it's Dad it's Dad in that bed and he's not moving, Dad please move please move please open your eyes* and the doctor said, "Your father's advanced directives were very clear about how we should proceed in the case of cessation of brain functions, but your mother asked us to wait until you got here."

He gestured to the machines.

After that, he kept talking, and Mom talked, and I think I nodded or shook my head, but it was all just noise.

The *click-hiss* of that machine breathing for Dad took up all my awareness as it kept moving and kept moving and kept moving until *click-hiss—click—*

It stopped.

The doctor pulled the taped lines away from my father's head, and took out his IVs, then took out that tube in his mouth. He even reached up and pulled out the antenna, and patted down the bandage around that spot. After he cleared everything away, the doctor stepped back and left the room.

I saw all this from way up on the ceiling, but then I dropped down from the ceiling, tumbling into my body like jumping off a high dive, but it hurt and I didn't want to be there and my mouth tasted like throw-up *please, please let me go back to the ceiling again let me just fly away I can't do this I can't stand this I can't I can't I can't.*

My eyes darted to the monitor over Dad's head, but the doctor had switched that off too. There were no numbers. There was no light on the screen at all.

I felt like I had been turned to concrete and plastered in place, but Ms. Wilson came back to my side of the bed and gently moved me forward. She picked up my hand and put it on my father's arm. Habit made my fingers move to his wrist, to that spot where I always checked Grandma's pulse. All the hospice teaching came back to me then, and the pamphlets I'd read, and yes, this was it, those *imminent* signs I had been looking for every day, every few hours, with my dying grandmother, but no, it wasn't supposed to be like this. It was supposed to be Grandma. It was Grandma's secrets I had been trying to learn, so I could help her find peace. Her, not Dad. It wasn't supposed to be Dad who died. How could it be Dad?

Tell them you love them. Tell them it's okay to go. Tell them you'll be okay. Forgive them, and let them forgive you.

No.

It wasn't okay for Dad to go. I wouldn't be okay. I'd never forgive him. I'd never forgive God or anybody else.

Dad's chest moved, then stopped, and stopped, and stopped, and moved again. The skin under my fingertips felt warm, but the pulse raced, then slowed, raced, then slowed, then went away and came back.

Tell him you love him.

I leaned forward and kissed Dad's cheek.

His chest moved up and down, but barely. Up close to his nose and mouth, I heard a faint rattling sound, like Dad had fallen into a well and gone underwater, and he was trying to cough, but he couldn't.

I kissed his eyelids.

They tasted like Vaseline. He smelled like antiseptic and hospitals.

Death comes too early—or too late. I hated death. It stole things it had no business touching. If death was a person I'd beat it and stab it and smother it and I wouldn't care if I went to prison for the rest of my life. Sunshine Hospice lied to us. You can never really prepare for death. You can't be ready for it.

Dad's mouth came open, and he breathed really fast.

Fish out of water, my brain supplied, straight from the hospice pamphlets I wished I had never read, because if I hadn't read those words, I wouldn't have known. I could have pretended for a few minutes or a few seconds that this wasn't happening, that it wouldn't happen, that a miracle might be waiting, and my father would sit up and shake himself off and grin at me.

"I'm sorry," I whispered in his ear, thinking about how I'd ticked him off and let him down these last few weeks, chasing hard after things that happened in the past, and how none of that mattered now, did it? It didn't matter at all. Nothing mattered.

What was the last thing I said to Dad?

I couldn't remember.

Did I tell him I loved him?

I started to cry. Mom was close to me, beside me, and she was touching my hair and Dad's head, and she cried too. Dad breathed fast and stopped. He breathed fast and stopped. The underwater sound got worse. I kissed him again, and his cheek felt cool.

He waved at me from the garden. He said, "I love you, baby girl."

312

"I love you," I told Dad.

"I love you, Marcus," Mom said. Then she repeated it over and over and over again.

Breathe-stop. Breathe-stop.

"You're the best, Dad." I pressed my face into his. "I love you so much. I'm right here with you, and I love you, and I'll always love you."

I wanted to believe he heard every word.

Maybe he did.

Maybe my whispers echoed in his heart and his soul, and they went with him to keep forever and forever, because as I said them, as I touched his face with mine and held his hand and cried with my mother, we watched Dad breathe for the very last time.

24

Absolutely No Guilt at All

MOM AND I SAT WITH Dad for another hour until we both finally believed there wouldn't be any more sounds or movements, that he wouldn't suddenly sit up and burst out laughing and say he was kidding and cover our faces with kisses and call me *baby girl* one more time.

The hospice pamphlets didn't talk about how eerie and wrong it would feel, to see Dad not moving at all, or how alive he'd look, or how we'd finally have to go and leave him alone in that hospital bed, even though it felt like tearing out pieces of our hearts.

Mostly, they leave out how much it hurts. That's what Dad had said about people who write about wars and civil rights and history—and death, too.

My father didn't want a funeral, so Mom signed papers for him to be cremated, and the last time I saw Dad, a nurse stood over him in the ICU room, quietly cleaning up tubes and bandages and everything left behind when death comes too soon.

Mom and I went home, and Ms. Wilson stayed with us, and I went through every basket in the laundry room until I found the still-damp, sweat-stained blue bandana Dad had waved at me from the garden. The one he waved when he said, *I love you, baby girl*. I put it in the old lockbox in my room, where I kept all my special things, along with Grandma's journals, and then I slept curled up with Mom. We didn't talk. It was like we both forgot how.

The next morning, food started to come, so much of it, and every kind, that Ms. Wilson had to stack up foil-wrapped squares and circles three deep on the counters, muttering, "Dear God, Southern people don't know what else to do for death but cook it away."

She started a list of who gave us what, and wrote people's names on the bottom of pans and dishes so we'd know who to give them back to. We had casseroles and soup and turkeys and hams and rolls and mashed potatoes and green beans and brownies and cakes and pies and cookies and enough fried chicken to start a restaurant chain. I didn't want to eat any of it and neither did Mom. It was Ms. Wilson who forced us into choking down chicken soup and rolls and ice water. The first few bites made me want to gag. After a few minutes, Mom said, "I can't."

She pushed back from the table. I followed her upstairs and watched as she went back to bed. Then I went to Grandma's room and sat next to her, holding her hand and taking her pulse while the Sunshine Hospice nurse bustled around. It was Cindy again, the one with the gigantic thick glasses and short blond hair. Ms. Wilson had called the hospice people and arranged for twenty-four-hour nursing until Mom and I figured out what we were going to do.

A bunch of new pamphlets about Sunshine Hospice's residential options lay on Grandma's bedside table. I figured that's what Mom might decide, to send Grandma to a residential hospice place away from our house until she passed. I didn't want that. I felt like my father had just vanished, and having Grandma go poof too would be too much.

Does Grandma know Dad died? Does she know he's gone?

Tears slid down my face. Grandma hadn't opened her eyes or moved on her own that I knew of, but she might have sensed something, since Dad took care of her every day. She hadn't been weepy or agitated, and her pulse tacked along at eighty, steady as ever. But I couldn't say our words. I couldn't tell her how, sooner or later, we're all gonna be okay, because I didn't think we would be.

The doorbell rang, and I jumped.

"Well." Cindy pushed her glasses back on her nose. "Guess folks are starting to come by to visit, since y'all aren't having a formal visitation."

My eyebrows pulled together, and I scrunched into the chair, holding Grandma's hand a little bit tighter. "What folks?"

"You know—your family, probably."

"We don't have family. Mom and me and Dad and

Grandma, we're it. We *were* it. Now it's just the three of us, Mom and me and Grandma."

Don't cry anymore. Not with Cindy. Don't.

She gave me a pitying look. "Then your friends and neighbors probably want to check on you and talk for a while."

I faded in and out for a second, slipping between the ceiling and being in my own self, and wishing I could just cry, hard and loud and forever. "But I don't want to see anybody. I just want to be left alone."

"Sorry, Dani," Cindy said. "Coming by to visit after a few days—and bringing even more food—it's just what folks do in Mississippi to help after somebody passes away."

I closed my eyes and the stupidest things to worry about trotted across my eyelids. "We're out of toilet paper," I mumbled. "And we don't have enough ice for visitors because the icemaker's broken. And paper plates and napkins and plastic cups, we don't have any of those either, because Dad thought they were bad for the planet."

"I'll tell Ms. Wilson," Cindy said, helpful as ever.

The next day, Mom stayed in bed, and I went over a to-do list with Ms. Wilson.

Memorial service—Your mom said schedule it later.
Life insurance forms—Your mom signed them and I mailed them.

Death papers from the military—Signed and delivered.

Toilet paper—Bought, and bought again, along with paper plates and paper towels and Coke and Pepsi and ice and water—oh, and tea. We have to have sweet tea. It's Oxford, after all.

At some point that evening, I realized Indri was at my house, and had been since—

Since—

Since Dad died—

She brightened up when I looked at her, like she had been waiting for me to notice that she existed again. "Who knew dying was so much work on everybody left behind?" I asked her. "Or that so many people could possibly come to my house? It's a good thing we got all that food. At least we have something to feed everybody."

"The fried chicken's good," she said.

I made a gagging noise and went to my room, and time trickled away all over again.

I didn't see Mac, but I got texts from him.

Thinking about you.

And, **Hope you're okay.**

A card signed by him and his parents. "So sorry for your loss." It had butterflies on the front.

And, Call me if you want to talk.

And, GG's been trying to drink herself to death. My folks dropped her off at a detox unit yesterday, hope it helps. The press is going nuts.

And, I'm here.

Good for him. He was there. I wasn't. I spent a lot of time on the ceiling, watching the world go by below me. People from the neighborhood and Mom's work and Ole Miss and the military base came and went. Dr. Harper often showed up and sat in my grandmother's room, talking to her about old times. I thought that was sweet, but I didn't want to see him. I didn't want to see anything.

When I wasn't on the ceiling, I was crying, or curled up with Mom, who wasn't teaching her class anymore, or going to her other job. She said she could decide when to go back to work, or if she ever would, thanks to Dad's good planning with benefits. That made no sense to me. If Dad was such a good planner, then how did he have a stroke and die?

Some days I felt mad at him, then I felt awful for feeling mad at him, and I wished he had wanted to be buried so I could go visit his grave and yell at him. Dad wouldn't have a grave. His ashes were in an urn, but Mom said she couldn't go pick them up yet. I was sort of glad about that, but ticked off too.

Yeah. I was losing my mind.

———

Ms. Wilson more or less moved in and slept on the couch. Indri stayed with me in my room, but she didn't bug me or anything. Mostly, she drew pictures of people's faces and the steady rain that fell against the windows for almost an entire week, and the cars in our driveway, and Dad's garden, where everything was starting to grow out of control.

We had like a bazillion tomatoes, so many the vines leaned over the metal stakes Dad had used to tie them up—and there was squash, and beans, and sunflowers, and peppers, and cabbage, and cucumbers, and tons of other stuff I couldn't even name. Sometimes I'd sit on the bench where I used to watch Dad work in the dirt, and play songs on his iPad, and stare at it all, and feel overwhelmed and guilty.

That jungle out there, it was Dad's garden. Mom and I should do something. Only, Mom didn't seem to be up for much, other than sleeping and eating a tiny bit of whatever Ms. Wilson slid in front of her.

A couple of weeks after my father died, Ms. Wilson was cleaning the kitchen while Indri and I sat at the table.

"Food's finally slowing down a bit," Ms. Wilson said. "But don't worry. I won't let you and your mother starve between now and when she feels like cooking again."

"That may be never," I said, and Indri gave me a sad look.

I was picking at a piece of fried chicken, and it didn't taste totally awful, even if it was battered with white flour instead of the unbleached whole wheat stuff Dad used when he cooked. My eyes moved to the clock, and I saw it was close to five in the afternoon.

How long had it been since Grandma had a proper meal, with family, like she was used to? Some nurses probably fed her, but she didn't know them. That wasn't right.

I pushed back from the table and stood, feeling a little less on-the-ceiling than I had in a while.

"Ms. Wilson, could you find the blender? I want to make my grandmother's dinner and go feed her. And I need Dad's iPad." I smacked my hand against my forehead. "Where did I leave that iPad?"

Indri and her mother gaped at me for a second, then got moving, and about an hour later, we had the folding table set up in my grandmother's room, and Sweet Honey in the Rock's "I Remember, I Believe" playing on the iPad, and I was feeding Grandma bites of fried chicken pudding.

"Do you want help?" Indri asked me.

"Nah, I got it," I told her. She was sitting at the table with Ms. Wilson, but Mom's chair was empty. We had given the hospice nurse a break, but Dr. Harper was with us, over at the desk against the wall, scribbling away on some paper he was writing.

"It's a good thing, what you're doing," he said without looking up from his work. "Most people these days don't see to family like we used to in our society."

I couldn't explain why, but feeding my grandmother blended-up green beans and mashed potatoes and fried chicken and brownies felt more important than anything else in the world right at that moment. I thought about ghosts and ghost stories—not the scary kind, but the just-a-little-bit-spooky-remembering kind. If I wrote a ghost story about my father, his worrying about Grandma eating enough would be a part of it.

Marcus Beans cared for his mother while she was dying. He fed her real food with a spoon, every day and every night.

A few seconds later, I added, *Marcus Beans served his country in three wars. Seeing all that death broke his heart, but it never broke his spirit.*

Would I want my father to be a ghost? I gave Grandma a bite of bean pudding, and she mouthed it without opening her eyes. No, probably not in a lingering, haunting, unfinished-business way. I wouldn't want Dad to be restless. But I wouldn't mind a presence. A sense of him. One of those "shivers" they talked about in books and television shows and movies about ghosts. Feeding Grandma—it was the closest I had come to feeling anything like that—or feeling anything much at all other than sadness—since Dad died.

The doorbell rang, and everybody in the room sighed. "I'll get it," Ms. Wilson said, and she got up and headed downstairs. She was gone a long time, and when the door opened again, it was Mom who walked in. She looked all rumpled in her shorts and T-shirt, with big, dark circles under her eyes, but at least her eyes were open.

Dr. Harper stood up and greeted her with a handshake.

Ms. Wilson came next, followed by Indri, then Mac and Ms. Manchester. She had her dark hair pulled back, and she was wearing a pressed white shirt and jeans with lace on the pockets. It surprised me to see her, but the person who came in last made me put down the spoon and turn away from Grandma completely.

Avadelle Richardson was in my house, in my grand-mother's room.

She looked . . . different, somehow, in overalls and a pressed white shirt a lot like the one Ms. Manchester was wearing. She wasn't wearing a fedora or using a cane, and her hair had been trimmed and combed into a strange white cap on her head.

Her cloudy eyes met mine—only they were less cloudy, and she nodded at me and didn't frown.

Mom came over to the table and sat at the place we had saved for her. Ms. Wilson and Dr. Harper stayed back, and Indri got up from her spot and went to stand with her mother. Ms. Manchester came to the table and pulled out a chair for Avadelle, who sat down beside me.

As Ms. Richardson went to my other side and sat in that chair, Avadelle studied my grandmother, her face showing nothing but concern and sadness. She reached out with trem-bling fingers and brushed my grandmother's cheek.

"Ruth," she whispered.

Nothing.

Avadelle leaned her face close to Grandma's. "Come on,

Ruth. Here I am. Go ahead and pop me one. I know you want to."

And I swear, my grandmother smiled.

Mom looked around the room, at all of us, at Grandma, and then at Avadelle again. Then she focused back on me. "This whole secret thing," she said. "You found out what caused the Magnolia Feud, didn't you, Dani?"

All eyes in the room turned to me.

That was a lot of eyes.

For a weird second, I felt like the whole room and all of Oxford and half the literary world was holding its breath. Avadelle looked uncomfortable, but she gave me a quick nod. Permission. Forgiveness. Whatever.

I glanced from her to Grandma, then at Dr. Harper, his pen hovering above the page where he'd been scribbling. My eyes shifted back to Grandma again.

She *was* smiling.

"No," I said, with absolutely no guilt at all.

Before anybody could ask anything else, I turned and faced Avadelle. "I know you weren't raised in the country, but do you know anything about organic gardening?"

25

SOONER OR LATER

———

**Excerpt from *Ghostology*,
by Dani Beans, page 1**

Once upon a time, my grandmother learned and taught and wrote, and my father came home from all of his wars and showed me that he loved me just about every day. Both of them survived bad things I've never had to face because they helped to make my world better.

The way I see it, Dad and Grandma climbed mountains. And I intend to start climbing right where they had to stop.

Don't worry. I know mountains can be tricky. When I get to the top of one, I'll see so many more. There will be big ones and small ones, close to me and far away, too. Some of those mountains will stretch so

far into the sky, I won't be able to imagine making it
up their steep, rocky slopes.

There's only one thing to do with mountains like
that: Start walking toward the sun, one step at a time.

SEVEN WEEKS AFTER MY FATHER died, my grandmother passed away peacefully, at home in Oxford, at our house, in her own room. Mom and I were with her, and Avadelle, and Indri, and Ms. Wilson, and Cindy the Sunshine Hospice nurse. We held her hands and stroked her face and rubbed her feet, and we made sure she knew she wasn't alone, and that we'd remember every wonderful thing about her, always. After she was cremated, we had a memorial for her and Dad at the same time, over on campus in the Grove, with pictures of them set on wooden picnic tables, tons of fried chicken and brownies, and items that reminded us of them.

Dad's table had a hoe and bandanas and his half-used bottle of spicy hair oil, his iPad and photos of him with Mom and me and Grandma, and pictures of him in his garden, and in his military uniform with all of its medals. Grandma's table had pictures of her teaching in elementary school, pictures of her with her family, and pictures of her with Avadelle, and photos of her standing at lecterns at Ole Miss, and copies of all the books and articles she wrote.

Dr. Harper had a talk with me after the service, about turning Grandma's time line into a book called *Mississippi:*

Putting It All Together. He showed me an outline, how we'd do it. It was Grandma's time line, pulled right out of her version of *Ghostology*. One more book by Ruth Beans, with Fred Harper and Dani Beans contributing. I checked with Mom, and she didn't have a problem with us taking on that project together. A nonfiction book about civil rights in Mississippi seemed like a fitting tribute to Grandma.

At the same time, it didn't seem like enough—or at least, not all I wanted to do. That's when I started writing *Ghostology*. It's a story about Grandma and Dad and me. It's nonfiction, but fiction, too. I decided to tell our story my way, in my own words, and Grandma's, too, and Dad's. The writing has been easier than I thought. I may have finally found my special talent, something like Grandma's, with a dash of Dad and a sprinkling of Avadelle, too. I never would have figured on that, or on Grandma turning out to be the muse I had been looking for.

I think Dr. Harper knows I learned some things about the Magnolia Feud that I'm not sharing. Maybe he's hoping I'll tell him the real story behind the legendary fight. Maybe I will. Maybe I'll put it in *Ghostology*—and maybe not.

Indri and Mac probably know I found out about the feud too, and Mom. Maybe even Ms. Wilson and Ms. Manchester. Nobody's asking though. For now, the secret belongs to Avadelle and me, and it doesn't feel like a bad secret at all.

Like Grandma said, when the time's right, I figure I'll know what to do with it.

On the second Saturday in September, Avadelle, Ms. Manchester, Mac, Ms. Wilson, Indri, and I stood behind our house in the cornhole pit Mom had made for us last week. One board was painted red and the other blue—university colors.

Indri made a toss. Her red bag sailed through the air and smacked down near the hole, but it didn't go in.

"How did I end up on this team again?" Avadelle grumbled, gripping her own red bag like she wanted to throw it at Indri's head.

"Random draw," Mom, who was refereeing, said.

Avadelle grunted like she didn't believe that for a second.

Mac tossed for blue team, a great big boarder—but his bag knocked Indri's into the dirt. He lifted both arms. "Yes!"

"Worm Dung," Indri said, but she didn't sound like she meant it.

I tossed my bag in a high arc, and it slipped through the hole without a single touch. "Nothin' but corn," I announced.

Ms. Wilson pitched a boarder, and Avadelle knocked her bag off with a solid overhand. Ms. Manchester tossed last, for blue, and she boarded too.

Mom checked her totals, grinned, and gestured to my group. "That's another victory for red. Blue, you suck. Maybe next week."

"This game is rigged," Ms. Wilson complained.

"In Dani's favor," Mac agreed.

"Mad cuz bad," I shot back.

"Yeah," Avadelle agreed, clapping me on the back so hard I almost face-planted in the pit dirt. "What she said."

Mom checked her watch. "All right. Everybody take a water break, then we have to get to work!"

Mom paced up and down in front of us, arms clasped behind her back and hands covered in too-big gardening gloves. She was dressed in frayed jeans shorts and a black tank top, with one of Dad's red bandanas tied around her neck. Her voice rang like a drill sergeant as she barked, "Okay, ladies. And gentleman. We have nothing to fear. It's an organic garden. Nothing in there can bite us."

Indri raised the hand not holding a gardening fork and harvest basket. "Wasps can. And bees and ants."

"And snakes." I shivered, gripping the gardening fork and harvest basket I had been assigned as I studied the gigantic four- and five-foot-tall weeds clogging the rows between Dad's raised beds. "Snakes definitely bite."

Mac, who was standing next to me, gave me a get-real look and shook his head, twitching his rake back and forth. "They'll run from you," he muttered. "'Cause you're really scary."

"Shut up." I menaced him with my gardening fork.

"I'd be more worried about Mississippi mosquitoes," Ms. Manchester said as she tucked a hoe handle under her arm and rubbed sunscreen with bug repellant on her freckled cheeks.

"Big as eagles," Avadelle muttered, leaning on a weed claw like it was a cane. "Carry off puppies and small children if you aren't watching them close enough." Her big floppy fedora hid her eyes, but I could tell she was smiling. Sort of. As much as Avadelle Richardson ever smiled.

"Nothing will bite us," Mom said—but she didn't sound completely sure.

The ground outside Dad's fenced plot had been spread with bags of composted soil and stinky, stinky organic manure. On each of the bags lay one of the organic gardening encyclopedias Ms. Manchester had ordered through Square Books, open to key pages and sets of instructions. I had Dad's iPad on the bench, playing Poco's "Keep on Trying." A whole cheerful playlist would cycle through until eleven thirty, when we went inside for the Ole Miss football game, because it was Saturday in Oxford, Mississippi, and, well—yeah. Football. Hotty toddy!

"Weeders first!" Mom called, and she and Ms. Wilson and Avadelle squared their shoulders and approached the no-man's-land of Marcus Beans's untended garden patch. They went in with grim looks of determination, seized hold of the first row of intruding plants, and started pulling. For really stubborn ones, Avadelle used the claw, then Mom or Ms. Wilson yanked up the stalks.

"Two piles," Mac called to them. "Seedy-looking weeds on the left to burn or pitch in the trash, and green ones on the right for compost."

When there was enough of a path, Mac went in to help rake up the mess into one pile or the other, and Ms. Manchester hoed at stubborn weeds they had missed. Indri and I were deployed to the raised beds with our forks. We used them to loosen dirt around carrots, potatoes, and onions that had already died back on top, then we pulled up the vegetable, knocked the dirt off it, and dropped it in the basket. If the plants still had green on top, we left them alone. If they were yellow-looking or spotted with blight like pictures we had studied in the books, we pulled them and threw them into the trash weed pile.

After a time, Indri moved a couple of beds away to pull up dead tomato plants and knock the dirt off those, too. Ms. Manchester hoed near my bed, and she said, "Next fall, we might be out here harvesting late lettuce, broccoli, Brussels sprouts, cauliflower, and cabbage, if we follow our schedule and don't screw it all up."

I wrinkled up my nose. "You can leave off the cabbage, thanks. That stuff stinks, and it tastes like green-flavored cardboard."

"Green-flavored?"

Dislodging a stubborn onion, I shrugged. "You know, gardeny-tasting."

She laughed. "I'm totally not looking forward to stirring manure and compost into these beds when we get all finished cleaning up—or coming by once a week to stir the steaming, rotting compost. But I think I can get the hang of it. Maybe."

"Compost will make Dad's famous 'good dirt,'" I said. "If there is such a thing as good dirt."

Dad's iPad switched to Patty Griffin's version of "Up to the Mountain." I dug up another plant, and the smell of onions and dirt and sweat made me smile, then made me tear up. I still cried a lot, and so did Mom. Sometimes it felt awful, but other times, crying felt good and right, and like plants in a garden might feel when rain falls after a dry bunch of days.

"When I show my kids pictures of my dad," I said to Ms. Manchester, "I'll tell them how he smelled—all gardeny, like cabbage, and onions, and dirt. And then I'll tell them how my Grandma Beans called me *Oops*. If that gives them chills and we feel Grandma and Dad there with us, that'll be a ghost story, right? The remembering kind?"

"Depends on how you tell it," Ms. Manchester said.

"Use a flashlight and yell to make 'em pee in their pants," Avadelle offered from behind a bunch of dead sunflower stalks. "Works every time."

Ms. Manchester rolled her eyes. "The finish is important, yeah. But I don't know about the pee thing, Mama."

I dug up another onion, and smelled my father, and got chills. I didn't really think Dad was a ghost, or Grandma, either—and I didn't know about Heaven, and whether or not it was real, or if people could look down on their loved ones after they died. What I did know was this: A bit of my father was in the onion in my hand, and would be in every onion we ever planted in his garden.

"My finish will be easy enough," I told Ms. Manchester as I loosened more dirt with my fork and found another onion waiting in the warm soil. "One day, when I'm ready to tell Grandma's story and Dad's story out loud, I'll use Grandma's own words to end *Ghostology*, and I'll say them whenever I do a reading."

"Sounds good," she said, fighting with an evil weed stalk that refused to be hacked by her hoe.

"Maybe by the time I'm all old and grown up and stuff, I'll be able to mean them again. I think Grandma used to mean those words. I really do."

Ms. Manchester waited. She liked hearing about Grandma, and all of her antics and sayings, so this was like practicing already with little pieces of stories. I didn't have a flashlight, but I had onions, so I held one up under my chin, where the tang of it made my nose burn and my eyes water with rain-tears instead of sad-tears.

In my best imitation of Grandma's voice, I said, "Sooner or later, Oops, we're aaaalllll gonna be okay."

Ms. Manchester stopped hoeing and gazed at me, sort of sad and sort of shocked. Then Avadelle peeked out from behind the sunflower stalks, her fedora tipped back where I could see her narrowed eyes and bright red nose and cheeks.

"Hmph," she grumbled. "Guess I have to admit you're right, Naomi. The kid *does* have storyteller potential."

"Snake!" Mom yelled. "Big snake!"

"It's more scared of you than you are of it," Mac said from somewhere behind a six-foot pile of pulled weeds.

"Prove it," Mom snapped.

"Don't move," Ms. Wilson said. "I'll chase it away."

"Somebody should make snake repellant spray," Indri insisted from the plot's far corner as she dropped dirt-covered carrots in her basket. "It's way past time for that to be invented."

Mac groaned, and Ms. Wilson chased the snake, and Mom pulled weeds, and Avadelle and Ms. Manchester tackled the dead sunflowers together, and music played on Dad's iPad, and I kept finding more of his onions.

"Sooner or later," I said, trying the words in my own voice this time. "Sooner or later, we're all gonna be okay."

Author's Note

This book was inspired by my early childhood in Oxford, Mississippi. I lived there until my father died when I was five years old. I started preschool there in 1968, and we stayed in Mississippi until I finished sixth grade. My early childhood played out against a tableau of societal change—the phase of the Civil Rights Movement that occurred between 1968 and 1976 (I consider the movement ongoing).

It frustrates me that less and less information about that turbulent time in history is passed along in textbooks and classroom discussions. I wrote this book to describe some of what I witnessed and experienced in my childhood. I also wrote this book because I fear we're forgetting and beginning to dishonor the movement toward equality bought— quite literally—by the blood of those willing to give up their lives so that we, as a nation, could move forward and include *all* of our citizens.

So much has changed in Mississippi because of those sacrifices since I was a child, and I wrote *Things Too Huge to Fix by Saying Sorry* from the present to look at some of those changes, but also to gaze without flinching at what hasn't changed. *Things Too Huge to Fix by Saying Sorry* is full of ghost stories, a traditional way of remembering and uncovering the past, of making sense of terrifying and often very sad events. I hope this book starts conversations about the past and those many events, about "then" and "now," about what we've gained, what we've lost, and the work yet to do to resolve inequality and dismantle institutional racism. I hope the story helps people remember and pay respect to the hundreds of names we don't even know—people who tried to live and succeed and thrive, humans just like each of us, who died for no other reason than the color of their skin.

Both friendship and betrayal comprise the core of this tale, and as I wrote it, I felt like I walked a difficult line, demonstrating how Avadelle appropriated Ruth's story even as I told my own through Dani's point of view. I'm very, very aware that as a white author in current times, my story *still* has a better chance of being published than Dani's story would, or her father's story, or Ruth's many writings. I carry Avadelle's privilege. I always have, and I always will. No matter how much I see or hear or know, that privilege will shield and protect me. I can step in and out of conflicts and struggles. I can get tired and walk away from many fights for equality. Dani, Marcus, Ruth, and Indri wouldn't have my opportunities. They wouldn't be able to quit the struggle, not even for a minute or a day.

How well I walked the line in my writing, only time and readers will be able to judge. I hope people talk about that, and I hope I listen, and others listen. I hope people who read *Things Too Huge to Fix by Saying Sorry* have these discussions, debates, and even arguments. I believe talking about these issues and taking deliberate action toward positive change are directions we can take to be more complete, more inclusive, more fair, more loving, and just—

MORE.

The facts presented about Mississippi history, the Civil War, the University of Mississippi, William Faulkner, the Meredith riot, the Civil Rights Movement, Alzheimer's disease, and the dying process are as accurate as I could make them given my personal experiences, clinical training, and available historical references. I also strove to be accurate about the appearance of the campus of the University of Mississippi and modern-day Oxford, though this was difficult due to the images of my early childhood in the 1960s and then my college years in the 1980s trying to peek through today's topography. The ghost stories I reference are also actual tales related to the town and university, with the exception of the screaming in the steam tunnel, which I created for the book. I also did my best with gardening facts, but I admit that I can kill plants just by looking at them too closely.

For those who want to read more about the topics in *Things Too Huge to Fix by Saying Sorry*, the following resources may be helpful:

NONFICTION

Andrews, Kenneth. *Freedom Is a Constant Struggle: The Mississippi Civil Rights Movement and Its Legacy*, Chicago: University of Chicago Press, 2004.

Beals, Melba Pattillo. *Warriors Don't Cry: A Searing Memoir of the Battle to Integrate Little Rock's Central High*, New York: Pocket Books, 1994.

Bullard, Sara. *Free at Last: A History of the Civil Rights Movement and Those Who Died in the Struggle*, New York: Oxford University Press, 1993.

Choices Program, The. *Freedom Now: The Civil Rights Movement in Mississippi*, Providence: Watson Institute, Brown University, 2012.

Dittmer, John. *Local People: The Struggle for Civil Rights in Mississippi*, Champaign: University of Illinois Press, 1994.

Doyle, William. *An American Insurrection: James Meredith and the Battle of Oxford, Mississippi, 1962*, New York: Doubleday, 2001.

Edmonds, Michael, editor. *Risking Everything: A Freedom Summer Reader*, Madison: Wisconsin Historical Society Press, 2014.

Freedman, Russell. *Freedom Walkers*, New York: Holiday House, 2009.

Levine, Ellen. *Freedom's Children: Young Civil Rights Activists Tell Their Own Stories*, New York: Putnam, 1993.

Levinson, Cynthia. *We've Got a Job: The 1963 Birmingham Children's March*, Atlanta: Peachtree Publishers, 2012.

Martinez, Elizabeth, editor. *Letters from Mississippi: Reports from Civil Rights Volunteers and Freedom School Poetry of the 1964 Freedom Summer,* Brookline: Zephyr Press, 2007.

Rochelle, Belinda. *Witness to Freedom: Young People Who Fought for Civil Rights*, New York: Dutton, 1993.

Fiction

Crowe, Chris. *Mississippi Trial, 1955*, New York: Dial, 2002.

Curtis, Christopher Paul. *The Watsons Go to Birmingham—1963*, New York: Delacorte, 1995.

Draper, Sharon. *Stella by Starlight*, New York: Simon & Schuster, 2015.

Nelson, Marilyn. *A Wreath for Emmett Till*, New York: Houghton Mifflin Harcourt, 2005.

ACKNOWLEDGMENTS

This book has been quite the journey for me. It touches many places I have wanted to write about, and gives voice to growing up as a child in Mississippi during a dark and yet explosively amazing period of change.

I appreciate encouragement along the way from many friends who have been willing to discuss, debate, and help me find the words. Thank you to Christine Taylor-Butler, Markeeta Wilkerson, and Jennifer Fritz for listening to me babble and struggle and try to put this into perspective. I really appreciate my agent, Erin Murphy, who kept saying, "You know, all this stuff you talk about from when you were little, don't you want to write about it yet?" And it has been wonderful to have an editor who didn't cover her head and scream, "No!" when I dove into this tale with all of its wild complexities. Sylvie Frank is brave and supportive, and most important, willing to listen, and able to help me listen when I forget to do so.

My stepmother, Bonnie Vaught, went intrepidly into the new Oxford (very different from the Oxford of my childhood and college years) and helped me with some locations and descriptions. My cousin, Camille Mitchell, hunted down restaurant info. A very sweet lady at the University of Mississippi, whose name I do not know, but who sits in front of the door to the Ventress Hall turret, answered my telephone questions with kindness and patience, and she never even laughed at me. And, as always, my family put up with me going silent and putting on headphones and playing the same music over and over for months as I wrote, rewrote, then tried again one more time. A book is never a solo effort. Many people contribute, whether they know it or not, and whether or not I remember to say THANK YOU.

So, um, THANK YOU. To all of you, and to anyone I might have forgotten, and always, always, to the readers. You get the biggest THANK YOU of all!

Turn the page for a sneak peek at
**Super Max
and the Mystery of
Thornwood's Revenge.**

Superheroes should never be grounded.

But if I had to be grounded, being stuck in my grandfather's workshop wasn't all bad. Toppy and I sat close together in the giant metal outbuilding, since I wasn't allowed to be on my own with tools and wires for a while—which was so completely bogus, because that fire was totally an accident.

Holding my breath so I wouldn't holler at Toppy about my punishment and get kicked out of the workshop, I snapped a connector onto the circuit board on my table. Toppy had one of our kitchen chairs clamped upside-down on his workbench as he used wood glue and finishing nails to stabilize one of the legs.

"Come on," he told the chair, his breath fogging in the chilly air. "Work with me." He tested the leg. It wobbled. He glared at it and adjusted his trapper hat. "Max, hand me the Phillips-head."

I grabbed the screwdriver from my table and rolled it over to him.

"Thanks." He gave my circuit board a quick once-over. "You about done with that thing? If we're out here much longer, I'll need to turn on the heat."

"One minute, maybe two," I said. "It's just a kit, and I didn't change much."

He went back to the chair, twisting the screwdriver and mumbling at it like it could understand him. I squeezed the red clown-nose on the top of my joystick. It honked as I motored back to my table. After that, it took me only a few seconds to snap the last circuit into place on the kit board, check the extra panel of LED lights I had added at the top, and then plug the main connector into my iPad.

I cued up a song and pressed play on one of Toppy's favorite Elvis tunes.

"You ain't nothin' but a hound dog," the King declared, and my circuit board lit up and changed colors in time to the music, just like it was supposed to do. Toppy let go of the chair leg and watched.

"Cryin' all the time," Elvis sang.

The little panel of lights I had added fired up and blinked SFC Stinks every four seconds.

Toppy's eyebrows lifted.

SFC Stinks.

SFC Stinks.

"That's—" Toppy started to say, but just then the little panel flashed again, twice as bright as it should have been.

I shielded my eyes. "Uh-oh."

Toppy squinted at the glare. The panel made a popping noise, and the last three letters went dark.

SFC St

Another flash of light made me wince.

FC St

A pop and a fizzy noise.

C

C

C

The last little bulb went supernova and cracked. Sparks shot from the edges of both boards. I leaned back as flames licked out from the added LED panel. The stench of burning plastic made me cough, but before I had to grab sand to smother the fire, it burned itself out.

Toppy came over to my workbench and unplugged my iPad from the smoking circuit board. He handed the iPad to me, then pointed to the extra wires I had used to attach the LED letter panel to the main board and the battery I chose to boost the power. They were smoking, too.

"You, ah, put a resistor in that LED panel you made?" my grandfather asked.

"I did," I said.

"Well, either you didn't wire it correctly, or the resistance was too low." Toppy patted my shoulder. "It drew too much current, so it shorted and blew the resistor. That's why your circuit board burned up."

I stared at the fried boards, miserable. Four weeks of allowance, poof. Up in smoke. Literally. "I'll work on my design."

"How about next time you want to make a blinking sign, you start with a circuit board meant to power blinking signs, not flicker to iPad music. And the right resistors, too."

I dug through my memory, trying to figure out where I'd messed up in my math. Those enhancements *should* have gone off without a hitch, even if the main board came from a kid's kit.

"You can't always make something haul the load you want it to, Max," Toppy said. "Not when it wasn't made to do that work."

I didn't answer, because I didn't agree, and I was sooooo close to working my way off grounding from the fire. The other fire. The big fire. The real—oh, never mind.

"Let's go, Max," Toppy said. "It's getting that time."

Like I said, superheroes should never be grounded—and superheroes definitely shouldn't be forced to watch sappy brain-eating holiday movies on the Sentimental Flicks Channel. SFC. Yeah, as in the big, blinking, flame-spitting **SFC Stinks** sign.

On the giant-screen television that dominated our living room wall, a girl squealed as a guy who just happened to be a secret prince rode up on his horse to return her lost puppy.

I groaned.

Toppy, who had ditched his down coat and trapper hat when we came inside, ignored my sound effects. He kept his bald head bent over the crossword puzzle on his worktable, but when I groaned a second time, he shot me a sideways glare. "Finish that report if you ever want to see your best friend again."

I bumped my joystick and backed up my wheelchair until I could look him in the ear. "This has to be child abuse."

"There are actual people who suffer actual abuse in this world." He scribbled a word into the puzzle. "Show some respect."

The threat of more days without seeing Lavender and more nights of my grandfather's heinous version of being grounded hung in the air between us. Movie credits rolled, and I muted the schmaltzy music, leaving the room quiet except for the pop-hiss of cedar burning in the fireplace and Toppy's slightly too-loud breathing. The air smelled like evergreen and winter, and the secret mug of Earl Grey tea with honey steeping next to Toppy's crossword book gave off a shimmery feather of heat.

With a sigh, I picked up my pen and scribbled a paragraph about the movie's ending, then slid my paper across the table toward Toppy. He took it and held it over his crossword, reading silently. The muscles in my neck tightened as his bushy white eyebrows lifted once, then twice. He tapped his pencil on the paper.

"Good insight about weak characterization. The Central Park Prince movies don't offer much in the way of literary merit."

I leaned hard against the back of my chair. "Literary merit? Who uses phrases like that in actual sentences in this actual century? No wonder you can't get a date."

"Wouldn't date on a bet." He kept reading. "And I'm not the nerd who can name every superhero in both the DC and Marvel universes."

"Hey, it's a useful skill."

"I'll be waiting on proof of that assertion without holding my breath." Toppy held up my report. "If I accept this as your final paper, we're agreed that you won't modify anything else in the house's electrical system without discussing it with me first?"

I squeezed the oversize clown-nose on my joystick tip, making it squeak. "If I had tightened the nuts on those wires, we would have been fine with my added fuses. I just wanted the breakers to stop blowing."

"Well, they're all tight now." Toppy's green eyes drilled into mine. "The three thousand dollars to replace the burned fuse box and repair the scorched wall was bad enough, but all that burned-up mess could have been the whole house. It could have been *you.*"

"I won't touch the house electric again," I conceded. My fingers trailed along my armrests, the leather covers currently painted with silver and gold runes I saw in a movie about faeries and King Arthur. "But my wheel-chair—"

"That chair is no different than your legs. You do what you want with your own body, Max. Don't let me or anyone else tell you any differently." Toppy pushed my paper to the side and almost went back to his puzzle, but he paused long enough to add, "Though I'd rather you not bust the thing trying to make it fly or float on water or whatever you come up with next, seeing as I don't have an extra ten thousand lying around to buy you a new set of wheels this year."

"Yes, sir," I said, my guilt rising like the heat off his tea. I hated how much my chairs cost, even though Toppy usually didn't make a big deal out of it, even when I broke something or fried some wires trying new ideas.

"And no, you can't have a tattoo until you're eigh-teen."

I sighed.

The phone rang.

Toppy and I both jumped and stared at each other. I caught the sudden sadness and concern on his face. The lines on his forehead deepened even as my stomach sank. Nobody would call at eight o'clock on a Friday night except for Mom.

My fists clenched on the arms of my wheelchair. "I don't want to talk to her."

Toppy held up one hand as the phone rang again. Caller ID flashed across the television screen, noting **Blocked Number.**

So, not a California area code. Not Mom.

Toppy answered the old-fashioned desk unit. "Yellow?" Pause. "Wait, who is this?" Pause. "Facebook? Bunch of cat pictures and whining, far as I can see." Pause. Then Toppy's head flushed a bright shade of red. His eyes narrowed, and his jaw set, and when he spoke, his normally mellow voice ground out in a low growl. "Now you wait one minute, Margaret Stetson Chandler."

I shot forward and bumped his chair with mine. When he startled, I leaned forward and grabbed the phone from his hand before he could say anything we'd all regret. Margaret Chandler was his least favorite person in the entire universe. She also happened to be Blue Creek's most revered businesswoman, owner of Chandler Construction, and the mayor. Which made her Toppy's boss.

"Hello, Mayor Chandler," I said, happy because she wasn't my mother. "Is there something I can help you with?"

"Maxine." Her voice switched from cool to warm as she spoke to me, then blazed right on to red hot. "You tell that—that—that *man* to take down what he posted. Right now, or I'll convene the City Council and we'll have his separation papers finished by morning. I will not have somebody speak about my business and my family—and my *hair*—in that manner!"

I pulled the phone away from my ear, looked at it, then realized I couldn't see whatever kind of confusion had infected Mayor Chandler through the mouthpiece. "I'm sorry to interrupt, ma'am, but are you talking about a Facebook post?"

"Yes!" She hollered so loud I heard her without the phone being back against my ear. "It's right there on his page, and every single one of his posts is shameful. You're a beautiful young lady, Maxine Brennan, and you know I adore you, but your grandfather is old enough to know better than to misbehave on social media. It's unbecoming for a city employee, and absolutely inappropriate for the chief of police."

I managed to get the receiver back against my ear without losing an eardrum to her shrieking, but it was a near thing. "Mayor Chandler, Toppy doesn't have a Facebook page. He doesn't have a computer at home, he doesn't have a smartphone, and he won't let me have one, either."

"Phones are for dialing telephone numbers," Toppy grumbled. He had already gone back to his crossword puzzle.

"How can you say he doesn't have a Facebook page?" Mayor Chandler sounded very skeptical, but at least her volume ratcheted down a few digits. "I'm looking at it right this very moment. Every post seems designed to make the town or me look foolish."

Wow. I briefly wondered if Toppy had taken up Facebook over at the police station, but just then, he bit at his pencil eraser, absorbed in trying to find an eighteen-letter word for who-knew-what.

No. Toppy and Facebook, that just wasn't happening.

"Just a minute, ma'am. I'll be right back." I put down the receiver, hit my joystick, and whizzed around to my side of the big drafting table, where my iPad rested on a custom stand Toppy built for me to hold it steady and at the exact angle I needed to be hands-free in my chair. I pressed my thumb to the fingerprint sensor, unlocked my screen, and pulled up Facebook. Then I typed my grandfather's name into the search bar, but got nothing.

I had to stretch to get the receiver, then work not to get tangled in the cord (no, Toppy wouldn't even do cordless). "Mayor Chandler? I'm on Facebook, but I'm not finding any page for Toppy Brennan."

"It's not under Toppy," she snapped. "It's listed under his real name. . . . Oh." She trailed off, the fire in her tone burning out completely. Once upon a time, a million years ago, Mayor Chandler had dated my grandfather. They were both in high school, before he joined the Army. They hadn't been together very long, maybe a few months, but long enough that Mayor Chandler knew Toppy never ever went by his legal name. "Interesting. I mean, that's unusual. I mean, why would—oh, never mind. I'm coming over."

She ended the call.

I hung up the receiver and put my hand on top of Toppy's crossword.

He glanced up at me, pencil poised over my third knuckle. "What was all that going-on about Facebook?"

"Mayor Chandler's coming over. We've got ten minutes, assuming she wasn't already in her car when she phoned."

For the briefest moment, Toppy looked like a mortified SFC heroine just after the hero shows up and catches her in flannel pj's. Because that's exactly what Toppy was wearing. Red-checkered no less. With matching red fluffy bunny slippers I had given him for his birthday.

"The mayor," I said, hoping to jar him out of stun.

"She's coming here. Right now. I'll get rid of the tea."

My grandfather was seventy-four years old with arthritis in both knees. I never would have known that when he exploded up from the worktable and blew out of our living room, dropping a few not-okay-for-school phrases on his way to his closet.

When Lavender and I were little, we played super-heroes *all* the time, when we weren't reading about them. She helped me etch my first ever Superman S into the back of the chair I had a few years back. After that, we welded a searchlight onto one of the push-bars, and I wired it to my battery and used it to stun people while I intoned, "I'm Batman" whenever somebody asked my name. Worked great until the bulb exploded.

Back when I still believed I'd be Super Max one day, I pretended my chair could go anywhere I wanted it to go, and turn into boats and cars and airplanes and spaceships. I had Batman cleverness, Spider-Man agility, Superman hearing, and Superman laser vision that caught every detail, every nuance of whatever we decided to investigate. Sadly, laser vision, real or pretend, didn't help much with examining Facebook.

"Smells like Earl Grey in here." Mayor Chandler wrinkled her nose as she settled on her knees beside me at the worktable. "My grandmother used to drink that stuff."

I couldn't see Toppy because he was standing behind my chair, but I know he must have turned red in the face. He didn't want anybody to know he'd swapped his coffee for tea. He thought it made him seem old. As fast as I could, I expanded the Facebook page she told us about and pointed at it to get Mayor Chandler's attention. I smiled, hoping my face looked completely innocent.

After reading the Facebook page for a few seconds, my smile gradually shifted to a frown. "Somebody went to a lot of trouble setting this up."

"Mmmhmm," Mayor Chandler agreed.

As we studied the Facebook page of Thomas Lelliett Brennan, Elvis crooned *Welcome to My World* in the background. Toppy's CD player, the one that looked like an old stereo, was on its last legs, and the disc hitched every now and then, skipping to different songs. "Anybody could have snapped that header photo of the Blue Creek Police Department," I said. "It looks pretty recent, like they took it from Town Square. And I'm sorry. I didn't choose this music."

"Yes about the picture, and I understand about the music," Mayor Chandler said. Then, "Lelliett?"

My grandfather stepped up on my right and cut her a side-eye.

"Family name," I told her, hoping the two of them didn't go from zero to brawl in ten seconds flat.

She pointed to the profile picture of Toppy, wearing his uniform complete with its bright blue hat. "This page has been updated since I saw it. That's new, and it looks like his departmental identification shot."

Toppy shifted from foot to foot. He was wearing pressed black slacks, shiny black shoes, and this year's winter sweater I bought him, the one with black shoulders, red stripes, and a snowflake in the center. He smelled like a pine tree. Every few seconds, he gave Mayor Chandler a once-over then looked away—then looked back again. Finally, he stared at the muted television as a secret princess galloped through Central Park on her white stallion.

"Public record, then." I frowned at a symbol in the upper right corner I couldn't quite make out, so I expanded it some more. "That looks like—hmm. It's like a drawing of a bird."

"An owl," Mayor Chandler said. "Carrying something."

I squinted at the dark lines and angles. "Thorns," I said. "It's carrying a thorny vine, or something. Oh! It's like a tattoo of the Thornwood Owl!"

Mayor Chandler's head automatically turned in the

direction of the mansion up the hill from our house. "Okay. That's a little strange."

"So is this," I said, pointing to the next photo on the timeline. It showed a young woman with blond curls so bright they probably made people see spots. She was wearing a really ugly striped dress and holding a baby.

The post read, **Heartless Widow Chandler won't escape Thornwood's Revenge.**

Mayor Chandler winced as I enlarged the picture. "That's from fifty years ago." Her hand lifted to her ash blond ponytail, blue eyes narrowing behind her small gold glasses. "Good lord, old photos should just self-destruct after a few decades." She sighed, then added, "*Blue Creek Gazette* did that article on my husband's construction business after we got that big contract with the state parks. I was already running the front office by then."

I glanced at her faded jeans and white sweater, and the bomber jacket with its worn elbows. She didn't wear cartoon-y makeup and striped dresses now. I was glad. She always looked pretty to me.

"She won't escape Thornwood's Revenge," I said. "Is that a threat?"

"Everybody's always citing that old legend," she said. "It's just another way of saying I ought to get tortured by a demon—or poisoned by a shallow-dug well. Wasn't that how Thornwood and his wife died?"

I had read every book about the Thornwood Manor haunting, most of them more than once. "Yes, ma'am." I popped open another window on the iPad and clicked the bookmark for my stored copy of the old Thornwood website, the one where people could schedule tours before the floor in the mansion's main room caved in and the city had to close down everything.

The Thornwood Owl bloomed into view, winging across a dark night sky with its evil-looking bramble clutched tight to its chest. It faded to a page about how Thornwood lost most of his fortune, turned into the meanest man alive, and then how weird things started happening at his mansion, like noises in the night and his prized possessions disappearing. The last paragraph of the history read:

> The coroner noted odd horizontal stripes on Thornwood's fingernails and his wife's also, hinting at arsenic poisoning. The Thornwood Manor well was found to be contaminated. Despite persistent rumors of homicide, a state surveyor pronounced the well to be shallow-dug and contaminated with natural arsenic. No doubt this was due to Thornwood's penny-pinching and bellicose management of his mansion's maintenance crew, who hurried in their duties to escape his berating.

In the end, Thornwood lived and died by his
own frequent assertion: In this life, a man well and
truly gets what he pays for.

"I don't plan to sip from an arsenic-laced well,"
Mayor Chandler said, "so we can move on."

I closed that page, leaving her old big-hair photo
front and center.

"Library has the *Blue Creek Gazette* going back to June
1, 1897," Toppy said. "Scanned it all into their computers. Whoever did this likely got your picture from those
archives."

Mayor Chandler and I both looked at him, because it
was the first time he had spoken since she got there. He
cleared his throat, and the top of his head turned pink.

"Do you have to go to Blue Creek Central to search
the archives?" Mayor Chandler asked. "Or can you do it
through their website?"

"They don't have anything but branch hours and
community events online." Toppy ran his fingers
through hair he didn't have, seemed to realize what
he was doing, then dropped his hand back to his side.
"When an officer needs something, they have to go on
over to the Third Street branch."

My iPad chimed with a message. It dropped down in
a black banner, tagged with Lavender's purple dragon
profile picture.